This Knot Intrinsicate

THIS KNOT INTRINSICATE

A Romance of the Canal

ARTHUR AUGHEY

SHORELANDS PUBLISHING

Published in the UK by SP (Shorelands Publishing) 2025

ISBN 978-1-7399568-5-1

Typesetting and design: Derek Rowlinson

Cover image: Sharon Glenn

Also available from Shorelands Publishing

Four Days in Villach
The Last Train to Hull
Between Hougham and Heaven

Dedicated to all those questing on the canals of Great Britain

Come, thou mortal wretch,
With thy sharp teeth this knot intrinsicate
Of life at once untie

William Shakespeare, *Antony and Cleopatra*

'Should you find, near or far, any lady in need of help or maiden in distress, be prepared to help them if they ask you to, for that is a matter of the highest honour. When a man doesn't behave honourably towards ladies, his own honour must be dead'

Chretien de Troyes, *Perceval: The story of the Grail*

CONTENTS

PART ONE: THE CHALLENGE

Chapter One

'WHAT the hell am I doing?'

Alex Perceval had pushed the tiller of *Knight Errant* the wrong way. He was taking the narrowboat towards the far bank of the Llangollen Canal rather than the towpath. 'On these beasts, left is right, and right is left' he told himself and pushed the tiller sharply in the opposite direction. *Knight Errant* returned to the centre of the canal but with the bow veering towards the towpath.

YouTube videos had claimed any novice was capable of serene cruising. This wasn't serene. It was like erratic weaving. No, not 'like', it *was* erratic weaving. Perceval cursed his ineptitude.

'Where the hell am I going?'

His over-correction meant misjudging the approach to a humped-back bridge at the canal turn. The near side of the boat nudged, then scraped along, the left sidewall while the bow bumped directly on the right. The juddering contact was deflected and cushioned by the tightly coiled and knotted fender rope. Even at this sedate three miles an hour, a mere gentle walking pace, Perceval was slightly unbalanced by the impact. Manoeuvring through the tight archway in this ungainly fashion, he'd forgotten another basic rule. Never cut a corner. Always think ahead, line up the boat and judge the turn from the mid-point. This beast was forty-nine-feet long after all.

'How the hell do I steer this thing?' he said out loud, steadying himself on the approach to another bridge.

Perceval bent down, adjusting the throttle lever until there was barely any forward momentum. Shifting from foot to foot, looking first left and then right, he tried to avoid a repeat of the previous scrape and bump. His alignment was only marginally better. He succeeded in navigating the bow through without colliding with the brickwork, but the stern took a hard knock against the concrete sill. Perceval shook his head in disgust, feeling reproachful as well as inept.

It was true that he'd only been driving this boat (was driving the right word?) for half-an-hour. He could comfort himself with the thought that it took time to master any particular art. How long had it taken him to drive a car confidently? Far longer than his brief time on the canal, a mere ninety minutes (including the instructions given at the wharf).

'You can't learn to swim without getting wet'. He remembered the words of the gym teacher admonishing reluctant pupils standing at the pool edge. It was a truth that didn't console. He didn't want to get wet. It wasn't poor technique, it wasn't lack of skill and it wasn't sheer incompetence which bothered him, at least not mainly. What he doubted right now was his will to fulfil the challenge.

He thought back to the handover at Whittington, the uncertain looks of the old man in his brown, oily overalls, flat cap slightly askew and pipe clenched in teeth (Perceval had never met someone who smoked a pipe), who'd explained to him in an anglified but unmistakeably Welsh accent, the basics of the boat and of canal-boating. He hadn't been the most expressive person and had gone through his demonstration methodically if not enthusiastically, for he was doing it as a favour to Perceval's uncle and seemed sceptical of his understanding. Perceval had to admit, he was right to think that.

'The basics are easy', the man had explained. 'You'll be steering with the tiller.' He put his hand on the waist-high rudder at the back of the boat. 'Always remember the boat moves in the opposite direction. When you push the tiller to the left the rudder will take you right, push to the right and the rudder will take you left.' It was in Perceval's nature to daydream and maybe the man could sense it, for he'd added immediately in an attempt at reassurance, 'The boat travels slowly so you'll have plenty of time to adjust if you do make a mistake.' He'd looked not at Perceval but along the length of the boat as if calculating the extent of Perceval's future misjudgements. 'Even experienced boaters can bump a bridge or get it wrong when misjudging a turn. Just keep moving gently and you'll have time to react. All you need is a steady hand on the tiller as the old saying goes.' His tone had been encouraging but Perceval hadn't been convinced. Nor was he reassured.

'Here's the throttle.' The man had tapped with the stem of his pipe the gear lever on the left of the transom. 'Push forward to move, back to reverse, but always put into neutral when you go from one to the other. You simply engage the throttle like this.' He'd pulled the lever out slightly towards him, pushed it forward, returned to neutral, and then pulled it back. 'Now don't forget you can't manoeuvre properly when in reverse, so be careful.' When Perceval had looked at him questioningly, he'd added. 'The rudder doesn't function in reverse.'

'Ah yes, I see.' He hadn't really but supposed it must be a basic rule of mechanics.

The man had given Perceval another sideways glance and from his trouser pocket produced a key. It was attached by thick string to a cork float. He held it up for Perceval's inspection. 'Here's the engine key. If you drop it in the canal,' he'd coughed, 'you can fish it out again as you can see.' He dangled the cork. 'But I don't expect you will.' These last words had been spoken softly and mainly to himself as he inserted the key into the control panel. 'You start the engine by turning the key like so to the middle position. This will show you if the battery and oil pressure are okay. Which they will be … I've serviced things myself. You wait for a moment and then you turn the key to the start position like so.'

The engine had throbbed into life and the boat shuddered. The power of the engine as it suddenly sprang into life had alarmed Perceval momentarily. 'The key will automatically return to the run position,' the man had explained. 'Then when you're ready to move – let the engine warm up for a minute or so – ease the throttle forward and off you go. The boat may seem sluggish at first but don't be too sharp when moving the tiller. Small adjustments are all you need.' He'd tapped the tiller again as if to remind Perceval of his earlier point. 'When you drive a car, you keep your eyes on the road. Same principle here. You keep your eyes on the canal and not on the tiller. Stay as far as possible in the centre of the canal. That way you'll avoid any mud or debris. When passing another boat always remember to keep port-to-port … that's left to left in other words. In the old days they said "hold in" when steering towards the towpath and "hold out" when steering away. And it was never "canal". It was always "cut". Times change.' Perceval had expected a sort of nostalgic tale of the way things were, but these remarks had been left hanging. 'And when you're passing a moored boat reduce your speed. You don't want your wash to disturb others, do you?

No, Perceval certainly didn't want that, imagining fists being shaken, insults shouted, and fingers pointed.

'Okay? Got it so far?'

'Got it,' Perceval had replied, suppressing his panic because he feared he hadn't got anything at all.

'Now then, when stopping, line yourself up to the towpath. Remember to put the throttle into neutral first and then push into reverse to slow down. Before tying up, approach as gently as possible before cutting the engine. Make sure the centre rope' – he pointed to the rope attached on the roof – 'is handy. Grab it when you step off onto the towpath to control the boat's drift and pull tight to secure. Like Frank Sinatra tells us, nice and easy does it every time.' Only then did the man abandon his instructional monotone, his Welsh accent coming through more strongly, his voice alive and his expression enthusiastic. 'Do you like Frank Sinatra? People your age have never heard of him most likely,' he asked.

'Who couldn't like Sinatra?'

In fact, Perceval did like Sinatra, or what he'd heard of his songs, so the response hadn't been his usual wish to keep other people happy and himself unchallenged. His mother had been a fan of Sinatra's. She'd been a fan of most singers of that generation or of any generation. Music had been her thing, her life really, apart from him. The only song which had come immediately to Perceval's mind was 'Fly me to the Moon'. He'd recalled his mother singing it quietly as she did the housework. God rest her soul, if there was a God, and if we had souls. 'My favourite is "Fly me to the Moon" If this boat can take me to Llangollen, I will be over the moon.'

The man had smiled, and his look had softened. He'd put his pipe back to his lips, but it had gone out and he'd thrust it into his pocket. He'd looked at his boots and then at Perceval. 'You'll do alright, I'm sure.' The image in Perceval's head at that moment had been the old black and white newsreel of Eisenhower encouraging airborne troops before they set off on D-Day. It had been nice of the man to be positive even if Perceval suspected he hadn't been honest.

'I'll just show you where I've put the windlass for opening and closing the lock paddles and you're ready to go. Any questions?'

There had been so many questions Perceval hadn't known where to start. Since it was in his character not to be troublesome and above all not to appear stupid, he'd replied, 'No, you've explained everything perfectly. Thank you.'

The sceptical look had returned to the man's face, but he'd moved on to show Perceval the windlass (there were two locks on this length of the Llangollen Canal he'd told him) as well as the switch for the light when going through a tunnel (there were also two tunnels he'd added). There had been an awkward silence once the keys were placed into Perceval's hand. He'd tried his best to look the self-confident young man and obviously failed.

'Look, it's a bit tricky to manoeuvre the boat from the wharf, so I'll give you a hand,' he'd said to Perceval's relief. Casting off the ropes and easing *Knight Errant* out into the canal as if driving a car out of a garage, he'd explained each move as he did so. The man glided to the grassy bank beyond the wharf where metal repair sheds stood, brought the boat to a stop and stepped off without looking back. 'It's all yours,' he'd said over his shoulder.

It was all his. And here he was, bumping into bridges and feeling less in control of his life than he usually did.

'Why the hell did I get myself into this?'

He knew very well why he got himself into this.

Chapter Two

AFTER living in England for three years, Perceval's deepest wish was to remain and make a life for himself there. He had no desire to return to Northern Ireland and to his mother. He'd studied history at Hull and, after graduation, had managed to find a temporary post, staying at his *alma mater* to work in admissions. The job was repetitive and unchallenging, but he enjoyed the company of the older women with whom he shared the office. He was always polite and courteous, never rude, never demanding. He was a companiable co-worker, his attractiveness lying in a genuine and gentle unworldliness. For the women in the office his reserve was considered charming, endearing, and it disposed them to protective fondness. It inclined them to make allowances for his dreamy forgetfulness, his bureaucratic errors and his lack of real interest in their own mundane or family affairs (though he was sensitive enough to feign concern when necessary). Their bond with Perceval wasn't motherly. Motherly love ('smotherly love', he called it unkindly) was an intimacy he'd left home to escape, an escape which released him to independence, though one which infected him with deep, filial guilt. He admired the stoicism and practical sufficiency of his female colleagues but above all, their good humour. Nor was he ever part of their social lives, apart from being on the edge of one Christmas party but leaving before the 'girls' (their self-description) went on to do some clubbing.

What was his relationship with these women? Perceval found it hard to categorise but when he did consider it, he always thought of cheeriness, a warm, relaxed, undemanding affinity based on mutual regard. Not being English but Northern Irish set him slightly apart, but Perceval didn't feel alienated or, as the academic jargon had it, 'other'. He thought his position could be best described as that of an 'outsider-in', accepting and being accepted. He considered it an acceptable bargain.

He supposed he was indulged because the women never really thought of him as being on the same level. They assumed his academic qualification would enable him to find something better, and that he was only passing through. It was how Perceval thought of things too. He retained a childish faith in providence, told himself that, in time, something worthy of his talents would present itself (even though he wasn't sure what his talents were, or what that worthy something might consist in). It was a comforting, though devitalising, thought, excusing him the effort to seek out that appropriate opportunity. Rather than his status being a source of resentment to others in the office, the opposite was true. He believed it pleased his colleagues to know they were more competent and efficient than he was, despite his academic record, and since he knew they were right to think this, he showed nothing but respect for and appreciation of their competence (living up, as best he could, to their view of him as 'a lovely young man'). Moreover, he treated each of his co-workers with equal charm, respect and distance, as though 'knowing his place', which meant everyone was happy, or so he liked to believe.

Of course, in female company, it was to Perceval's advantage that he was tall, lithe and good-looking. His eyes were blue and clear, his facial features sharp but not overly angular, his jawline strong without being prominent. In this regard, he took after his father, albeit without the tough manliness the photographs of his father revealed. His complexion was clear (he'd avoided the torment of acne unlike less fortunate schoolboys) and here he took after his mother whose skin never betrayed her age, remarkably so, given her addiction to cigarettes. His hair was dark and slightly tousled, remaining so whether he brushed it or not. Perceval gave the impression of someone thoughtful and reserved, but kind and certainly not cold. Handsome was the word his mother had used. Though he'd discounted the partiality of the maternal eye, Perceval's own eyes, and his own experience with women, confirmed her judgement.

No mention of a steady girlfriend, or any evidence of one, had encouraged the women to assume a melancholic hinterland to his daily good humour, perhaps an unrequited love, a sorrowful parting, an emotional wound not yet healed, the average fare of romantic fiction. It was obvious to them he wasn't gay. (The openly gay IT technician, who called in to the office periodically to fix computer malfunctions or glitches in the system, had assured them of that one day, brazenly, almost spitefully, in his hearing, a declaration which had pleased Perceval no end). The women weren't entirely wrong. Perceval did yearn for a time in the recent past when his life appeared meaningful, a 'before' which cast a long shadow on 'after'. He knew his yearning was a refuge and a barrier. It was a refuge in his uncertainty about the future but a barrier to his confronting that uncertainty, defining him as well as confining him.

Perceval recalled a line from *The Dream of John Ball* by William Morris quoted by one of his history tutors: 'fellowship is life and lack of fellowship is death'. Morris had put into a simple slogan how, at university, Perceval had experienced life for the first time. He was able to give himself over to collective belonging and to relax into the liveliness of like-minded company. At school, at least by the collective indices of Northern Ireland belonging, there was no doubt he was firmly inside one community and not the other. And yet the fact that he was a fatherless boy with an overly protective mother set him apart, an 'outness' compounded by his innate reserve and cultivated bookishness. Fortunately, he was physically strong enough to avoid being bullied as a swot and good enough at sports, especially cricket, for his intellectual aloofness to be accepted by his schoolmates, albeit with an edge of resentment. However, Perceval never truly felt that he belonged.

At university in England, this changed. The experience of academic immersion with like-minded students on his course was the intellectual backdrop to the absorptive friendship he'd found as a member of the university's cricket team. What alchemy inspired this camaraderie? What charm fashioned this fellowship? What secret sustained it? It was hard to say. There was something rudely masculine in the game, expressed through shared physical action and mutual dependence, implicitly understood as a bond of loyalty and honour, celebrated in rituals of post-match storytelling and, almost without fail, drinking. He used to think such communion their one true religion – cricket – with its rituals, liturgy, devotions, laws, spirit, festivals, saints of the game, and with its sins and redemption.

If the male bonding of sport provided an earthy connection, he experienced at the same time a pure longing for an ideal woman (the speculation of his work colleagues was true in that respect at least). This ideal was an illusion, of course, and said more about Perceval's immaturity than it did about the woman of his adoration. If the masculine earthiness of sporting comradeship was all about physical action, this feminine idealisation was all about emotional inertia. Jenny, his ideal woman, was the wife of the cricket captain, and, so Perceval believed, it doubly required him to resist what he most desired.

Jenny was tall and slim with long copper hair. She was also a few years older than Perceval and more mature. For young men between youth and adulthood, wrestling with self-doubt and ambition, trying out identities confidently or diffidently, Jenny was a measure of assurance. She reminded Perceval of a Pre-Raphaelite beauty, ethereal, striking and intelligent. But that simple wedding ring on her finger fixed a line he dared not cross, nor did he wish to cross it. His mother's sepulchral devotion to the sacredness of wedlock was too powerful for him to deny, as was her view that to behave dishonourably in any way was to betray himself.

Nor did Jenny try to draw attention to herself. She never flirted, never toyed with emotions, never teased. She never encouraged anyone, least of all Perceval. It simply wasn't in her character. She didn't need to. Something in the way she carried herself, her poise, her self-possession, was magnetic. Jenny would give you her full attention, make you feel valued. She was free-spirited, independent without disregarding others, possessing autonomy the limits of which both she, and her husband, seemed to respect implicitly. Every man adored her but not, he believed, with the paradoxical effect it had on him (or intuited it had, for young men would never admit such emotions to each other, however comradely they were).

Here was Perceval's paradox which he was naïve enough to think unique. For him, Jenny was all *too* real, an embodiment of grace, style, wit and fascination, someone in whose presence he felt more alive, as though things around him had a clarity they hadn't had before. And yet also for him, she was all *too* unreal, and when not in her presence it was difficult to believe someone like her existed at all. She was a hopeless longing eclipsing desire itself, was a devotion without possible consummation and, seeking her in other women of his age, usually, as far as possible, with a similar Pre-Raphaelite look, he found only disappointment.

Of course, he *had* known other women, student affairs in which he played his part with whatever charm and wit he possessed. But these relationships had no roots. And here was a further paradox. Though they were real enough physically, they were without substance passionately. Did he prefer an ideal love unrequited to love returned? Was Jenny his loss or was she his escape? Those questions he didn't wish to ask. He had loved her twice over, as ideal and as impossibility. Consequently, he doubted himself emotionally and felt romantically inadequate, cowardly in love, gallant only in longing, and hiding a timid spirit behind a lively imagination.

And yet ... to experience intellectual fraternity in study, comradeship in sport, and desire in idealised love had been the best of times. After he graduated, the fulfilment of the first, the solidity of the second and the reverie of the third, the tethering of different worlds, were undone. He should have seen it coming and prepared himself. A measure of his innocence was that he chose not to see it coming. He didn't prepare himself for 'after'. And so, Perceval's short idyll had dissolved and that closely woven fabric of his student days, now his 'before', unravelled as mysteriously as it had appeared. What seemed to him a condition perfectly virtuous, indifferent to time and circumstance, had proved frail, flawed, and insubstantial, as if made by a lesser god. William Morris had been right to say that lack of fellowship was death. To Perceval, 'after' did feel like a sort of death, however congenial his female colleagues at work. And this they sensed too, if they did not know why, and it informed their touching protectiveness.

As the termination date of his employment approached, Perceval was called in by the Assistant Director of Admissions and told that it had been decided to make his post permanent. If he wished to consider re-applying, she told him, his experience and favourable record would 'stand him in good stead' at interview. The Assistant Director explained that the administration 'pathway' in university life was one with opportunities of advancement to positions of 'leadership' for graduates with 'initiative', the 'right skills-set' and the 'requisite aptitude for teamwork'. Perceval listened politely to this litany of management-speak and behaved with suitable deference to and gratitude for the good news. At the same time, he knew that the woman sitting behind the large desk was someone who had achieved distinguished status through her own ability, someone who took her responsibilities seriously, someone who had high standards and expected them of others, above all, someone who took pride in the ethics of her profession, even if she were bending them ever so slightly in his case. And Perceval was intelligent enough not to be seen to connive in this ever so slight compromising of probity. When he left her office, he was sure the Assistant Director had appreciated his straight-faced demeanour and thought it stood him in even better stead. He felt as if he'd already passed the test.

Was this the 'something' he'd expected to 'turn up'? He liked the idea of his life being fated, an idea which removed the need for agency on his part. What optimism he possessed lay in a sort of fatalistic determinism, the equanimity of accepting that the course of life was already decided. Perceval turned over the advantages and disadvantages of the Assistant Director's words. His current role lacked intellectual stimulation, and Perceval wasn't without pride or self-worth despite his adaptable and accommodating character. He didn't want to think that in a few years' time he would regret being unambitious. Bureaucratic routine, especially its demand for practicality, might depress him and lead to despair. These objections represented the gap between fading youthful irresponsibility and anticipation of the mundane responsibilities of adulthood. He wasn't sure he was ready yet to cross that gap. On the other hand, what was being offered was not a rut to grind out an uninspiring existence but, as the Assistant Director suggested, a career with promise for advancement (if you're not in you can't win had been a mantra of his cricketing days). Perceval had been offered the chance to win advancement of some sort and at least it was preferable to the uncertainty of remaining in the 'job market'. Why not settle for 'less' since he'd no idea what 'more' should look like. He decided he would grind it out in Admissions for a while, accumulating experience like building an innings and then, when his eye was well and truly in, he could move things along. That made sense to him. Initial caution on the sticky wicket of life might set the groundwork for later success.

Then he got the message from home.

His mother had taken seriously ill, and he needed to return as soon as possible. Dutifully, that's what he did do. His colleagues in the office wished him well, possibly hoping their own sons and daughters would be equally dutiful when the time came. Perceval felt their collective goodwill, their 'we will miss you', had been sincere.

Chapter Three

His mother had never been physically strong, but her lack of bodily wellbeing was more than compensated for by mental resilience. She'd married Perceval's father relatively late in life, she in her late thirties and he in his mid-forties. She'd been a legal secretary though her real passion had been singing, in choirs, in small bands, even solo. His father had been a sergeant in the Royal Ulster Constabulary, long divorced from his first wife who couldn't endure the stress and insecurity of his job. They'd met when his mother was in the band hired for a private police function and married soon afterwards. The birth of a healthy baby boy had been an unexpected blessing. Perceval never got to know his father. Sergeant Philip Perceval was murdered when off duty by two members of the Irish Republican Army, shot in the back when he'd stopped off at a supermarket to pick up a pack of Pampers. For once, and fatally, his father had ignored the rule of not establishing a predictable routine.

Thereafter, Perceval and his heartbroken mother formed part of that substratum of society in Northern Ireland called 'victims'. She never stopped suffering from the loss inflicted upon her, never overcame the enduring grief of happiness so quickly and violently snatched away. Tragedy defined her, this brutal bereavement preserved in self-imposed exclusion. And she never forgave those who'd committed the crime. No one was ever convicted, even though, as his mother learned later, detectives were certain they knew who had been responsible and who had ordered it. From a well-placed agent inside the IRA, the word was that, as the 'peace process' was gathering momentum, the murder of Perceval's father was a signal to militants that the 'military campaign' was still active as well as a reminder to the Government that the IRA should not be underestimated. This calculated cynicism made the deed even more evil.

The murder had two effects on Perceval's mother. She remained obedient to the vows she'd made and to the love professed on her wedding day. Now, that love was given to Perceval alone – protective, caring, selfless, exclusive, sacrificial. It helped to still his mother's sorrow if not remove it, to soothe her anguish, if not quell it. Was it a crime in heaven for her to have loved so well and so briefly? She believed so and lost her religious faith too.

This submissiveness to fate was matched by disdainful rebelliousness against a world which had destroyed her happiness, a Falstaffian contempt for the rhetoric of public service, obligation, or conscience, and a boiling contempt for sophistries of so-called civil society, the do-gooders, the 'creeping Jesuses', the 'poor mouths' and the 'big mouths' never off TV and radio. Only when it came to his own behaviour did his mother ever talk of 'character', 'honour', and the virtue being true and honest. Perceval found his mother's commentary on the world refreshingly corrective to his own naivety and not the wearying negativity it might have been, for her cynicism was entertaining and often funny. It also meant Perceval had no need to cultivate his own hard-nosed contempt, for his mother's was adequate for them both. And she'd warned him not to ask questions because people were given to falsehood, told him to avoid intruding too quickly into the affairs of others lest you be loaded with their problems, and not to give advice for you could never be sure it would be taken the right way. In her sorrowful retreat from sociability, his mother's wisdom was unfailingly mordant, and she would quote in justification Kipling's line: 'Them that ask no questions isn't told a lie', adding, 'And a good silence never harmed anyone.'

Above all else, she was determined her son should never be seduced into joining the police or the military (and in this she succeeded). One death had been enough, one joy destroyed sufficient, and official gratitude was worthless. It was worse than worthless. Slovenly thinking and comfortable complacency in peacetime, she told Perceval many times, would surely combine with the worst elements in society to diminish and ultimately demean his father's memory. And from what he could tell (though he was not a political animal) his mother had been right. When bad is embedded, much worse is left to come, and nothing can ever come to good, she was convinced. And her judgement of the times, which he accepted, had been one reason for his wishing to escape Northern Ireland. It was also the reason why his mother, however much the fact pained her, did not stand in his way.

Why had she remained in Northern Ireland all her life? Perceval never asked that question. It wasn't that it meant she could visit his father's grave. He recalled her saying she knew he was there no longer. Like everything else in her life, the grave was a familiar place made alien by absence. She would sing softly some lines from Eric Clapton's 'Tears in Heaven' and Perceval, as a child, would look up to her in awe as her voice faltered through trembling lips. As an adolescent, he would look about in embarrassment. As a young man, he would stand rigidly in solidarity, despising himself for not being able to cry with her. He had no heroic heart nor, he feared, a tender one. Maybe his mother couldn't imagine being anywhere other than where his father had been and her memories of bliss, as well as sadness, were in the deep core of that pitiless land.

After Perceval's return, she survived longer than doctors anticipated or he expected, long enough that he had to forgo that full-time post in Admissions. Thankfully, his mother hadn't suffered dementia or Alzheimer's, and he was glad, for his own as much as for her sake. What killed her were the cigarettes she'd started smoking again after his father was murdered, cigarettes she'd quit smoking when she'd become pregnant. You could say they were a comfort in her loss, just like the music of all kinds she loved. You could also say cigarettes symbolised a denial of the world and its public pronouncements, two fingers to authority, to conventional wisdom, as well as the platitude to 'think of the children'. Anyway, she never smoked in the house, always on the front porch or in the back garden, cautioned him against tobacco or drugs of any kind, so the child had been thought of, and had been spared. Perceval admired his mother's grand rejection, for it revealed iron in her soul which he didn't possess. Even in her final days, she'd asked him to wheel her into the garden for a cigarette, encouraging a final rebellion against the authority of her doctor, a shared defiance which they'd both appreciated.

'What difference does it make now?' her voice had whispered in short breaths. Despite the frail body, the sunken cheeks, the dull eyes, her determination remained fixed. 'What difference does anything make?'

These questions Perceval couldn't answer.

His mother had given herself to memory and now she was gone.

At the funeral he was the grieving son, and the grief was genuine. Perceval played the role of the mature young adult, for he imagined people expected it of him. He accepted the condolences of some old comrades of his father, a couple of his mother's acquaintances from whom she hadn't retreated completely, a few neighbours, and the rector of the local church from which she was estranged but who had been decent enough to visit when she was ill. Few relatives attended which wasn't surprising. His mother, like him, had been an only child. During the Troubles most of her family had lost contact, and others had left the country. He hadn't recognised a cousin who introduced himself, pretending that his mind was distracted by events, apologising profusely, and his dissembling appeared satisfactory.

His father's family attended in numbers and Perceval was glad to see his Uncle Frank, one of the very few with whom his mother had kept close and who had, off and on, acted as a father-figure to him. He too had been a policeman and knew the score. When Perceval was eleven, Uncle Frank and his wife Jean had said farewell to Northern Ireland to move to England. They had no children, he had retired on a decent pension, and they wanted to live a completely different life. And they lived well.

Perceval had visited them as a teen during the summer holidays in their new home near Padstow in Cornwall, once with his mother and twice on his own. It was a traditional stone-built cottage with a slate roof and thick whitewashed walls, large bay windows, exposed wooden beams and an inglenook fireplace. It was in a beautiful location and must have cost a lot. They also had a small boat in the harbour which his aunt had learned to sail and from which his uncle would do some angling or in which he would idle with a can of beer. He must have concluded that his wife doing the sailing was a challenge to his masculinity (though he would never have used such a term) for later he'd bought a narrowboat after seeing on television an episode of *Great Canal Journeys*. The two of them travelled the waterways in spring and autumn. On these journeys, so his uncle told him, his aunt relaxed with a glass of wine while he skippered.

Uncle Frank had come over to the funeral without Jean. 'She not up to travelling, I'm afraid. It's her heart. She sends her deepest sympathies, hates to think of you having to cope all on your own.' He smiled feebly. 'Can't you just imagine her getting the sandwiches, slices of cake, cups of tea, maybe sneaking out the odd brandy for mourners old and infirm? She'd be in her element.'

His uncle had aged visibly since Perceval had seen him last, his former sturdy physique less robust, his gait less confident, and his presence less imposing. 'Your mum could be a difficult woman sometimes, you know,' his uncle told him. 'But she did a great job bringing you up. She couldn't have been prouder of you. And rightly so.' He put up a hand to prevent Perceval challenging him. 'You can be proud of her too.' He then squeezed Perceval's shoulder and said no more about his mother or about Jean. And Perceval didn't ask.

Now he was alone and in possession of the family home along with the money his mother had saved over the years. He told himself there was an opportunity, a breathing space, to get his bearings again (wasn't that the term?) and to think seriously about his future. These trite thoughts came up against his innate lack of will, his inclination to vacillation, and his temptation to drift. A few months had passed already since the funeral and he'd done nothing, made no decisions, aware that inaction was also a form of choice. Perceval felt returning a spiritual indolence, a smothering from beyond the grave and despaired at shaking himself out of his lethargy. At the age of only twenty-four, he found it hard to imagine the best years of his life were over.

Chapter Four

O<small>N</small> a wet morning in August 2024, Perceval confronted the   prospect of another aimless day. His employment black hole, he had discovered, was academic over-qualification (that degree in history now seemed not a glittering prize but a curse) and lack of practical experience (he'd never taken casual work during university vacations, returning instead to Northern Ireland to spend time with his mother). That's why finding the temporary clerical post at university had been such a morale booster. Now that he did have work experience and was sure he would get an excellent reference from the university, he felt he should be more attractive to a prospective employer. Yet he had found nothing.

He supposed he could always use some of his mother's savings, travel the world, and gather experience of a different kind. At this thought, Perceval had to laugh, knowing he'd only take his inadequacies with him. He could imagine solitariness intensified and discontent magnified. Travel had its romance of discovery, of forging new relationships, but he believed such things would never happen to him. Though he might be independent, he had little spirit of adventure. As he half-heartedly doomscrolled through job boards on his laptop yet again, Percival's mobile rang. It was his uncle Frank.

'Hello?' Perceval was inhibited about using either the word 'uncle' and certainly the word 'Frank' which he thought disrespectful somehow.

'Hello young man. You busy?'

'Not really. Just … you know.' Perceval closed his laptop, wondering what was coming next. He had an intuition it wasn't good news.

'Sorry for calling you up out of the blue like this.'

'It's good to hear from you.' Perceval said these words sincerely but heard his uncle scoffing. It was typical of the man. 'What is it?'

'I've got some bad news and maybe a bit of good news. I don't know …'

'Oh no, what's the bad news?'

'It's Jean.'

'Oh no!' Perceval repeated genuinely shocked, at the same time despairing at the possibility of another funeral, a mixed emotion that made him feel despicable.

'Before you start getting your hankie out, she's still with us.'

It was his uncle in matter of fact, nothing to see here, move along, constabulary mode. He paused, perhaps uncomfortably aware of insensitivity about Perceval's mother, but leaving unsaid any apology. 'Jean's going into hospital for an operation. It's her heart. I'll spare you the details. She's going privately this time. I know we're supposed to worship the NHS on principle and all that but … well, some things are more important than principle.'

'An operation? Is it serious?'

'All operations are serious when you get to our age. To use the jargon, her condition isn't life threatening. But you know she's had poor quality of life recently.' He left unsaid Jean's inability to attend his mother's funeral. 'We have a limited number of years ahead of us and I want us to enjoy them as best we can. Simple as that. So, no expense spared. I want the doc to fix her up. I'm taking a punt on myself staying one hundred per cent. Even sixty per cent will do me fine.'

'Right,' Perceval said softly, relieved not only for his aunt's wellbeing but also for his own convenience. He struggled to find an appropriate question to ask. Luckily, his uncle went on.

'Jean feels the same as me. It's a risk worth taking. We've lived with worse risks as you know all too well.' Percival did know all too well. 'These consultant chappies always cover their backs against claims, but Mr Green says he wouldn't recommend the op if Jean didn't need it and wouldn't benefit from it. I suppose we should trust him.'

'Hmm, I suppose so,' Perceval replied, but he could hear his mother saying uncomplimentary words about 'the medical profession'. He paused. 'So, the bad news is Aunt Jean needs an operation, and the possible good news is she will be fine afterwards. Is that what you're telling me?'

'Yes and no.'

'No?'

'We never bothered to take out private health insurance. That's the other bit of bad news.'

'Oh …'

'Don't ask how much the op is going to cost because I'm not about to tell you.'

Percival didn't ask, merely groaned sympathetically.

'You remember *my* boat?'

'The canal boat, you mean?'

'Yes, *my* canal boat. Well, I've sold it to help cover the cost of the operation. It will mean not having to dig too deeply into our savings.'

'That's terrible …'

'A man in Wales bought it. We haggled on the phone, but in the end, he offered a fair price. And that's possibly good news for you, Alex.'

'You've lost me now …'

'I have a favour to ask. Don't think you have to agree. I understand you may have other things on.'

'I'm not sure what you're asking me.'

'I'm asking you to take the boat to Llangollen.'

'Where's Llangollen? '

'In Wales, obviously.'

'And where's your boat?'

'Whittington.'

'Where's that?'

'Shropshire, quite close to the border. A friend we made on our canal trips let me moor it there as a favour. Plus he promised to give it the once over. I've cleared the boat of our personal stuff already, no need for you to worry about that.'

'Llangollen? Is it far?' Perceval was imagining weeks.

'It's about twenty-five miles thereabouts.'

'How long will that take?'

'Two days at least, four at most.'

'But I don't know the first thing about canal boats or any boats for that matter.'

'You don't have to. You don't need a licence, and you don't need experience. People hire these boats all the time. My old mate Rhys at Whittington says he'll show you what's what. Just point it in the right direction and set off. The canal is the last of the old freedoms. You should enjoy it before they take it away … like everything else.'

'Can you not do it? Or your friend at … Warrington, was it?' He knew this sounded churlish, almost an adolescent whine.

'Whittington. You know, like the Lord Mayor of London, Dick Whittington, the one with the cat. You studied history, didn't you? I can't do it because I'll be in London at the hospital with Jean. Rhys isn't available because he's got too much on. Besides, I thought you might have time on your hands, maybe looking for a bit of an escape from being stuck at home. Clear your head. It would be a great experience for you, a real adventure … you never did come along with us on the canal. Remind me. Why was that?'

'You were always on your boat during term time.'

'Yes, that's true. I forgot. Anyway, I think you'll love it as much as we did. Consider it as a short holiday. Look, why don't you take your girlfriend along?'

'There is no girlfriend at the moment.'

'Well, what about a get-together with your cricketing friends from university, the ones you were always talking about? There's nothing like a lads' outing to raise the spirits.'

A little defensively Perceval replied, 'I'm not sure that's possible for any of them, work commitments and all that.' He was certain that his old friends, who had been such a big part of his life, a few of whom kept in touch fitfully, would never sacrifice time or domestic comfort for a few days with him on a canal. The magical spell of comradeship had been broken and, more to the point, he wouldn't know how to ask them.

'Never mind. I trust you can handle the boat on your own. I knew nothing about it when I started out, apart from what I'd seen on TV – and *they* always have film crews along to help, don't they? I suppose I learnt the hard way.'

'And was it the hard way?'

'Piece of cake, Alex, wee buns.'

His uncle's swift re-assurance didn't convince him. 'When is all this supposed to take place?' Perceval asked

'I need the boat to be in Llangollen by the 9th of November. That's Remembrance Sunday by the way. The new owner is ex-service, Welsh Guards, and he'll be there for the service and march past.' His uncle laughed. 'He'll be the big bugger with the medals so you can't mistake him. Look, it's not *Mission Impossible* I'm asking – but if you do decide to take it, you know I'll be grateful. As a novice, you'll probably need three or four days to get there. Or take as long as you like, see a bit of the countryside. It's beautiful … romantic too. And think of all those young women you'll meet along the way.' He laughed. 'Just make sure you make it to Llangollen Basin by the 9th of November.'

Perceval felt he couldn't refuse. He wanted to, of course. He thought he'd learn the hard way only by making a complete mess of things. And he knew that between saying yes and setting off on his uncle's boat, a black cloud of disquiet would hang over his days. 'I'm less worried about the boat and more worried about my own ability,' was his final negative marker.

His uncle laughed again. 'Let me do the worrying about the boat! Do you think your Welshman will be pleased with me if you deliver a complete wreck? He'll be wanting his money back and I'll be the one in hospital, not Jean.' He chuckled at the thought then became serious. 'It will save us a lot of money if I don't have to use a private delivery service.' There was a silence. 'Look, Alex, I wouldn't ask if I didn't believe you are capable. You're a smart lad and I know you can do it.'

Perceval swallowed his reservations. 'Okay. I *will* do it … I hope those aren't famous last words.'

'Good lad. Knew I could count on you.

'I'll … I'll work something out.'

'Thanks, it's much appreciated … by both of us.'

A few days after the telephone conversation, a large envelope arrived with a letter from Uncle Frank.

Alex

Thanks again for helping us out. I am very grateful and so is Jean of course. Settling the problem with the boat was one of those gaps in our best laid plans. You know I wouldn't have asked if it wasn't important. As I said, it would have been difficult (not to mention expensive!) to get a private company to do it over that weekend.

I've enclosed our old map of the Llangollen Canal. You can see the route is straightforward and that I've scrib-

bled a few notes of my own about pubs and also about kayakers. I panicked the first time in case I motored over them. Plus you'll have two locks and a couple of tunnels to deal with. There won't be much traffic on the canal since it's off season in November and there should be no queues. One of the great words I learnt is gongoozler. It means a person who likes to watch activity on the canal, especially at locks. In my experience, they aren't backward at coming forward if you need help. But if you've found someone to go with you, the locks are straightforward to negotiate. Get the other person to do all the work.

I've included a useful booklet about canal boat basics (all simple stuff). I found it useful at any rate. You can also get some good instruction on YouTube. But if you're still worried, I picked things up very quickly and so will you. There'll be a few snags, but that's life, isn't it? You're a university man and have a good head on your shoulders. And whatever you do, don't drive at night. That's a big no no. Take your time. You can't go much faster than walking pace even if you want to.

Now I've also enclosed a cheque for expenses. I can't have you being out of pocket. You can get flights from Belfast to Liverpool, train to Gobowen and a short taxi ride to Whittington Wharf from there. And there'll be something left for 'provisions' of the solid and the liquid kind.

When I spoke to you about the canals as the last frontier of the freeborn, I should have said that the drink-drive limits are the same as on the roads. Though I have to say, I never saw a cop on a towpath with a breathalyser.

Best wishes from us and have a good journey. If I think of anything else, I'll call, and you can do the same if you're unsure about anything. Thanks again for doing this.

Best wishes

Uncle Frank

Perceval imagined all kinds of snags. But he knew it was about trust and duty. It was the expectation of him rising to the occasion, a request he couldn't deny. He traced with a finger on the map the route to Llangollen. It was daunting to his inexperienced eye. Yet the challenge held – he couldn't say why – a kind of promise.

PART TWO: THE CARDS

Chapter Five

S o, on this late afternoon in November, on this stretch of the Llangollen Canal, a true pilgrim soul would meditate on the sweep of the canal before him cutting through a rolling green landscape. He would consider the trees in their late autumnal barrenness scratching a slate-grey sky, wonder at the tranquillity of sheep grazing along sloping banks, and enjoy the enfolding stillness of this Shropshire pastoral, a stillness broken only by the gentle chugging of *Knight Errant*. A pilgrim soul might well be poetically inspired by these impressions. Perceval wasn't. He didn't have a pilgrim soul, or so he believed.

Evening was closing in. Light was fading. It was half-past four already and it would be dark soon. Under no circumstances, he remembered, should he be cruising at night. If it felt like he'd only journeyed a short distance, this feeling wasn't wrong. He'd arrived in Whittington too late to make serious progress today, Tuesday, having misjudged the time of his train connection from Liverpool. There was nothing for it but to find a mooring as quickly as possible.

The weather was surprisingly mild for November. There was little wind, and the still air carried a faint scent of damp soil and fallen leaves. Perceval had prepared himself for the canal by wearing his old tan waterproof parka over a heavy woollen jumper and thermal vest. On his head was a close-fitting beanie and around his neck a thick Merino gaiter. Underneath his cargo trousers he'd an added pair of joggers. Only moments ago, he'd considered himself overdressed. Not now. As the low sun set, as daylight dissolved and gloom descended, a sudden chill penetrated the extra layers and made him shudder. Perceval had the strange sensation that *Knight Errant,* once beyond the two bridges he'd blundered through, had crossed an unseen boundary. It felt like he wasn't moving between fading day and falling night but he was at an auspicious borderland, a frontier between the known and the unknown, the familiar and the unsettling. And an eerie desolation compounded his unease. The trees which arched over the towpath now appeared sinister, the water darkly forbidding, and his abandonment appeared absolute.

As if from nowhere, he heard a sound, soft though unmistakable, above the chugging of his engine. It was the chiming of wind-bells, haunting but oddly soothing. Then he smelled woodsmoke and was immediately comforted. He'd thought himself alone, indulging childish disquiet about being lost in an unforgiving land but his spirits rose at the sound of these chimes. Bizarrely, he felt he'd been rescued. As he manoeuvred *Knight Errant* around a long sweeping turn, he saw ahead a moored narrowboat and decided to tie up to it as closely as he could.

He cut back on the throttle and slowed down to the gentlest of glides. As he neared the other boat, he heard a woman start singing, her voice gentle, the melody joyful, and it stirred in Perceval a memory of his mother, how she would sing each day to keep her pain at bay. ('Music may have the charm to soothe a savage breast,' she'd told him. 'But it hasn't the charm to cure a broken heart'). As he neared, the singing stopped abruptly. Had the woman heard his engine and paused, perhaps out of curiosity, to observe who was passing? He hadn't detected any movement on the boat, and the singing began again. The voice had a beauty that even Perceval, with his tin ear, found moving. He wondered who this woman was, if she was singing only for herself or for someone else. Or was she singing for him? Was this voice a siren of the waterway luring him to his doom, the sweet Lorelei of the canal? For a second, this thought made him hesitate, then he smiled at the absurdity of it.

Knight Errant was painted plainly in red and everything about it was utilitarian. There were no artistic frills or flourishes, and Perceval thought it typical of his uncle. This other boat was different. Green and midnight blue, along its sides the colours were accented with hand-painted floral motifs in crimson and ivory. Perceval noticed the name *The Flower Maidens* inscribed at the stern in flowing, golden script, bordered by intertwining small leaves and blossoms. Wooden flower boxes with colourful blooms were placed along the roof and bow deck. Curtains were drawn back, and lighting inside allowed him to glimpse a homely interior, making out plants on shelves, books in a tall case, polished wood, a standard lamp, soft furnishings, and a few paintings. Everything looked cosy and inviting. Steady wisps of smoke curled from a metal chimney, and the roof was stacked with chopped wood and bags of coal. A pair of bicycles was also strapped on top, along with other odds and ends he didn't recognise.

Perceval wished to be embraced by the light and warmth of *The Flower Maidens*, to find an escape from the responsibility of *Knight Errant*, if only for a short time. He wanted the woman singing so sweetly to care for him, not romantically, but sympathetically, to provide solace, to cheer him, and tell him everything would be alright. At the same time, he wished to prove his worth, to show his self-reliance, to give the impression of a practised boater who needed neither solace nor reassurance. He wanted to demonstrate his youthful strength and confidence, to prove he was capable and needed no one to mother him. Wasn't that the manly thing, the heroic thing? Both wish and pretence were measures of his ingenuousness. That he did know.

When *Knight Errant* was almost beyond *The Flower Maidens*, Perceval noticed in its bow another woman reclining on a soft leisure chair, a tartan blanket over her legs, and smoking a cigarette. So, there was someone else (the clue, he realised, was in the boat's name) and this someone would be his first gongoozler. He felt under pressure to make his mooring a good one. Remarkably (he couldn't quite believe it), his approach was almost copy-book. He got the angle right and he got the speed right, minimised the impact against the soft bank and, reversing the throttle correctly, brought the boat to a halt flush to the towpath. How did he do that? Perceval couldn't help drawing out a jubilant, sibilant, 'Yes!' He looked back to see if the woman in the bow of *The Flower Maidens* had witnessed his triumph but couldn't see her in the gloom. He could only hear once more, fainter now, that sweet voice singing.

Perceval reached along the roof to grab the centre line, but it was too far for him without a risky shimmy along the narrow gunwale. His only option was to jump onto the towpath. When he leapt, he felt the damp earth beneath his feet and almost slipped. Quicky, though off-balance, he was able to snatch the centre line before *Knight Errant* drifted from the bank. Tugging firmly, he heaved in the boat, surprised at how easy it was to manoeuvre and hold its bulk. This section of the canal had mooring rings set at the edge of the towpath and he ran the centre line through one of them. Perceval pulled it taut and knelt to loop the rope around the ring a few times. Good enough to hold, he thought, now to secure bow and stern. He looked sideways to *The Flower Maidens*, wondering again if anyone was watching. He heard no singing and could see no one on deck.

He moved to get the bow rope, uncoiled it, and hauled its length over the side. Perceval stretched the rope to another ring forward of the boat to make an angled mooring. He worked quickly to hook it around the ring, trying to recall the instructions about tying a boatman's hitch, something about winding, looping, tucking and finally twisting through. The winding bit he got alright, he fumbled with the looping, but he couldn't tuck or twist properly. When Perceval pulled the rope to test its tautness, it worked loose again. He set about retying, but he couldn't get the sequence right. *Knight Errant* began to drift out towards the centre of the canal. Noticing the centre line hadn't held either, he abandoned the bow rope to grab it.

He used all his strength to bring the boat back and knelt to re-fasten the centre line as best he could, praying it would stay put this time. He walked towards the bow once more, running over in his mind the sequence of making a successful hitch. It still eluded him. He briefly wondered if he could tie a knot like the one on a shoe. He knew the idea was ridiculous and tried several times to get the hitch right. Finally, his frantic winding and twisting seemed to hold fast. He jogged to the stern, stepped on the deck, cast the rope onto the towpath and jumped down after it. Perceval searched along the towpath for another mooring ring and found one. He looked along the boat.

'Please no! No, no, no!'

Knight Errant was drifting again – more than drifting – it was gliding free from the bank altogether. Both of his improvised knots, centre and bow, had loosened. Perceval ran back to catch the bow rope before it slithered into the water. He snatched it and hauled back. As he did so, the stern began to drift out from the bank. Dropping the bow rope, he moved to the centre line again, caught in a hapless dance, a theatre of farcicality. What now? All he could think of was to repeat the same manoeuvres, working by trial and error. Fail again, maybe fail better? Darkness was falling quickly and Perceval imagined himself spending his first night on the canal sitting on the towpath, centre line in hand, helpless and hopeless.

He went to the stern once more and knelt, feeling the dampness of the bank seep through his trouser leg. Flustered as his fingers fought to find a successful pattern, he sensed a presence close by. A black Labrador was sitting still and watching him. Perceval could have sworn the dog's look was one of sympathy or perhaps benevolent curiosity and its presence made him feel better. 'Hello boy.' He reached out his right hand for the Labrador to sniff, and then patted his head. 'Do you know how to tie knots? I don't and could do with some help.' The Labrador, still sitting, wagged its tail, probably expecting Perceval to give it a welcome treat.

'Toby! Come here!'

It was a woman's voice, her accent unmistakeably Welsh, authoritative, the sort of voice you responded to immediately. And Toby did respond immediately, running and then circling behind a tall, wiry, middle-aged woman with crew cut silver hair. Despite the cool of the evening, she was dressed in brown cargo shorts and a white short-sleeved T-shirt, over which was tightly zipped a blue gilet. Around her neck she wore a dark-blue snood. Even in this fading light, Perceval noted her skin was leathered and weathered.

'Having trouble?' she asked curtly, standing over Perceval. Her eyes were a piercing blue but not unkind he thought.

'Can't get these ropes right.' Perceval tried to keep his voice light, his tone insouciant, but he knew his words must sound pathetic.

The woman nodded at the name on his boat. 'It's usually the knight who comes to rescue the damsel, isn't it? Ah well, we live in different times. And all the better for it, don't you think?'

Perceval stood up holding limply the stern rope. He noticed the centre line unravelling again. He couldn't think of a suitable response.

'I'd say you need some help.' The woman moved past him purposefully while Toby, sniffing Perceval briefly, lost interest in the drama, turning his attention to the trees and hedging beyond the towpath. The woman seized the centre line and gave a smooth but powerful heave, returning *Knight Errant* to the bank. 'Here take this,' she ordered as she held out the centre line to him. 'Now hold it tight. Keep the boat steady.'

Perceval scrambled into position like a young recruit obeying a sergeant major. He felt like saluting.

Picking up the bow rope, the woman looped it around the mooring ring, no fumbling, no hesitation, with practised skill, and secured it firmly. 'Keep holding,' she said walking to the stern and repeated the job. Giving the stern rope a final yank, she returned to the bow and did the same. 'There, all safely done'. Perceval remained rigid, still holding the centre line as if his life depended on it. The woman came over and put her hand gently on his arm. 'It's okay. You can let go now. Give it here.' Perceval's freeze thawed and he handed her the line. She laid it on the roof and dragged its edge towards the transom. 'Make sure to keep the centre line within reach,' she told him. 'Makes it easier to keep control when you step off.'

'Thank you,' Perceval stammered. 'I don't know what I would have done ... I was never in the scouts, you see. I never learned how to tie knots properly' and gave the woman his best boyish smile.

She shrugged off Perceval's gratitude, rubbing her hands to remove some of the grime from the ropes. 'Be prepared is a message you need to take to heart,' she replied brusquely. Looking directly into his eyes, she appeared touched by his shame. 'Learn your knots,' she added gently. 'You won't always have someone there to rescue you.'

Yes, he thought to himself, knots wouldn't dare come undone for her. 'This is my first time,' he said and immediately knew it sounded wrong, for there was a mischievous flicker of amusement in the woman's eyes.

'A virgin,' she said dryly.

He had to laugh. And so did she. Perceval put his hands up.

'I really did make a complete mess of it, didn't I?

The woman folded her arms and gave him a long assessing look. He sensed that she would like to banter suggestively, make a few laddish remarks about his ignorance and lack of experience. Instead, her expression became serious once more. 'Alright,' she said. 'Look and learn. Follow me.' Perceval followed to inspect the knot she'd made at the stern. 'Two things about a good hitch you need to know. First, you don't want the knot slipping loose. Second, you don't want the knot difficult to undo. Now pay close attention.' Self-consciously he moved to watch over her shoulder as she knelt, undid her knot, and once more looped the rope, tucked it under, twisted and pulled decisively. It was simple but efficient. 'Right,' she said, standing up and stepping back. 'You do it.'

Perceval bent down, determined to get it right. He copied her movements as best he could, loop, tuck through, twist, and pull. He failed and looked up at her dejectedly.

'Again,' she commanded, taking a hand-rolled cigarette from her gilet pocket. Lighting it, she said to herself rather than to Perceval, 'This could take some time, I think.' Perceval tried again, failed again, and hit a palm against his forehead. 'Okay. I'm betting third time lucky,' the woman said laconically, and exhaled a stream of smoke over his head.

He set to, working more deliberately this time, tongue at the edge of his lips. The knot held. Perceval looked at the woman with a mixture of delight and surprise.

'Good boy,' she said, and Toby came over to see what he was being praised for. 'Not you, Toby, our young friend here.' Toby looked disappointed but wagged his tail and went back to sniffing the hedges. 'Undo it and tie again,' she ordered. When Perceval had done so successfully and stood up, she inspected his work then gave a small nod. 'Not bad. Not bad at all. For a virgin. Now go and do the same at the bow.' Perceval hesitated and the woman raised an eyebrow, as if daring him to argue. He didn't. He untied the knot she'd made and redid it first time. 'See,' she said, taking another drag of her roll-up, speaking as she exhaled. 'It's entirely your own work now. These things matter. I can officially confirm you are no longer a virgin. You're a man.'

Perceval sat back on his heels and laughed. She was right. For the first time in this mooring fiasco, he felt as if he knew what he was doing – or ought to be doing. The woman finished her roll-up, extinguished the butt on the damp earth, and put it back in the gilet pocket. As she turned to leave, she smiled. 'I have to say, it's a good feeling for an ageing damsel to save a young knight in distress.' She called to Toby who returned obediently, and they turned to go back to *The Flower Maidens*.

'Thanks again,' Perceval said with absolute conviction, though part of him winced at the reversal of damsel and knight. The woman lifted a hand in a casual wave but didn't look back. He stood to watch her go but she'd only taken a few steps when a voice carried down to them.

'Bron, ask the young man if he's on his own.'

At the transom of *The Flower Maidens*, another woman leaned nonchalantly over the guard rail. Her accent was unmistakeably English, Home Counties Perceval suspected, possibly London, and certainly well-educated. It was difficult to tell in the poor light, but she looked about the same age as his saving damsel, though much heavier, smaller, with silver-streaked waist-length hair tied in a thick, single plait, wearing what appeared to be a chiffon dress, a fringed woollen shawl draped over her shoulders.

Perceval heard his saviour sigh, as if this sort of thing happened all the time and to her to personal inconvenience. She turned and asked with what he sensed was a touch of exasperation, 'I take it you *are* on your own?'

'Yes. Yes, I am.'

She turned, rather theatrically cupped hands to her mouth,

and called back, 'Yes, Jo, he *is* on his own.'

'Well then, Bron, can you ask him if he'd like to join us for dinner later?'

Bron didn't ask but turned to look at Perceval and tilted her head, waiting for him to respond. Toby sat looking at him too.

Perceval had been caught off guard. He hesitated, feeling awkward and unsure of himself. But it didn't take him long to make up his mind. He thought of the provisions he'd managed to pick up at a small convenience store in Whittington. (Provisions, he remembered, had been the perennial concern of Jerome's *Three Men in a Boat*. Unlike theirs, his weren't 'substantial' but decidedly meagre). He'd asked the taxi driver on the journey from Gobowen to stop in order to buy groceries (another reason why he'd turned up late to collect *Knight Errant*). There wasn't much to make a decent meal and he considered he deserved something substantial after the stress of his day, in particular his mooring fiasco. And hadn't his mother told him never to refuse good food when it was offered? 'Eat well' was her advice for a young man, to which she'd added, 'and always be sure to look after the woman who cooks it.' She was of a generation never to expect a man to make the dinner. The prospect of a warm meal, something hearty and filling, was too tempting. Still, he didn't want to impose.

'I'd love to … but only if it's not too much trouble for you both.'

'He says he'd love to, but only if it is not too much trouble,' Bron relayed to Jo.

Jo simply waved away Perceval's hesitation, as if the idea of it being 'too much trouble' was utterly ridiculous. Bron turned back to him, her expression one of resigned forbearance, not only, it seemed, with Perceval but also, and mainly, with Jo. She looked at her watch. 'We'll expect you in an hour, then,' she told him as she strode away towards *The Flower Maidens*, Toby racing ahead. She stopped, turned around, and said, 'No need to dress for dinner. For your information, I don't knot bow ties.' She paused then added, 'For you or for any man.'

When Perceval stepped back on *Knight Errant* gutted of all homely personality and saw the rucksack he'd dumped in a corner, his bag of groceries still on the table where he'd left it, the solitude was palpable. The prospect of sitting at table, eating heartily, talking but mainly listening, perhaps joking (he knew he could be funny when he needed to be), was irresistible. Perhaps making these two women laugh now and then would be sufficient recompense for his intrusion. Or were those thoughts patronising? It was difficult to tell these days. Jo's invitation felt like a reprieve, a reprieve from this space lacking warmth and life, the emptiness not in the boat alone but also inside him.

He plucked out the bottle of red wine from his groceries. He couldn't arrive empty handed, and this plonk would have to do. 'You shouldn't come with nothing but your appetite,' was another of his mother's sayings. He would apologise for his small offering, smile agreeably, and hope indulgence of youth, along with a spirit of hospitality, would cover for the inadequacy of his gift.

Chapter Six

WHEN Perceval climbed up the steps from the cabin onto the transom of *Knight Errant,* he was surprised by the crow black, bible black, night. He wasn't yet in Wales, but Dylan Thomas's description seemed apt.

His mother's house … No, he reminded himself, it was *his* house now. There was no escape from the responsibility of property ownership, well, until he could sell it. That house was deep in the East Antrim countryside. His mother had bought it after her husband's murder, bought it to escape Belfast with all its painful memories, bought it, more importantly, so that her son would not be affected by either sectarian violence or be seduced by 'serving his country with honour' in uniform.

Even in rural Northern Ireland, Perceval had never experienced darkness like this before. Nor had he ever sensed such vastness of the night. At home there had been streetlights, lights from nearby housing, even the reflected glow of distant urban illumination. The light of modern life had always been with him. Here on the canal, it was a night in which everything was inky black, no stars and no moon above. The dim, indistinct glimmer from *The Flower Maidens* didn't lighten, only seemed to deepen, the darkness. Perceval felt momentarily embraced by a sense of eternity, by immortality and then, just as swiftly, by the sense of all time collapsing and his life vanishing into nothingness. It disturbed him momentarily and he hesitated before jumping to the towpath, fancying he might be plunging into the void.

Walking the towpath, following the scent of wood smoke, he was cautious of his step and fixed his eyes on the shrouded form of *The Flower Maidens*. He doubled his caution as he got closer in case he tripped over a mooring rope and went head-first into the canal.

'You're punctual.' It was Bron sitting in the bow deck recliner and smoking another roll up. She stood, and he noticed she'd swopped the gilet for a heavy fleece but was still wearing cargo shorts. Her words startled him, and he stopped dead. 'I was posted here to keep an eye out for you,' she said then paused. 'Jo had a vision of you falling in the canal.'

Perceval thought this concern a kindly coincidence. From Bron's mildly mocking tone, he suspected her words carried a reproach for his earlier fumbling incompetence with the knots. Maybe he was being too sensitive? He thought it best to de-flect any implied rebuke by acknowledgement. As his mother always told him, the best response was one which indicated graceful acceptance, one which would make further comment seem boorish. 'After my disaster earlier, I'm not surprised,' he replied. 'It would be doubly embarrassing if this time you had to dive into the water to rescue me.'

'Dive in?' Bron guffawed at the idea. 'You think too highly of yourself. I'd have fished you out with the bargepole.'

Did he detect a touch of contempt? Or was it Bron's lingering resentment at her evening being disturbed for his sake? Perceval couldn't tell. However, her tone changed almost immediately, became welcoming, and Perceval decided it was just her way. 'Wait there and I'll take you onboard,' she told him. 'The hatch can be a little hard to push open, needs a bit of grease. I'd better do it. Don't like the thought of Jo struggling with it … or you straining your back.' She stepped onto the towpath and put her hand companionably on Perceval's shoulder. He relaxed, grateful for her apparent approval. It was the sort of validation he experienced when his cricket captain congratulated him on bowling a decent over. He followed her onto the transom. Bron opened the doors and put all her strength into shoving the hatch forwards. 'Our young man is here, Jo,' she called into the boat. She turned her head to Perceval and asked, 'We can't call you "young man" all evening. What's your name?'

'Alex.'

'Alex is here,' she called more loudly.

There was no response and Bron made a face, at once indulgent and exasperated. She stood aside for Perceval to go down the steps into the galley and he manoeuvred himself cautiously, bottle of wine clutched to his chest in one hand, the other held out for balance. He didn't want another humiliation by stumbling and reached the bottom of the steps without mishap.

Jo wasn't to be seen. Perceval had expected her to be the one cooking, had a vision of Jo in a pinny, perhaps singing to herself like earlier, absorbed in the preparation of their meal. What seemed like a thick stew was simmering in a pot on the gas stove, a familiar sight, for Irish stew was one of his mother's regular dishes. However, the aroma was unfamiliar, more herbal than meaty, more piquant, but no less appetising. There was another pot beside the stew containing a clear soup. Perceval's stomach rumbled. He hoped Bron hadn't heard and didn't look back in case she was smirking.

The galley was neatly organized with pans hung from hooks, knives set in a wooden block, herbs ordered in racks, and fresh vegetables arranged in wire baskets. Clay jars and multi-coloured tins stood on latticed shelves, recessed above the stove. Every surface was spotless. What a contrast, he thought, to *Knight Errant* and its lifelessness.

A more dramatic contrast was the saloon with its colours and fabrics. The ceiling was covered with an ornately hand-dyed silken tapestry decorated with motifs of flowers, vines, fruits, all intertwined with geometric patterns. Its interwoven sequins reflected light from two standard lamps with tasselled shades. The effect was astonishing, as if this narrow interior was so much wider, higher, feeling dreamily open to sky and stars. The floor was layered with overlapping rugs, some faded and some bright. The narrow passageway to the bathroom and bedroom was hidden behind rainbow-coloured beaded curtains.

Along one side was a cream two-seater sofa, over which was draped a burnt orange blanket, and onto which cushions of different shapes and colours had been thrown, with apparent randomness yet also with a touch of artistry. A bookcase of reclaimed wooden shelving stood just to one side of it, filled with paperbacks haphazardly arranged, some upright and some horizontal, amongst which were inserted what looked like old sketchbooks and notepads. On top of the bookcase sat a small brass reading lamp with a domed shade and beside it a small piece of blanched driftwood.

On lacquered wooden panelling hung a couple of framed paintings, a few ink sketches, two black and white photographs, as well as a tiny mirror with ornately fashioned edges. Small shelves held pot plants whose names Perceval couldn't try to guess. A modest table had been set for dinner in the centre of which a beaten brass tray held a lighted candle. Radiating warmth was a small cast-iron stove blackened from much use, its stovepipe angling to the right then extending upward through the roof. A mild, though pleasant, trace of wood smoke remained. Beside the stove, chopped wood as well as kindling were piled in a woven basket. And next to the basket, Toby lay on cushioned bedding, by his ears a soft, much chewed toy rabbit. The interior was bohemian no doubt, yet surprisingly domestic, ordered, and well-appointed.

Perceval remained standing uncertainly, the bottle of wine held tightly to his chest.

Bron sighed and called again. 'Jo. Alex is here'. Then to Perceval she muttered, 'I don't know what she's up to. Unlike you, punctuality isn't one of her strong points.'

He felt this was a source of grievance but rather than mis-judge her meaning, Perceval didn't say anything, just made a face suggesting tactful sympathy.

Bron went to pull over the hatch cover and close the doors. She took off her fleece and hung it on a hook in the cupboard beside the stairs. 'Give me your jacket, Alex, and have a seat. I really don't know what Jo is up to.' He handed it over along with the bottle of wine. 'Thank you,' Bron said, 'there was really no need. I'm going to finish making dinner. Can I get you something to drink while you wait for madame to make her entrance?'

Perceval was about to answer 'yes' and sit on the sofa when the bead curtains opened with a swish and Jo appeared. Bron's word 'entrance' was appropriate, for there was a distinct theat-rical flourish to it. Jo didn't put one hand to her hair, the other to her hip, and sway like a singer or dancer pausing before coming fully onstage, but that was the impression Perceval got nonetheless. Between sitting and standing, he was caught off balance, and not only physically.

'Finally,' he heard Bron mutter from the galley. 'Jo, this is Alex.'

Jo gently placed her hands on Perceval's arms as he straight-ened up. 'No need for any introductions,' Jo declared. 'I feel like I've known you for ages.'

Perceval had no response to those words, though he could hear Bron groan softly. Delicately, Jo grazed her powdered cheeks to each side of his. He sensed a subtle scent of sandalwood, recognising it straightaway because a former girlfriend at university had sworn by its alluring and seductive characteristics, claiming it was the perfume of choice for the adventurous woman. The allure and the seduction had been short-lived in his case since her idea of adventure had been to dump Perceval as soon as possible for someone else.

'Oh, your face is so cold, Alex' Jo said. 'We will have to do our best to warm you.' She took his hands in hers. 'Oh, you *are* cold.' She gently stroked his fingers. 'Come and sit closer to the stove.'

Perceval was slightly overwhelmed by this attention, but gratefully comforted.

Jo had let down her hair and it cascaded to her waist. Perceval found this extraordinary. Most middle-aged women he knew had shoulder-length bobs and most dyed their hair. Jo's hair was natural, uncoloured, and its naturalness, surprisingly, made her look much younger, almost ageless. She was dressed in a long flowing skirt with a patchwork of colours, dark blues and reds, patterned with flowery motifs, complemented by a loose, embroidered blouse in dark blue, a choice of clothing which served to accentuate her voluptuousness. Around her neck was knotted a short, light blue silk scarf. On one wrist was a chunky turquoise bracelet, and on the other a leather amulet. On the index and small fingers of each hand were heavy silver rings, while on her wedding finger, by contrast, she wore a thin, delicate, plain gold band. Jo's eyes were blue green, and the word which came to Perceval's mind was 'wise'. She projected a calm, knowing presence, which was indeed, like her scent, alluring and seductive, though not in an erotic fashion (for Perceval anyway). Nevertheless, he couldn't resist her aplomb and vivacity. In truth, he'd never met a woman who'd made such a dramatic impact on him. She pushed aside the cushions on the sofa, and they sat together.

Bron stepped from the galley and handed each of them a glass of chilled white wine.

'Thanks, love,' Jo said, smiling radiantly at her.

'Dinner will be ready soon,' Bron told them.

'Thank you,' Perceval said, smiling at Bron as charmingly as he could. Actually, right now he felt like a usurper, imagining how Bron must delight in her companion's exclusive attention.

Jo touched Perceval's hand briefly, and he felt the metal of her jewellery on his knuckles. 'Bron's such a wonderful cook. Her dishes are so delicious.' She ran both hands over her hips. 'As you can see, they are *too* irresistible for a rather sedentary person like me.' Perceval didn't challenge her comment, only made a slight shake of the head. He couldn't think of what to say. In fact, Jo's presence made him speechless. 'Bron, of course, can eat like a horse and it makes no difference to her figure whatsoever.' Jo looked over at her tall, vigorous companion with a blissful expression. 'She likes to keep active, walks a lot with lazy bones Toby here, and she does all the heavy labour on this boat. If only I could persuade her to stop smoking ... by the way, what do you think of *The Flower Maidens*?'

Perceval looked around to give himself a moment to think of a pleasing answer. 'I love it,' he said, truthfully but unimaginatively. He wasn't only captivated by the harmonious, bohemian décor, and the intimate mood it created. He was also taken by the intimacy of the life lived within it, the harmony of the contrasting yet complementary personalities of these two women, their shared purpose, their evident trust and ease. It was the kind of connection with a woman he desired, if only he could find her. Unlike the world he inhabited – the vacancy of his dead mother's house, the aimlessness of his present situation, his own lack of agency – this world seemed calming, yet purposeful, restful, yet vibrant.

'I find it enchanting,' he tried to be more poetic, 'it's like a beautiful sanctuary, all these wonderful touches'- he circled his hand to encompass the artefacts in the saloon – 'they are like the harmony most of us strive towards but never find. Or the harmony we thought we once had, maybe only dreamed we had, but have lost.' He stopped abruptly, for his unaccustomed

eloquence surprised him and he didn't know where it was headed. He feared he might sound like an ass, or even worse, a pseud
(and he pictured his old cricketing mates guffawing loudly).
Perceval heard Bron tapping a spoon noisily on a pot – which
may well have been her guffaw – but Jo closed her eyes as if in
contemplation then opened them again.

'You are a very perceptive young man, Alex. Yes, *harmony*. It
is exactly what we, Bron and I, have tried to create. I'm so glad
you can sense it. But I detected as you spoke some dissonance
in your own life, a disappointment unresolved perhaps, or a
still painful ...'

'Jo, please don't analyse Alex before dinner,' Bron called from
the stove, tapping the spoon again with a note of finality. 'It
will spoil his appetite ... and mine too.' Jo huffed, but only
playfully, Perceval imagined. 'Alex, I hope you're hungry,' Bron
announced. 'Lady *and* gentleman, perhaps for one night only,
please take your seats. Dinner is served.'

Chapter Seven

'WE rarely have the pleasure of entertaining young men, Alex,' Jo said as Bron ladled out a first course of soup.

'What Jo means is that we *never* entertain men, young or old,' Bron added.

'So, this is your first time too?' Perceval said to her.

'Don't get smart, Alex,' Bron replied, but her tone expressed a hint of appreciation.

'What's this? Have I missed something?' Jo looked at them in turn.

As Bron sat down, she touched Jo's arm with a tenderness Perceval hadn't seen from her before. 'It's a private joke between Alex and me.'

Jo still looked perplexed.

'It's my first time on the canal,' Perceval explained. 'So for me everything here is for the first time. If it hadn't been for Bron's help it would probably have been my last time too.'

'Oh, I see.' Jo didn't pursue his answer further. 'I am so pleased. It was your fate to meet us ... I knew it. And tell us, what brings you to this place all on your own? Your accent is Northern Irish, isn't it?'

'Before you extract his confession, Jo, what do you make of my soup, Alex?'

Perceval took a spoonful and tasted cautiously for he didn't know what to expect. The soup was smooth and spicey. He was so hungry that a bowl of Heinz would have been good enough, but this was truly delicious. Warmth spread through him and he nodded appreciatively. 'It's wonderful reviving. I congratulate the chef.' He glimpsed Jo beaming at his words but thought he might have gone too far for Bron, whose face registered neither approval nor disapproval of his compliment. 'What is it?' he asked.

'Spiced carrot and red lentil. I added a little ginger and turmeric. To make it especially "reviving" as you say.'

Perceval decided his words had been well-chosen.

'Ah, endurance, clarity and resolve,' Jo added. 'What you need, Alex, for your journey ahead.'

'Yes, that's exactly what I *do* need.'

'Yeah, yeah,' Bron said. This remark wasn't to Perceval but to Jo, as if she'd heard such interpretations of her cooking many times before. 'Try some of my Welsh wholemeal bread,' she said, offering Perceval the plate.

Perceval did so and bit a piece as he took another spoonful of soup. 'That is so good. I love the slight treacly flavour,' thinking he was beginning to sound like a guest on *Saturday Kitchen*. (It was one of the TV shows his mother liked to have on while she fussed around the living room, stopping now and then to take mental note of a recipe or a cooking technique, though Perceval never noticed any variation in the meals she served up. A soup such as this one would never have made her menu).

'Molasses,' Bron told him then looked at Jo.

'Patience and the virtue of taking things slowly … rather like life on the canal.'

'I suppose,' Bron said, as if Jo's response was the one she'd expected.

Perceval gave them a brief explanation of the reasons for his journey to Llangollen and his doubts about doing it successfully.

'I find your sense of duty admirable, don't you Bron? And we both hope your aunt's operation goes well.'

Bron nodded, then asked, 'And you really have no idea whatsoever of boating, its customs or techniques?'

'Only what I gathered from YouTube and a short booklet

my uncle sent me. And a man at Whittington Wharf gave a brief demonstration and that's it ...' Perceval broke off. 'No there was one thing I did know and even so it's only as a joke. '

'Go on,' said Bron, 'Tell us the joke.'

'You really want to hear it?'

'I wouldn't ask if I didn't,' Bron replied.

'Oh yes, do tell us,' Jo added eagerly.

'It's not very good but ... okay then. Picture a pirate ship on the high seas. After some time, the crew begins to question the strange behaviour of their captain. Each morning, before giving them orders for the day, he disappears into his cabin to consult a paper locked in the desk. They suspect it must be a treasure map. They can think of no other explanation and believe the captain is keeping its whereabouts from them. Their suspicion grows until finally they conspire to mutiny, throw him overboard, steal the map, and keep the treasure for themselves. Next morning, when the captain calls them together, they seize him, tie him up, and toss him overboard as planned.'

Jo gasped, put a hand over her mouth, 'Oh, no,' she said and Perceval stopped.

'It's only a joke, Jo, for goodness' sake.' Bron shook her head. 'Go on Alex.'

He cleared his throat. 'They rush to the cabin, break open the drawer, and snatch the paper. But it's not a map. It's only a sheet of paper with a sentence of four words. Since only one of the crew can read, he's handed the paper. He looks at it and looks up at their expectant faces. "What does it say?" they ask him. The pirate crumples the paper and throws it away. It says, "starboard right, port left" ... so you see, I did know at least what starboard and port mean.'

Jo laughed loudly, 'That's a start at least.'

'That's a good one,' Bron said, and Perceval considered her words true praise, as good a compliment he was ever going to get.

The joke had been told to him on the phone by his uncle. It was the first time he'd been able to tell it and was glad it had such a good reception.

'I think that tale deserves more wine,' Jo announced and refilled their glasses. 'Were you not able to get someone to come along and help you?'

Perceval tempered with excuses his failure to rally his old cricketing mates: 'the timing was difficult for them, hard for them to get off work'. In truth, he'd never asked. His uncle's financial need excused the absence of a Northern Irish helper: 'it would have been expensive for two return journeys'. He also felt he needed to explain the absence of a girlfriend, not wishing to appear a complete loser: 'of course, it's not the sort of thing you can ask a girlfriend to do in November'. He reassured himself, put in this way, that he hadn't dishonoured their hospitality with lies, and merely stated what he believed to be the truth. They seemed satisfied with his explanation.

Having cleared away the soup dishes, Bron returned with the main course, the crock of vegetable stew. She dished out generous helpings onto flower patterned dishes.

'This is also scrumptious,' Perceval said to Bron. 'I've never eaten vegetarian food so good.' (In fact, he rarely, if ever, ate vegetarian food, and didn't know if baked beans really counted). 'It's barley, beans and mushroom, yes?'

'With toasted walnuts for a little bit of extra crunch,' Bron told him and turned once more to Jo.

Jo closed her eyes and said, 'Resilience even in the darkest moments, and hard-won wisdom, gained through experience.'

'I never imagined food to have any meaning, apart from filling my belly,' Perceval laughed.

'Oh, everything, even the smallest thing on this earth, has meaning, Alex. Don't you think so?' Jo asked.

'I suppose you're right. It's just I've never given it much

thought, that's all.'

'Let Alex enjoy his food without worrying about the meaning of life,' Bron said.

They ate silently and enjoyably for some moments. Perceval thought he should ask about their life together, though he never liked to pry. 'Can I ask if you live on *The Flower Maidens* all year round?'

'Yes, we do. We haven't always done that of course,' Jo said. 'Today we are romantic rovers of the canal, water gypsies as they used to say, free and elusive spirits, intimately in tune with the changing seasons.'

'It sounds like a poetic way of life,' he said.

'It can be a hard way of life at times,' Bron added, not looking up from her food.

'What did you do before?'

'Sometimes it's hard to remember "before" because life is so idyllic now.' Jo paused as though struggling to recall this 'before' they'd once lived. 'I taught literature at a college in Lewisham. Do you know Lewisham?' Perceval shook his head. 'No matter.' It seemed like it mattered no longer to Jo either. 'Teaching became increasingly taxing and unrewarding. Life in London became increasingly stressful and demanding. It was more so for Bron than for me. She was a police officer in the Met, if you can believe that.'

Now that Jo had told him, Perceval could well believe it.

'It was the fault of watching too many cops and robbers on TV as a kid,' Bron said. 'You can blame *The Bill*. Have you ever seen it? Don't think it's been on for years.'

Perceval said no, he'd never seen it. The series fell into that category of 'daytime television' which, according to his mother, was the mark of the nursing home and never to be mentioned in her presence. He added that his father and uncle had been policemen in Northern Ireland and Bron's eyes widened slightly, as though she was seeing Perceval with fresh interest. Neither of the women said anything about the Troubles, for which he was grateful.

'It was a crime that introduced us in the first place, you know,' Jo said, reaching across the table and touching Bron's hand. 'You see here the long arm of the law, Alex,' she laughed.

Bron remained impassive and shrugged, as though she'd heard the line many times before. Perceval told Jo *that* joke was a good one, much better than his one about the pirates. That admission really did please her.

'My flat was broken into and Bron was one of the first officers on the scene. We've been together ever since. You see how fate brought us together.'

'You were right the first time, Jo. Criminals brought us together.'

'There's a divinity that shapes our ends, rough-hew them how we will ... I think we should give Shakespeare the final word on this, Bron,' Jo said, as if instructing a contrarian student. And Shakespeare did have the final word for there was a silence before Bron spoke directly to Perceval.

'I know you'll read stories that life on the canal means freedom, peace and quiet, a simpler way of life and brings you closer to nature, all the old hippie stuff.' Bron gave a quick glance at Jo. 'I don't deny it.' She gave her another quick glance. 'For me, I wanted to escape the abusiveness, the coarseness, the lack of respect I experienced every day. Not just us cops. It goes for anyone in authority, even for teachers. On the canal you'll encounter the old-fashioned civility I thought we'd lost in this country. You get bad people here as you do anywhere, but very, very rarely. If you are searching for Merrie England, Merrie Wales even,' she smiled, 'this is where you'll find it. Anyway, it's what *we* found. Together.'

'Bron and I, we found the silver apples of the moon and the

golden apples of the sun.'

Bron didn't remark on Jo's fancy, but neither did she challenge the romance it conveyed. Instead, she asked, 'Have you room for dessert, Alex?'

'Of course, he has,' Jo spoke for him, once more filling his glass with wine.

This time Bron brought glass dishes filled with hot stewed apples and raisins, topped with fresh cream. She looked at Jo as she set them on the table. 'Well?'

'Sweetness, though fleeting, we must enjoy it while we can,' Jo responded.

'Amen,' Perceval, slightly drunk, said with such gusto that Jo and Bron smiled indulgently.

These silver and golden apples were sweet, and he enjoyed them immensely. In fact, he had never enjoyed a meal so much, not only the food but also the ambiance, the genial atmosphere, the company. When they'd finished dessert Toby, who, until he'd heard spoons clinking on glass dishes, had slept peacefully by the heat of the stove, stirred, rose, yawned, stretched and looked with pleading brown eyes at Bron.

'We haven't forgotten about you, Toby,' Bron said, bending over to scratch his ears. She carried the dessert dishes to the galley sink and Toby followed expectantly. Bron gave him his dinner in a large metal dish and Toby ate with such an energetic appetite that it shifted his bowl across the floor, finally banging it into the fridge door.

Perceval announced that he must help with the dishes and, despite their (he judged half-hearted) refusal, insisted on it, putting this unaccustomed firmness down to the wine he'd consumed. He was surprised how quickly they were able to complete the task of washing (Bron) and drying (Jo and Perceval) the pots, bowls and cutlery of three courses. In the time it took, Bron expanded on the practicalities of life on the canal, Jo rhapsodised about its joys and Perceval provided some superficial details about what was presently going on in his life. He was surprised how much he was enjoying himself in this feminine world. Only Toby excused himself once his dish was empty and returned to snooze on his bed.

When everything was cleared away, Bron put on her jacket. From one of the shelves by the steps, she took a blue baseball cap, around which was fixed an LED headlamp. 'I'll take Toby out for a walk now. Alex, you stay on, have another glass of wine and I'll see you later. As Jo told you, we rarely have the company of a young man.'

'Or any man,' Jo added.

'Or any man,' Bron repeated firmly.

Perceval was about to say his farewells and go too, but the thought of his empty boat made him hesitate.

'Don't run off,' Bron interpreted his hesitation. 'Jo will keep you company.' Bron put some more wood in the stove then from a shelf she took down an oblong tin, examined a couple of roll ups, and put them in her jacket pocket. Putting the collar and lead on Toby, she took the dog out to the canal by the foredeck.

Unsure what he should do, Perceval stood uncomfortably in the middle of the saloon, starting slightly when Jo put a hand on his arm. She raised her other hand demonstratively.

'I know just the thing for you,' she said. 'I think you'll find it very helpful.'

Chapter Eight

A tarot reading? Perceval had never had a tarot reading before. His mother's residual Sunday school view of life had seen to that. After his father's murder, disillusionment with her own 'before' meant she stopped going to church as regularly as she once did, finding little solace in the liturgy or meaning in the sacraments. Unlike Chesterton's remark that losing your faith in God meant believing in anything rather than nothing, Perceval's mother was never seduced by esoteric mysticism, never tempted to access a spiritual realm 'beyond', and never wished to discover what was written for her in the stars. Her own communion with the dead was intensely personal. He remembered a remark when they were watching television and a documentary on Aleister Crowley was announced. 'Oh, turn that rubbish off, Alex. Why am I paying my licence fee for this nonsense? Mediums, fortune-tellers, tarot card readers, they are all deceivers. It's all stuff and nonsense. There's no good in it, there's no truth in it. Never turn to mediums or necromancers and don't seek them out, they are an abomination. Really it is the Devil's work.'

Perceval had promised easily because spiritualism of any sort he considered mumbo jumbo. His own religious faith (perfunctory and cultural rather than deeply felt and personal) was sufficient because he could keep it at a distance, stored safely in church and bible, accessible if and when needed (like his mother's funeral rites and burial). He was superstitious enough by nature, though, and suggestible about otherworldly things. However, his mother's words returned to him now as Jo offered him a reading.

'I had a feeling over dinner that you were burdened by something in your past, something perhaps you were not fully conscious of.' Jo put her head to one side and looked at him like his greatest desire should be to explore with her this dimly perceived trouble. He was taken aback and withdrew from her slightly. Perceval could tell she was conscious of his uncertainty, and he considered his reaction both discourteous and ungrateful. Would his mother not expect him to show appreciation and to acknowledge indebtedness to Jo's kindness? What had he got to lose? He didn't think his soul was going to be forfeited or his spirit imprisoned in the hull of *The Flower Maidens*.

'Sorry, only your suggestion took me by surprise. A tarot reading would be another first for me. Bron was laughing at me for being a canal boat virgin ...'

'Oh, she would, that's the sort of thing she does.'

'... well, I'm a tarot card virgin too.'

'You know what they say, Alex. There's a first time for everything.'

'Do they also say it's the first reading that counts?'

'That's up to you to find out,' Jo beamed.

From a narrow chest of drawers beside the sofa, Jo took out a blue, velvet-soft, merino cloth, spread it across the table and smoothed it out. She told Perceval to sit down while she fetched her cards, returning from the bedroom with a latticed wooden box, engraved with moon and star and which, to his eye, looked old and worn. Jo sat down close beside him and their arms touched briefly. She opened the box, extracted the deck of cards which was wrapped in a white cotton cloth and set it the full deck in front of them.

'Alex, I'm not a fortune teller, I'm not a medium, and I'm certainly not Mystic Meg,' she smiled, her voice playful rather than solemn. 'The cards are about helping you think more clearly about yourself, to encourage you to ask questions about your own journey, in life as well as on this canal. Let's hope you can find some answers.'

'My mother always told me not to ask questions,' Perceval said, thinking these words sounded silly. 'You know, like the old saying "whatever you say, say nothing". It's a way of avoiding trouble, I suppose.'

'That's one wisdom in life for sure,' Jo replied, without elaborating on whether it was an appropriate wisdom. 'Remember, Alex, the cards can never lie because you' – she touched his hand, and he felt again the metal of the rings on his knuckles – 'are the one reading *yourself* into *them* and *their* message into *your* life. They provide a mirror to reflect on who you are, what may ail you, what may drive you, what you wish for, what you fear. Rest assured, I'm not a priestess awaiting your confession. I'm only helping you to see more clearly what, at some level, you know already.'

'I see,' Perceval said, but wasn't certain that he did.

'Yes, you *will* see. Now, ask yourself a question you wish to answer, a general question, a why, where or how question.'

Perceval nodded. He thought to himself he might as well ask two for the price one. He asked: 'How can I navigate *Knight Errant* successfully to Llangollen? What will I discover along the way?' He took a moment, thinking this would show Jo he was taking the reading, and her, seriously then looked to confirm he'd done what she'd told him to do.

'Good. Now shuffle the cards as you would any other pack.'

This was something he did know how to do. His mother had been keen on gin rummy and, until he went off to university, sometimes Perceval had played with her on long winter evenings. She'd told him she and his father used to play it, and he couldn't deny her that pleasure, even if, to his shame, he thought it rather macabre. Having shuffled the cards, Jo ordered him to cut the pack three ways and reset them how he wished.

'Now, fan out the cards in front of you, face down. Look at them carefully and concentrate on your question.'

Perceval did a mental shuffle of his own, back and forth between his two questions.

'We can begin the reading. Pick one card, one which seems to leap out at you, and slide it forward.'

'Just one?'

She nodded.

None did leap out at him and, rather than appearing to act randomly, for Jo's benefit again he let his hand hover above the cards, this way and then that, before sliding one out. Jo picked up the card and then looked at him with a smile. She set the card face down then turned it over. 'You've drawn the Fool.'

'My mother used to say that in our violent and corrupt world it's better to be a fool and remain innocent than to be clever and become corrupted.' It was true. She had said that.

'Your mother sounds like a smart woman, Alex. The card isn't about foolishness as the world knows it, so your mother knows what she's talking about. It is *not* a sign of wisdom always to be wise as the world knows it. The card symbolizes a beginning, for you if you wish to take it. Yes … as the card shows, you are stepping into the unknown and that is, or can be, unsettling. It's not about the canal journey alone but something deeper in life, for you, like me, like all of us, are part of its unpredictable dance. The Fool embodies the eternal recurrence of beginning afresh. The Fool, as you see, is a youth. Is the little dog at his heels warning against or encouraging this new beginning? You notice the youth's small knapsack, telling you that he, or she, carries little baggage. You know, not encumbered by much experience.'

'Well, physically I suppose that's right. I came here with only a rucksack. And I guess I am inexperienced. But I'm not sure if it's quite right emotionally.' Perceval was uncomfortable about saying anything further about his past and his eye caught the little dog leaping at the Fool's feet. 'Maybe the dog is Toby. He was like a herald of rescue to me earlier.'

'You could say this little Toby,' Jo tapped the card, 'represents your intuition, a warning or an encouragement. Maybe he prevents you walking off the cliff? Maybe he encourages you to be adventurous? Do you see the Fool is holding a white rose and wearing a laurel wreath? These suggest innocence is not mere naivety but also its own kind of knowledge in itself, potentially leading to success.'

'It didn't feel that way earlier when Bron saved me from disaster.'

'Alex don't be defeatist! You will gain knowledge as you go along. Look at the card again. It's saying you're on the edge of something new and not just on this canal journey. You are about to make discoveries, about yourself, about life. The card is telling you to be open to others and to trust yourself, to have faith in your own intuitions. The fool is taking a risk, yes, but you need to take a risk sometimes to find what you're searching for.'

'I'm not sure what I *am* searching for.'

'Exactly, Alex! It's about finding clarity, even if it seems "foolish" to others, even if the path is uncertain. But remember that success and failure are sprinkled over life like dew drops.'

'So, it doesn't mean I'm a fool to have embarked on this canal journey?' He almost added 'without knowing how to tie a knot'.

'Call me not fool till heaven hath sent me fortune,' Jo whispered.

When Perceval looked confused, she explained, 'Those are the words of the court jester, in Shakespeare's *As You Like It*.' She tilted the card slightly for emphasis. 'People are too ready to judge and write off others without a thought. You can even do it to yourself … as a canal boat virgin.' She smiled and tapped his hand once more. 'I repeat. Sometimes you need to have confidence in your inner qualities, Alex. Don't write *yourself* off. Heaven, I'm sure, will send you fortune, but only if you're willing to seize it.'

'The Lord helps those who help themselves, you mean?'

'Yes, you could very well say that. Indeed so,' she laughed, paused, and put her hands together as if in prayer. 'Choose two cards this time,' she told him. 'Slide them out one by one as before. Let's see if they provide some further guidance, shall we?'

Perceval went through the motions of selection, though more genuinely this time. He pushed his chosen card towards Jo. She turned over the first and then the second, putting a hand on one, then on the other, as if extracting their meaning into her body.

'Hmmm,' she said and pondered the two cards a little longer. 'The second card represents what tests your journey. The third is what you might do about it.'

Perceval waited, curious now, his vanity in play.

'Our natures are paradoxical, Alex. The cards you've drawn reveal a paradox. All things keep continually running into mystery. You can tell me if I'm wrong … or not say anything, as your mother might advise.'

'What's the paradox? '

'The first card is the Eight of Swords. As you see it depicts a blindfolded woman surrounded by swords and imprisoned by them. Of course, as you know, prisons can be mental as well as actual. And they're not only for us women! "The mind is its own place and in itself can make a heaven of hell, a hell of heaven". That's Milton. And he was right. Your mind shapes reality, Alex. Of course it does. Your thoughts are the key to whatever confinement you may feel. Do you feel stuck? No, don't answer.' She held up her hand. 'Reflect on it. For maybe in life you overthink, fearing failure, doubting your own judgement, relying on others to take the initiative, hesitant to commit to anything because you can't foresee all the consequences?' She paused and tapped the first card once more. 'Perhaps, like the Fool you should become the agent of your own fate and challenge your comfortable limits?'

'And the other card is different?'

'The Knight of Cups.' Jo smiled. 'The young knight on the white horse with a golden chalice, everything calm and steady, romantic and dreamlike, free too, his eyes on the cup aloft … you as the Knight Errant perhaps? The card is associated with idealism and emotional depth. As you see, he's not charging aggressively but moving forward gracefully, His demeanour suggests introspection, charm and sensitivity. Possibly he is a listener, someone who understands and is trustworthy, but can be lost in reveries … or impractical, someone not good at tying knots perhaps?'

Perceval laughed. 'That does sound like me, the last bit anyway. The bit which suggests I'm totally useless.'

Jo held up a hand again. 'Don't be so negative, Alex. This card is possibly how *others* see you. You strike me as sensitive and attentive. But let's see what the following card has to say.'

She invited him to select the fourth card. He did so, and she turned it over.

'Ha!' she said. 'Just as I thought. The Five of Pentacles. Alex I'm not surprised. Here's another of your paradoxes.'

'I never considered myself so complicated.'

'We are all complicated. Perhaps you don't wish to admit your complications. The Five of Pentacles represents the outsider, someone who feels alone despite the presence of others. It tells me that, though people like and trust you and, despite believing you a companionable Knight of Cups, you, yourself, never quite feel part of things. Like the woman figure in the Eight of Swords, you feel yourself excluded … or maybe you exclude yourself? You can feel yourself emotionally lacking, on the edge of the comfort others feel, or appear to feel, observing, but not fully experiencing, their sociability.'

'I did feel part of things, once,' Perceval said, more to himself than to Jo.

She studied the cards together for a moment. 'Alex, you have charm, and you have courtesy. You are honourable, decent, and likeable, you are "clubbable" as toffs used to say. You know all this, and yet you feel on the outside looking in. Others warm to you, but you feel yourself cold.'

Jo had said at the beginning that the cards didn't lie. They only held up a mirror to those who wish to look. Perceval did feel he was looking into Jo's mirror and could see himself more clearly than before.

'Is your "keep your distance" default – and this may sound presumptuous of me – preventing you finding love?' Jo asked. 'Has your experience of "before" made you think that emotional connection is impossible?' Perceval was on the brink of mumbling words he knew would embarrass him but Jo was intelligent enough to prevent him. 'Don't answer me directly,' she whispered. 'Only think about the questions. Now, the Five of Pentacles depicts two desperate figures struggling past a warmly lit building. They are *literally* out in the cold. Maybe help exists, but they can't see it, you can't see it? The Knight of Cups tells me you have much to offer, even if you don't think yourself worthy. Remember, Alex, there's no need for you to be an outsider in your own story. It's your journey ahead, you are the one making his own way, impressing people you meet, as you've impressed Bron and me.' Perceval raised his eyebrows at this. 'Oh yes, you *do* impress. Don't deny it, Alex, so why not give more of yourself? And take more from life too ... sorry, that's me back talking like a schoolmistress. But a schoolmistress can be right, you know!'

'I don't doubt it. And thank you.'

'You're not finished yet, young man. One more card to draw and then I'll let you out of detention. This time close your eyes and think of your future.'

Perceval did so, touched a card and Jo extracted it from the rest. 'What did I get?' He opened his eyes and was excited now.

Jo shielded the card from him. 'And this is how your life *might* unfold. You won't solve all your problems or resolve your paradoxes. They are who you are, after all. The question is this. Will you permit yourself to be open to life? This canal journey, about which you feel doubt and anxiety, is an opportunity to find out. Think of it as your quest .When you get to Llangollen, and you will, I expect you'll be able to judge things much better.'

'And the card is?'

'The Lovers. Young people, even old people like me, are delighted to see The Lovers. Who doesn't want love, Alex! But it's really about choice and engagement with *life*. Passion, yes, relationships, yes, but there is vulnerability too, all the random tempest of the emotions. Love, to be realised, requires *you* to make a choice. It requires *you* to show compassion.' Jo touched his hand again, and Perceval nodded but said nothing. Instead, he looked to Jo for an interpretation. She held his eyes for a moment which made him uncomfortable.

'Wisdom and love, Alex. Don't we wish they were found together and not at odds? Do you know Shelley's line? "The wise want love; and those who love want wisdom"?' Perceval shook his head. 'Well, that line captures the paradox in our nature which your cards symbolise. Shelley uses "want" in the old sense of what we "lack". Wisdom can leave you yearning for the immediacy of love, while love may overwhelm judgment with emotion and make you act irrationally. Shelley knew that wisdom and love in isolation are incomplete.' Jo looked to the cards again. 'Maybe you do feel it wise to observe life rather than be involved in its messiness? Or maybe you do feel adrift and desire life to be shaken up a bit?'

'You know when you were talking earlier about your life "before" and after, how "after", being with Bron, on the boat like this, was so much better than what you both knew?' Jo's face showed genuine pleasure that he'd remembered her words.

'For me, it is the opposite. When I was at university, I found a world that I loved. It was also a world that I felt I could grow wise in. Today I feel that I lack both love *and* wisdom.'

'"Let us not burden our remembrances with a heaviness that's gone",' Jo said. 'I'm sorry, Alex, I'm probably boring you with all these quotes. It's my "before" as a teacher haunting me,' she laughed. 'It's Prospero in *The Tempest*. I hope there will be no tempest before you reach Llangollen.' She laughed again. 'The message of the cards is that you shouldn't *allow* regrets about something lost to burden your present. Rather than clinging to the past, however beautiful, you should seek renewal. Can you accept that some things are gone for good? Not necessarily for the better, Alex, but just gone?' Jo intuited his indecision. 'Your decisions need both heart and reason. Don't lack wisdom and don't lack love, Alex. Don't be trapped by your misgivings. Do take courage from your own abilities. Most importantly, be the agent of your own fate.'

When she'd said these things, Jo's eyes shone brightly, like she'd completed a difficult task. Just as suddenly, Perceval had the impression her energy was spent. She grasped both his hands like someone fearing they were about fall. She let go, sat back, and, placing both hands face down on the tablecloth, signalled finality. 'I hope you found my reading interesting,' Jo said quietly, picking up her glass and draining the last of the wine. 'And remember, Alex. These paradoxes I talked of, they aren't character flaws. They are who *you* are, sources of strength as much as sources of weakness. As Bron showed you how to knot your mooring rope, your contrasts can weave together to provide stability. You can be rooted without becoming stuck, open without being aimless.'

'I will remember,' he told her. 'Thank you.'

Shortly after Jo had cleared away the cards and table covering, Bron came into the saloon with Toby. The dog went straight to his bed, curling up like a cinnamon bun, and Bron began poking around the embers in the stove. In the time she'd been away (and Perceval was surprised it had been over an hour) the previously toasty temperature had dropped considerably. For once, he hadn't noticed the cold. Bron threw in some kindling, waited for it to catch fire then added a couple of logs. When she stood up, she told them she'd been sitting out on the bow deck for the last minutes of the reading, not wanting to disturb, and apologised for overhearing Jo's final words.

'Alex, I thought you might appreciate this,' Bron said. She pulled from her jacket pocket, a small strand of rope which she'd tied into a knot and handed it to him. 'It's a memento of our meeting, a memento of Jo's reading, and a memento of *The Flower Maidens*. There are some things in life you shouldn't untangle and some you should. Remember what Jo told you. To be attached doesn't mean you can't be free.' Bron smiled at Jo then seemed unusually self-conscious about saying something half-way philosophical. In a matter of fact tone she added, 'And when you walk back to your boat, remember not to trip over the mooring ropes ...'

'Ah, so wonderful of you, Bron,' Jo exclaimed, and to Perceval she said, 'Alex, it is your knot intrinsicate!' Both looked at her, uncertain what she meant. 'Forgive me. It's Shakespeare once more. We would say today deeply interwoven, inextricably entangled.'

'I love that word,' Perceval said. 'Intrinsicate. I must commit it to memory.' He cradled Bron's gift in the palm of his hand. 'This knot intrinsicate. You've been so kind to me. I really don't know what to say except thank you both.'

PART THREE: THE QUEST

Chapter Nine

Aᴛᴇʀ the warmth and comfort of *The Flower Maidens*, *Knight Errant* was chill and barren. He thought Jo had been shrewd in her reading of the cards and even more so in her reading of him. Then again, he had possibly disclosed to her enough about himself for Jo to intuit the peculiarities (or paradoxes) of his character. Were they peculiarities, though? He recalled their Latin teacher who used to say, when a pupil gave an apparently unique excuse for not handing in home-work, '*Homo sum, humani nihil a me alienum puto*' adding for edification to the miscreant, 'That's Terence by the way. And yes, I have heard your excuse before.' Maybe Jo read cards on the same understanding of human nature. And they didn't lie because Perceval had traits everyone shared. Nevertheless, he did feel more confident about the journey ahead. As he fell asleep, he didn't believe, as his mother had warned, he'd been party to the Devil's work.

During the night, though, he feared his mother may have been right. Despite the light duvet he'd found onboard, despite his need to curl up like Toby's cinnamon bun, despite keeping on his socks, despite all these ways of warding off the cold, Perceval sweated profusely and uncharacteristically through an anxious night of alarming dreams.

One found him in a fog so profound that he couldn't anticipate the shape of the canal ahead. He bumped off bridges, steered into banks, and scraped against mysterious obstructions in the water. When he reached a lock, he couldn't shift the gates no matter how hard he tried. The paddles were rusted, and his windlass was broken. In the meantime, the ropes holding *Knight*

Errant had slipped loose and he could only watch helplessly as the boat was dragged by the current into a vortex of churning water. Meanwhile, a host of gongoozlers, men and women, stood at the lock laughing at his distress.

This was followed by a dream about a tunnel. As he entered, its walls shrank, stopping the boat dead. He was trapped and could see no way of exiting. In another, a boat approached on an open canal, but Perceval lost control and threatened to collide head on. The other skipper cursed him and thrust a bargepole forward like a jousting knight. Perceval was hit full on the chest and catapulted into the canal. Even when he woke, sweating, not sure of where he was, and fell back to sleep again, the dreams continued relentlessly, a series of repeated humiliations. When he finally awoke fully, he felt unrested. Checking his watch, the time was already 9.30 and Wednesday beckoned.

After a lukewarm shower, he pulled on his clothes, slid open the hatch and climbed the steps onto the transom. *The Flower Maidens* had gone. Perceval thought he might have heard its engine starting or the boat chugging by. He would have liked to have said farewell, or at least to wave a greeting as Jo and Bron went by. All was silent and the world was hushed. A few ducks swam back and forth noiselessly, no one passed on the towpath, and in the fields, sheep safely grazed. He supposed it was for this kind of quiet people gravitated to the canal. But right at this moment, and like the sensation of embracing darkness the night before, he found it eerie. A sudden breeze blew through the branches of the trees and brought down a shower of dead leaves. It sounded as if they were whispering to him. Perceval wondered what secrets of the earth they were trying to tell him. Were they whispering the word 'fool'? Or were they telling him 'have courage'?

The morning was overcast, leaden, but the air was fresh. His mood changed with a cup of tea and some toast. He felt revived, thinking the nightmares may have exorcised his terrors and, hoping he wasn't tempting fate, Perceval felt eager to resume. The engine fired promptly into life. First success of the day, he told himself. He grabbed the centre line as Bron had advised and stepped off *Knight Errant*. Attaching it to one of mooring rings, he undid the ropes bow and stern and tossed them onto the decks. He'd coil them later. He undid the centre line and stepped back onboard. Second success of the day. He engaged the throttle in reverse and slowly moved off from the bank into the middle of the canal. Once clear, he put the engine into forward gear and pushed the tiller correctly to swing the boat straight. Third success of the day. The water's surface rippled at the boat's passage. The only sounds were the gentle lap of water against the hull and the steady chug of the engine. Perceval began to relax. His hand formerly tense, rested more easily on the tiller. Yesterday *Knight Errant* had seemed like a questing beast which, in his nightmares he had failed to tame. But right now he had things under control, or believed he had.

He passed under a bridge without mishap and rounded the bend onto a straight stretch of water. The banks here were reedy rather than tree-lined, though the water remained dappled with dead leaves, agitated only by the turning of the propeller. Beyond the banks, verdant Shropshire lay in early winter somnolence, rising only slightly to the horizon. It was still autumn, dressed in faded golds and ambers, not yet the pewter greys of winter. This was an English landscape shaped by measured lines of cultivation and civilisation, yet beyond it was the suggestion of something wilder and untamed.

Quite soon he did see another boat coming towards him. Port to port, he reminded himself and gently steered *Knight Errant* towards the right bank, easily enough because the canal at this point was much wider than before. As he neared, Perceval reduced speed. There was a portly middle-aged man at the tiller, wearing a wide brimmed tan bush hat and beside him, leaning against the rail, a middle-aged woman in a matching bush hat. They waved to him, and he waved back. As their boats crossed, the man called out. 'We've just come through the lock. There's no boat behind. The wife saw you as we came out and left the gates open.' The woman gave another wave as if to confirm that not only was she the wife and but also that she'd done what her husband said.

'Oh, thank you. I was worried about going through on my own.'

'There's an old boy there,' Perceval heard the man call as the couple headed away. 'He'll give you a hand. He helped us.'

'Nice man,' the wife shouted, 'but a sad story.'

Perceval raised his arm in acknowledgement of the information, wondering what she meant.

Approaching New Marton Bottom Lock he could see the gates still open as he'd been told. Slightly forward of the lock at the bottom of a grassy slope was a landing and standing at its edge was a man, small but sturdily built, grey bearded, dressed in an olive army jacket with matching fatigues, on his head a black woollen beanie. He waved for Perceval to come towards the mooring point. Cautiously, Perceval swung across the canal and corrected sharply to line up *Knight Errant* to the bank, reversing throttle to bring the boat to a halt. Yet another success.

The old man came alongside and nodded a greeting. His face was deeply lined and weathered. Straggling from under his beanie fell strands of greasy silver hair. His eyes were morose, and he gave Perceval an appraising look. 'Need help with the lock?' he asked. The words were said expressionlessly, and Perceval couldn't detect an accent. It was obvious the man believed the answer to his question could only be yes. His uncle had warned him to be careful of people offering help with lock gates. 'Often they didn't know what they're doing and can get you into trouble. They may be well-intentioned, but we all know where good intentions can lead, don't we?' he'd reminded Perceval on the phone, sounding at that moment just like his mother. However, Perceval was prepared to take the risk on the kindness of strangers or, rather, the competence of strangers. After all, the man had been recommended to him, and he wagered he'd been lucky in all things this morning already, so why not now.

'That would be great, thanks.'

'Hand me your windlass, then,' the man said.

Perceval took it from the shelving just inside the hatch and leaned across to hand it over. There were two windlasses on the boat. If he did a runner, Perceval reckoned he'd still be okay.

'Take your boat into the chamber.'

His direction assumed Perceval was familiar with the process, an assumption at once pleasing and slightly alarming. He thought he should be honest. 'This is my first time going through a lock,' he admitted sheepishly.

'Let's hope you live and learn, then.' The words were said with a poker-face. The man gestured for Perceval to head on and strolled up the slope, swinging the windlass. By the time he'd steered to the entrance of the slimy, stone-walled chamber, the man was already at the gates. Despite Perceval's watchful manoeuvring, *Knight Errant* bumped its way in to the lock chamber.

'Watch out! Careful now!' the man called above the engine's throb and when Perceval had come to a halt, he added 'Touch your throttle now and then to make sure you don't drift back onto the sill ... or get caught on the front gates.' He moved with surprising spriteliness to close first one and then the other lower gates. 'I'm going to open the paddles now,' he called. 'I'll do it slowly at first. Keep the boat steady as the water comes in.'

It didn't take long for the water to raise *Knight Errant* to the upper level and the man opened the top gates. Perceval exited smoothly and pulled over to the mooring, thinking he should probably give the man a tenner.

'The top lock is only half a mile on. I have my bike here and can go ahead. I'll help you through again.' The man wasn't asking. He was telling. He cycled to the mooring and handed back the windlass. 'Saves me carrying it,' he said.

'Thanks, I really do appreciate it.'

'It keeps me busy.' The man wobbled off slowly on his bicycle which looked like he'd found it abandoned somewhere and fixed up.

When Perceval reached New Marton Upper Lock, he discovered a beautiful old whitewashed lockkeeper's cottage shaded by weeping willows. The lower gates had been opened already as before and he was able to glide in easily this time. His assistant was waiting there and Perceval passed him the windlass.

'Same again,' the man called, closing the gates behind *Knight Errant*. And it was the same again, but smoother this time. As the boat emerged through the upper gate, the man pointed to a bridge close by the lock and told Perceval to moor up at the water point on the far side. 'There are few boats this time of year. You're only the second one I've seen this morning. Don't imagine you'll be in the way of someone wanting to fill up. Wait there and I'll bring over your windlass.'

Perceval tied up to bollards on the towpath by the water point with a mixture of relief and pleasure. He remembered the little keepsake Bron had given him and took it out of his pocket. What had she said? Attached as well as free? Life felt that way today, for sure. He saw the man pedal over the bridge and freewheel down towards him. Perceval searched for his wallet in the inside pocket of his jacket. He cursed when he realised the only banknotes he had were Ulster Bank. They were sterling, legal tender and all that, but there was always the chance, as Perceval knew from experience, that shops here might not accept them. He would make the offer anyway.

'Your windlass,' the man said, dismounting from his bike, and handing it over.

'Thanks a lot. Look, I really should pay you for all your help.'

The man put up his hands. 'No money,' he said emphatically but without any edge of offence. 'The most insupportable evil is that of doing nothing. And you've given me the opportunity to do something.' The man paused and said, 'You're not from these parts.'

When Perceval told him where he was from, he said. 'I'm not from these parts either. I'm from Manchester originally. But I like these borderlands … they suit me, especially when you're on the margins like me.'

Perceval didn't know how to respond. Then he recalled Jo's words about being compassionate. 'That doesn't sound too good,' he said as compassionately as he could.

'I usually take payment by people listening to my story and asking them a bit about themselves. It helps me think that I'm still part of the world.' This wasn't said as a joke, Perceval realised. 'The couple, the ones who went through the lock before you,' the man went on. 'They're on a second honeymoon. Both have retired and decided to start as if afresh. That's a nice story, don't you think?'

Perceval nodded, 'I do, yes.' If it had been him (which he couldn't imagine right now), he and his wife (whom he couldn't imagine either), second honeymoon or not, would be in a good hotel, somewhere warm, and not on a narrowboat on the borders of England and Wales.

'You can make me a cup of tea, and I can tell my story,' the man went on. 'It won't take long. And you can tell me what brings you alone to the Llangollen Canal in November.'

Chapter Ten

'I'M sorry I can offer you only tea,' Perceval said as he set down the mug on the table in front of the man. 'I'm low on provisions.'

He waved away Perceval's apology and held out his calloused hand. 'My name is Tristan.'

'Alex.'

'So, tell me, Alex, what brings you to the Llangollen Canal?'

Perceval gave him a summary of his uncle's request. Tristan didn't look at him as he spoke but at his steaming mug of tea around which he'd cupped his hands. It made Perceval slightly uncomfortable. He wondered if it had been wise to invite him onboard. How was he going to get rid of him politely? And as he spoke, his eye drifted to the heavy windlass left on top of the galley cupboard, a self-protective instinct his upbringing had encouraged. He finished his story by joking, 'I hope fortune rewards me for my good deed.'

Tristan grunted. Still contemplating his tea, he shook his head and for some moments he said nothing. He exhaled slowly, making Perceval uneasy once more, and his glance strayed to the windlass again.

'You're young, Alex. A hard lesson you'll find is there is no reward for doing good. There is only punishment for doing bad … or for the bad that people accuse you of doing. Let me tell you a story which may change your mind about notions of good and bad.' Though he spoke directly to Perceval, it seemed that Tristan's eyes were fixed on a vision far beyond him. 'I didn't always live as I do now. I didn't always look as I do now. And I'm not really all that old, though people assume I am.'

Tristan ran fingers through his beard then indicated his soiled clothing. He held up his rough hands with their grimy nails. 'These were soft once, clean and spotless, sensitive with the delicate assurance of the expert.' He cupped his hands around his tea again. 'I'm sure you must have wondered – who's this sad old bastard with nothing better to do than hang about the canals looking for company?' He saw that Perceval was about to contradict him. 'Don't feel obliged to be polite. I have no illusions about the judgement of the world ...' He smiled ruefully. 'Just hear me out if you will.' He took another sip of tea. 'Believe it or not, I was at one time a doctor, a partner in a private practice in Didsbury. Do you know Didsbury?' Perceval shook his head. 'Let's say it is on the affluent side of Manchester. It was a great place to live. It was a great practice to work in. I was good at my job, well respected by colleagues, and trusted by my patients. I had a loving wife, two beautiful children who never wanted for anything, and the sort of house estate agents would call "high end". You could say I was a pillar of the community, on the parent-teacher association of our kids' primary school, a churchwarden if you can believe it. You could also say that in my life and in my career, I always made the right choices. I never did a wrong thing and never strayed from the straight and narrow.' Tristan took a deep breath. 'Have you ever seen the film *Brief Encounter*?'

Perceval had seen it because his mother loved it. On Amazon he'd found a ridiculously cheap DVD and bought it for her birthday one year. It had been, as they say, one of his better decisions. She'd been delighted in such a girlish way, and he was glad she had no idea how little it had cost him. They'd watched it together that same evening. He'd been put off by the cut glass English accents, but could appreciate the sentimental storyline. His mother had wept at the end. He had never forgotten her telling him this film reminded her of his father. 'My brief time with your father was taken away from me, from us,' she'd spoken through her tears. 'But he had no way of coming back. I had no way of coming back, either.' That night Perceval had learned the meaning of *lacrimae rerum*, a phrase from Virgil which the Latin master hadn't been able to get the class to understand. What he said to Tristan was, 'I have seen it, yes.'

'I don't suppose you remember Doctor Harvey's line about GPs needing a sense of vocation, a "deep-rooted, unsentimental desire to do good"?' Perceval shook his head again. 'That was me. I had an unsentimental desire to do good. That was how I saw my vocation too. I still do. Before, others thought it of me too. After, when I met Iseult, it all changed.' Tristan put up his hands immediately those words were out of his mouth. 'Don't get me wrong, Alex. In my own mind *nothing* had changed. I still desired to do good. I thought I *was* doing good. But that's not how the world saw it. The world denounced me for doing wrong. It didn't feel that way at the time. It doesn't feel that way now either. Who should trust the wisdom of this world, Alex? You're young and don't realise how cruel it can be. The world has a lifetime of trouble for you when it mistakes false for true. It will destroy you for loving and will celebrate you for hating. And like Job, I have suffered so much. Suffering never ennobles or refines. It only breaks you, and no doctor can heal your broken heart. You could say I was done to death by slanderous tongues. Losing my vocation was a form of death.'

Tristan said nothing for a while. Perceval wasn't sure if his 'after' was too painful to relate and was about to say something banal but his instinctive caution stopped him.

'Iseult was a patient,' Tristan continued, 'who'd come to me with a persistent problem which hadn't resolved after numerous visits to her NHS doctor. She was seeking a second opinion. When I listened to her speak of her symptoms and after I examined her, I was certain her condition was serious. I referred her to a consultant who confirmed my suspicion. Her diagnosis was terminal. I was only providing professional care and the kind of human sympathy which such professionalism requires. I treated her like I would any other patient. And yet … it was her wonderful spirit in facing death so gracefully which touched me. Our conversations went beyond her medical condition and the little that could be done. She was a classical musician. I used to sing in the church choir. We talked about music as much as we did her treatment. Here's the truth. Her dying created new possibilities for living, for both of us, however short her life would be.' He broke off and looked at Perceval. 'Do you like classical music, Alex?'

He felt too ashamed to admit his ignorance of classical music and lied. 'Yes, of course.'

'If music is the food of love, Alex … we all know that old line. It can express feelings in the way that words can't.' This was something Perceval really did understand. 'Shakespeare was wise enough to know that too much might dull the passions. In our case there was no "if". Iseult and I did fall in love. Not in a reckless, wanton way for that was impossible, but in a soul-deep way that neither of us could have expected or would even have chosen if things were different. Iseult was divorced, had no children, no family that she could call upon. I wanted to make the rest of her short life as beautiful as I possibly could. I knew what people might think but I couldn't help it. Love has its own gravity, and I couldn't resist.' Tristan paused and said more quietly, 'Then came "after". What you see today is what "after" created.' He pushed the empty tea mug away. 'You seem a bright lad, Alex. I'm sure you can anticipate most of what I'm going to say. I did what I thought was right but what everyone else thought was wrong. I was accused of violating professional ethics, of taking advantage of a vulnerable woman, of betraying my wife and children. A local newspaper made out that I was a sort of serial philanderer and Iseult may have been one of many. I mean, how obscene is that? No one accepted the truth. I lost everything, family, career, everything. I lost Iseult too, of course.'

How could Perceval not feel sorry for Tristan? Yet how could anyone express that sympathy sufficiently? There are wounds which never heal. He was his mother's son and he said nothing.

'And this is how you find me, Alex, haunting the canal alone. This is how you find me, outside normal society, living like a hermit and choosing solitude as a fitting punishment for doing right. The world does not forgive compassion. It can erase a life dedicated to doing good. And what remains? Penance I have done and penance more to do.'

'How do you manage?' Perceval meant the practicalities of existence for he knew too well the emotional misery of such a life.

'A local farmer lets me live in a run-down cottage that's part of an old stable. His son had an accident working on the engine of a tractor. By chance I was passing, looking to beg work. I attended to him, possibly saved his arm, and the father let me stay. I do odd jobs, sometimes I give the farmer and his family medical advice for free. But at some point, I'm sure, he will turn the cottage into a holiday let. He's spoken of it already. That's where the money is these days, so who can blame him?'

On the towpath, a man and woman cycled past, laughing companionably. Perceval's thoughts followed them and his only wish was to be underway again. But the memory of leaving his mother for England, that paradox of liberation and guilt he felt, returned and he felt shame for wishing rid of Tristan.

'Here's the moral of this story if moral is the right word,' Tristan concluded. 'In the ill-fortune which the world brings, the most unfortunate man is the one who once was happy. Do the right things all your life, Alex, and one act, however well-intentioned, however much of a good deed you believe it to be, can destroy your life. Fate is a heartless trap.'

Both sat in silence for some seconds. The image Perceval had now was of the Five of Pentacles he'd drawn from Jo's pack. In front of him sat the beggar cast out and hungry for human sympathy.

Tristan shrugged. 'I know you're probably eager to be off and I won't stay any longer.' He stood up and stamped his feet as if to get circulation back into his legs. It was indeed cold on the boat, Perceval realised, shivering suddenly himself. 'There is much evil in this world, too much … there may be hope for others. But not for me. Take care of yourself, Alex. And good luck.'

Perceval waved to Tristan as he cycled off over the bridge and onto the towpath towards the lower lock. Was he hoping for another opportunity to tell of his fate? Would others have the consideration to hear him out? If they did, would they feel as Perceval did now? Would they feel relieved of another's burden but thankful for the blessings of their own minor problems? As he undid the centre line and jumped back on *Knight Errant*, he thought of his own unmoored existence, his solitude, his lack of love, his drift. Wasn't the knot Bron had given him a symbol of connection. Wasn't her gift a truth he now carried with him? Unaccountably, *paradoxically*, Tristan's tale had given Perceval hope.

Chapter Eleven

On his uncle's map, he traced with a finger the line of the Llangollen Canal towards the town of Chirk. It was too far to reach today, he thought, but at least getting close was an objective. He was hungry, but what remained of his groceries didn't appeal. He would push on. There were a few pubs ahead and he was sure they would have more appealing options (he could almost taste the fish and chips and savour the pint of beer he would order). He smiled at the thought and shouted, 'Anchors aweigh!' to an empty towpath as he pulled out from the watering point.

The afternoon was hushed in a grey stillness, the clouds low, unbroken, and the light pale. It had become unseasonably mild as late autumn bled slowly into winter and Perceval was grateful for the absence of rain. Branches along the bank stirred in a gentle breeze and only a few leaves weaved and fell. He felt as if the day was holding its breath and expecting something of him. To one side of the canal, marshy land gave way to rolling ground, beyond which, on the far horizon, he could now see low hills. That was Wales, he presumed. On the other side was lush pasture empty of grazing animals. He did spot a few horses standing idly by wooden fences, some with blankets and some without. The countryside appeared somnolent, not exactly melancholic, but meditative.

In his own dreamy, reflective mood Perceval was on autopilot, a sign, he thought, of new-found confidence. Rounding a gentle bend, he saw a boat coming down. Port to Port, he reminded himself, adjusted the tiller and realised he'd pushed the wrong way again. He pushed desperately in the opposite direction, over-corrected and had to pull back to avoid the bank. He managed just about to be in line as the appropriately named *Narrow Escape* passed by. Its skipper, partially obscured by a protective canvas canopy, ignored him entirely, either out of contempt or possibly to avoid having to acknowledge Perceval's embarrassment.

His concentration had been lulled and a cricketing memory returned. A coach had told the team that commitment, belief, even energy, may not always be there but the important thing was discipline. 'So long as you maintain discipline,' he'd said, 'commitment, belief and energy will return. Self-talk,' he went on. 'Self-talk. When you begin to wilt, say to yourself: "Focus! Focus!" Okay, lads,' he'd concluded, 'that's what you got to hold on to – your discipline.' Perceval told himself to hold on to his discipline. He would tie up soon, have a sleep, and then get himself a good dinner. He consulted the map again and pleased to see he had already covered a fair stretch of the canal since Marton Locks. A canal bank pub had been circled by his uncle and Perceval decided he'd try to tie up to it as close as possible.

Suddenly, he was shocked by a scene of unexpected devastation. Not only shocked, but unusually for him, dismayed by a profound sensation of mourning. The serenity of the tree-lined banks had been brutally interrupted by an execution (or so it looked to him). There was a gap where only stumps remained, trunks laid down like fallen bodies, branches severed and splintered, the ground littered with sawdust, a jarring openness, defiled and bare. He saw utilitarian housing built on the rise behind the felling, these buildings standing like the tanks of an occupying army, arrogantly in possession. What a wounding of the land! What a scar on the landscape! How could this possibly be allowed to happen? He didn't know. The desecration made him angry. But it was a hopeless anger, really a form of powerlessness. What he'd seen left him feeling hollow, 'unmanned'. This sympathy for nature was new for him. But he needed to keep his concentration and tried to shrug off his present disquiet.

Passing under a road bridge, Perceval saw two boats moored in front of him and wood smoke floated up from their chimneys. He slowed to glide by the first boat, painted black, all its blinds pulled. Between it and the next boat there was a gap long enough for *Knight Errant* but, given his misjudgement earlier and lingering sense of powerlessness, he thought he wouldn't attempt any complicated manoeuvre. He went past the second boat, painted in British Racing Green become grubby, and found ample space to moor before the canal turn. Below the towpath was a row of cottages nestling behind hedges and wooden fencing. On the far side, a gaggle of white geese wandered across low-lying wetlands. Perceval pointed the bow towards the bank and pushed the tiller to bring him level. 'Keep her steady,' he said. An accomplished berthing, he thought to himself. Discipline and self-talk really do work.

He jumped off, grabbing the centre line as he did so, but could see no rings on the bank to tie up *Knight Errant*. He had to leap back on board to get a hammer along with two mooring pins. *Knight Errant* bobbed slightly but thankfully didn't drift. Perceval grabbed the rope from the bow, leapt back onto the towpath and started hammering in the first pin. As he did so, he thought he heard a woman shouting. He paused then started hammering again. This time he was sure he heard a woman shouting. He stopped once more and looked around. He could see no one. He was about to strike a third time when a voice from behind one of the fences cried out. 'Can't you hear? I said don't bloody well hammer those pins into the bank!'

Opening a cottage gate was a stocky woman of about sixty wearing a worn cardigan, equally worn knee length skirt, thick woollen stockings, and Wellington boots caked with mud, her grey hair tied back untidily, her demeanour one of outrage. Behind her was a little brown terrier, which looked just as threatening as she did. The woman conveyed solidity, a sort of immovable strength, her voice clipped and sharp. She was clearly not someone to be trifled with (another of his mother's phrases). Perceval's stomach knotted as he expected a surge of righteous outrage.

Standing over him now, the woman folded her arms and glowered. Her look wasn't only admonishing but also conveyed an assertion of right, as if Perceval had committed a breach of longstanding custom. Though unnerved, he didn't think this woman heartless or vicious. Her eyes conveyed tenderness absent from her voice. What he read in her manner was impatience with ignorance and unwillingness to suffer fools, however naïve they may be. At least he hoped that reading was correct.

'I'm terribly sorry,' he said. 'I didn't know.' Reprising his default excuse, he added, 'It's my first time on the canal.'

She sighed with what appeared to be long-suffering exasperation. 'At least you're not one of the weekender crowds,' she said, relenting a little (at least, he hoped she was relenting). 'Some of them haven't a clue ... or a care. Are you on your own?'

Perceval stood up, answered yes, and put on the look of someone keen to learn, but innocent of the ways of the canal.

The woman unfolded her arms, as if indicating a momentary truce in hostilities, and scrutinised him more closely. 'You're accent. Is it Scottish?'

Perceval had been asked this frequently since living in England. To his ears, his speech sounded decidedly un-Scottish. 'No, I'm from Northern Ireland but I've lived in England for the last few years.' He also explained to her the purpose of his journey to Llangollen. His correction and his explanation appeared to satisfy her curiosity and she nodded at *Knight Errant*.

'I take it you've got mooring clamps on board.' Her tone was practical and no longer confrontational.

'Mooring clamps? I'm not sure. But there seems to be everything …'

'They'll be in your locker. Normally just inside the cabin. They're metal, same as your pins, only they hook to the piling here on the bank.' She walked to the canal edge and pointed to the metal sheet running the length of the bank. 'They're much safer anyway than your pins. They won't work loose. I've seen that happen in my time with pins in the bank.'

Perceval's boat began to drift out at the stern. The woman picked up his centre line from the towpath and pulled it tight. She was strong, he had to admit. 'Go on and have a look. I'll keep you secure.' She nodded to his abandoned attempt at mooring. 'Take out that pin and take it with you,' she ordered.

Perceval did as he was told. He pulled out the pin with some effort, apologised a second time and got onboard. On the storage shelf he found two galvanised steel hooks. He'd seen them before but never knew what they were for or how to use them. Had he been told by the man at Whittington? Probably, but he couldn't recall. He held them up for her to see. 'Are these what you mean?'

'Yes. That's them. Clip one onto the piling where you were going to tie up a moment ago and thread the rope through.'

Perceval knelt by the canal edge and fussed with the hook, made a few attempts to attach it, but failed. The woman let him struggle for a while before she stepped towards him. The dog followed and sniffed at Perceval before turning away, obviously unimpressed, just as Toby had been the night before.

'Here, let me do it,' she said. 'You hold the boat.' The woman took the clamp from his uncertain hand, thought for a moment about the correct positioning, knelt with some effort, and fixed the hook firmly in place. She gave it a testing tug. 'There you are.

No chance of that coming undone. Now tie your rope through.'

When she'd got back to her feet rather unsteadily, Perceval handed over the centre line to her again. He threaded through the rope and knotted it firmly. 'Sorry,' he nodded at the centre line in her hands, 'Sorry for all your bother.'

She waved away his apology. 'Do the same again and we'll both be happy.' Her tone was almost indulgent now.

Perceval had no problem this time and he sensed that he had passed another test. As he took the centre line again, he wondered if she, like Jo, had been a schoolmistress in another 'before'. 'Thank you,' he bowed his head as graciously as he could without appearing unctuous.

'Those pins you were hammering in,' she explained. 'We've had flooding recently. Erosion of the bank is bad enough without boaters adding to the damage. As you see, these cottages lie below the level of the canal. Any damage to the bank only makes things worse.' Perceval thought at one point she was going to apologise for her initial rudeness, but she didn't. 'You can see I had good reason to shout at you.' Now that she had explained, he could see no reason why she should apologise. As the woman strode back toward her cottage, calling for her dog to follow, Perceval noticed a hand-painted sign hanging on the gate: 'Fresh eggs and local honey for sale'. They had become neighbours, if only for a night, with his boat almost tied to her doorstep, and, after the way she'd helped him, Perceval considered it right to make a peace offering of sorts, however small. It was a practical way of saying thanks, of apologising, but also a way to add to his food supply.

'I see you sell eggs and honey,' he called after her.

The woman stopped and turned around. 'Hens are mine. Bees are mine. You won't find better anywhere, Supermarket stuff is rubbish,' she replied.

Perceval had the impression she was issuing a challenge. 'That sounds perfect. Can I buy some, if that's alright? It would be good to have something fresh.' When he said those words his stomach rumbled, whether audibly or not he wasn't sure.

The woman's expression changed again. Maybe she had heard his hunger speaking. Her look became sympathetic, almost maternal. 'Wait here,' she said.

Chapter Twelve

A few minutes later, the woman returned carrying a half-dozen eggs and a pot of honey, the first in a recycled carton and the second in a small, re-used jar. She held them out to him. 'That's one pound fifty for the eggs, three pounds for the honey, four pound fifty for the two.'

Perceval looked in his wallet and remembered he had no Bank of England notes. And there was no way he could use his debit card. Fearing how awkward this would be, he felt in his pockets for loose coins and fished them out. He found four one-pound coins and two fifty pence pieces. He gave thanks for the good fortune of The Fool and put them in her hand. 'Keep the extra fifty pence. It's small recompense for your help. I really do appreciate it.' Immediately, he felt this might have been the wrong thing to say and the woman would consider herself insulted. Luckily for him again, she seemed genuinely touched. She put the coins into her cardigan pocket and folded her arms, this time a gesture affable and not combative.

'Just as well I was in the garden to keep you right.'

'I didn't realise I was doing anything wrong.' He shifted awkwardly. 'I just assumed that's how people tied up.' He hesitated. 'This is the second time in two days a damsel has rescued this knight in distress.' He pointed to the name *Knight Errant*.

The woman thought that was funny and said so. Perceval stood cradling the carton of eggs in one hand and his jar of honey in the other. On the canal a few ducks bobbed over towards the towpath where they stood, while the white geese on the wetland came waddling to the canal. It looked like the woman's presence was their prompt. She must have guessed what was on Perceval's mind.

'I feed them,' she said, not with self-congratulation but as a matter of fact. 'The ducks and the geese and the birds. I feed the hedgehogs too, not that there are many of them left. Do you know how much of our natural habitat's been lost in the last twenty years? The destruction just goes on and on.'

'I saw the trees cut down back there on the canal,' Perceval said. 'There was violence to it, you know. I was genuinely shocked. In fact, I felt angry.' He hesitated to become too emotional but thought what the hell. He needed to get rid of his lingering rage. 'It was as if nature was crying out and no one could hear it, like something sacred had been defiled. I felt powerless as if I might as well shout into the wind.'

'Oh, I'm very angry about that too. Don't get me started ...'

Perceval could see it was too late. He had triggered something elemental in her, he feared.

'Have you heard of the term "nature-depleted" before?' He shook his head. 'It's the term scientists use to describe our country's status as one of the most ravaged on the planet, not only flora but also fauna. Did you know that?' He shook his head again. 'That's generations of habitat loss accelerating each year. Oh, you wouldn't believe what's happening. You hear politicians talk of Britain being world leading in this and world leading in that. Yeah, well we're world leading in destroying nature. You never hear them boasting about that. World leading! My arse in parsley!'

Perceval snorted at the phrase and almost lost grip on his jar of honey. It was his mother's favourite expression when she heard politicians on TV making high-flown statements, exactly of the kind this woman excoriated.

'Yes, you may well be scornful. Who can believe anything they say these days? So much wildlife under threat – think of what they've done to the badgers – so much acreage vandalised

… we're turning the countryside into a sterile land and our oceans into sterile waters.' She had a fit of coughing which made her bend over for a few moments. When she straightened up, her cheeks were flushed, by the effort of hacking. 'I must give up smoking, I really must,' she said. 'Do you know that over ninety percent of our meadows have been lost in the last seventy years? That's seven million acres of wildflowers. That's the size of Wales plus half of Yorkshire. Just imagine!'

He knew, in her presence, he should think it was bad, so he shook his head in disbelief. Truth to tell he *did* find her comparison hard to believe for he knew a bit of Yorkshire.

The woman broke off to glance at the geese and ducks swimming back and forth at the bow of *Knight Errant*. 'There was a song when I was a girl. It was by Joni Mitchell and called "Big Yellow Taxi". Maybe you've heard of it?'

He had heard of it. His mother had been a fan of Joni Mitchell. He remembered, as he got ready for school one day, her singing 'Chelsea Morning' as she washed up the breakfast dishes, looking through the kitchen window's yellow curtains into the back garden. She'd sung the song brightly enough but even as a boy Perceval was attuned enough to her feelings to know what lay behind. And he couldn't help but sense the sadness in the words, 'Oh, won't you stay?'

'Then you'll know the lines about taking all the trees and putting them in a tree museum, the birds and the bees being killed by DDT, and paving paradise to put up parking lots. And it is all so true. We *don't* know what we've got till it's gone! And I tell you, it's going, going, and faster than you could ever imagine.' She took some pellets from her skirt pocket and cast them onto the water. There was frenzy amongst the geese and ducks at which she looked benevolently. 'Modern farming methods are a disgrace! Battery cages. Animals pumped full of antibiotics and hormones. Cows kept indoors instead of on the fields. You know, industrial farming has caused more pain and misery for sentient creatures than anything else in history. And those big fishing trawlers are devastating the oceans. Such suffering we inflict should break everyone's heart. But people close their eyes and hearts to it. And for what? Monumental food waste and obesity?' She guffawed 'This land which used to be teeming with wildlife is soaked with pesticides and our rivers are full of sewage.' She threw some more pellets into the canal. 'When we destroy nature, we destroy ourselves. We *are* destroying ourselves!' She paused for a moment, as if trying to remember something, then looked at Perceval. 'Have you heard of Simon Armitage?'

'The Poet Laureate you mean? Yes, I've heard of him.'

'He wrote a poem where he asks if you could say the word and everyone in the world disappears leaving only the world, would you say it.'

'I've not read it.' Perceval hadn't read any poems by Simon Armitage. He only knew he came from Yorkshire.

'Well, *I* would say it. I would … if that doesn't sound inhuman or apocalyptic.' She threw some more pellets absent-mindedly towards the birds. 'The true horseman of the apocalypse is human arrogance, and mankind trots along behind it. Humans have the most astounding notions of their place in nature and this universe, as if everything turns on their selfish needs, however cruel, and however stupid.'

Perceval shifted the jar of honey and carton of eggs, uneasy because he'd never thought critically before about what she was saying. This woman's moral seriousness made him aware of his ethical lack. She cared in a way that made his indifference feel shameful, almost criminal, even if her last words did sound apocalyptic. He felt he should say something, but he could only repeat himself. 'When I passed by those felled trees, I could only think the land was wounded. I don't know why I thought that, but it was what came to my mind.'

There was a flash of surprise in the woman's eyes. She put a hand on her hip, a similar stance taken by a former history professor about to make a key point. 'That's an old truth,' she said. 'The woodland chopped, the hillsides stripped, the land *does* wound. And it also *remembers*.'

Perceval was confused. 'What do you mean it remembers?'

'Have you ever read the poem "The Sleeping Lord" by David Jones?'

He shook his head, 'No I haven't.' The truth was he didn't read poetry at all.

'My husband and I are fans of his. We came to this part of the country, to the Marches of Wales, to this borderland, because of the mythology of his poetry and the hope it brings.'

'What hope is that?'

'However separated we may be, English, Welsh, Scottish … and even Irish like yourself, the legendary tradition he re-worked with is common to us all. And what is wounded can be restored.' She paused for emphasis. 'The sleeping Lord is King Arthur,' she said. 'Or maybe it's some other godlike monarch, waiting to rise when the land is in need of him … or her.' She pointed to *Knight Errant*. 'It could be a questing knight like you?' She laughed when Perceval looked dumbfounded. 'I'm being flippant. Think of it, though. Jones saw the land as living. If it suffers, we suffer. Do you see the significance now? We have broken faith with our land. It is being wounded re-peatedly. Those trees you saw cut down, the way we treat our animals, how our landscape is despoiled, the flooding here I told you about, on and on. The lives people have today blind them to it all. They are cocooned in centrally heated homes, air-conditioned offices, they move about in planes, trains and automobiles, little do they see of nature that is theirs. And the digital age, IT, AI, and the all the rest of it, is even further removed from the nature. Like everything else they do, people consume the countryside without a thought. And every time, we wound not only the land but also ourselves.'

'I never thought of it that way,' Perceval said. It was one of the many ways he'd never thought about things. 'So that's why you choose to live here? '

'The only thing for us, for everyone, is to live simply again. The truth is, we need to go backwards not forwards.'

'This may seem a naïve question but wasn't this canal the modern age in its day? Wasn't the industrial revolution a product of these canals?'

'I suppose you've got a point. And yet modernity abandoned them, didn't it? Don't you see? Exploit, extract, discard, that's what it's all about. There will come a point when we'll be extracted and discarded on this earth, the whole of humanity and our civilisation. If I could only say the word …'

'But the canals were restored, weren't they, just like this one?'

'You mean we re-awaken the things modernity left for dead?

'Yes, I suppose that's what I do mean, or what I should mean.'

The woman laughed and Perceval took her relaxed manner as a small victory. 'I know how I must seem to a young man like you.' She waved vaguely toward her cottage. 'You probably see all this and say to yourself: "Ah, they must be hippies, old back-to-mother-earth types, who probably spent the eighties in a commune." I wouldn't blame you if you did.' Perceval did his best to look as if he couldn't possibly have entertained that notion. And he hadn't. 'You couldn't be more wrong if you did,' the woman continued. 'We are Church of England, and we always used to vote Conservative. But not the ones today who have no interest in conserving anything, it seems to me'

Perceval felt emboldened to risk a witty comment. 'Let me get this straight. So, your alternative lifestyle is an alternative to the alternative lifestyle?'

She laughed loudly. 'Exactly! No drugs, no free love, maybe only a bit of rock and roll.'

'A counter-counterculture.'

'That's us in a nutshell. Or maybe that should be in an egg-shell.' They stood quietly, enjoying this pleasant moment between them. 'I'd better get on,' she said. 'And I'd better let you get on. I hope you like the eggs and honey.'

'I'm sure I will.' He hesitated to go and asked. 'Do you know where the pub is? My uncle has marked it on the map. I thought I'd give it a try.'

The woman gave the impression she didn't fully approve of his intention, but he also sensed she judged it was none of her business. 'I'm sorry,' she said, 'if I sounded like a prophetess of doom. I hope my words didn't spoil your day. The pub is around the corner,' she pointed along the towpath. 'You can't miss it. Only be careful on your way back if you have a few pints. There are no lights along the canal. Don't go headfirst into the water.'

Chapter Thirteen

Perceval roused himself from a deep sleep. For a moment he had no idea where he was and lay still until he remembered. Switching on the light above the bed, he checked the watch on his wrist. It was seven o'clock. He'd intended to lie down for a short nap, but that had been over two hours ago. Perceval's dreams, normally fleeting and prosaic, had again been vivid.

He'd been walking along a towpath which gently rose and fell under his feet, as if the land was alive and breathing. Suddenly before him he saw a figure half-buried in roots and moss. It was a knight in armour, unconscious, wounded, but still breathing. He was afraid to go to the warrior's aid and lacked the courage to awaken him. Fighting through a thicket of briars, he stumbled on a ruined chapel. Inside, he found a knotted rope lying on a candle-lit altar and close by, he heard a woman's voice. It wasn't Jenny's voice. It wasn't Jo's voice. It wasn't Bron's voice. It wasn't the voice of the woman at the cottage. It wasn't his mother's voice either. The voice was youthful, intelligent, playful, and he fell in love with its sweetness. He longed to see the woman's face, but couldn't. The voice spoke to him, 'You must ask.' He didn't know what the question was, and he looked about him, not in panic, but in expectation. He heard the voice again saying, 'You must ask'.

He sat up and noticed he hadn't thought to pull the curtains. Anyone strolling along the towpath could have looked in and seen him. Did they imagine him to be a wounded knight? He smiled at the idea. Fully conscious, only the sweetness of the young woman's voice remained to cheer him. The sleep hadn't subdued his hunger. He swung his legs off the bed, stood, and stretched. He boiled a kettle to have a quick body wash and change his clothes, though he hadn't much choice in the matter.

In deep darkness, Perceval walked cautiously around the canal turn, meeting no one. It was only when he got close to a road bridge that lights from a beer garden spilled across the towpath to where a narrowboat was tied up. The boat was unlit, so he assumed the crew must be at the bar. Very convenient, he thought, within staggering distance of home and no possibility of falling into the water. He went up the steps from the towpath and discovered there wasn't a garden, just extensive wooden decking with tables and benches. He imagined it would be pleasant to sit out with a drink on a balmy summer's evening and watch the boats go by. No one was out this evening, and he didn't blame them. The air was damp and cold.

The double glass doors of the pub shut softly behind him, sealing out the night's chill and he was embraced by warmth. This pub must have undergone recent, corporate chain style refurbishment. The wooden bar, painted blue, appeared to have been left untouched for it looked original, and behind it a whole wall was stacked high with bottles of spirits. This part of the pub was brightly lit and, on the wall in a recessed space with soft chairs and a sofa, a large TV, on mute but with subtitles, was showing a game show. Only one man lounged in an armchair near the screen. He wasn't watching the show but looking at his mobile. Two couples of Perceval's age, all four dressed in jeans and T-shirts as though it was still summer, leaned across a table covered with empty bottles and glasses, their conversation punctuated by shrieks and bursts of laughter.

Sitting on a soft chair nearby was a large man in a heavy roll-neck sweater and waterproof trousers swirling the dregs of his pint of lager, looking around, it seemed, to order another from a passing waitress. Perceval wondered if he was the owner of the adjacently moored boat, alone like him and seeking refuge, perhaps enjoying the laughter of the young couples, laughter which made him feel in touch with life, a bit like old Tristan. Beyond this lounge was an annex, less brightly lit, where he could see couples dining. Perceval was ravenous and went to the bar.

'So, what'll it be?' the barmaid asked without looking up at him, distracted as she was by waitresses coming and going through the kitchen door to the side.

Perceval studied the labels on the draft pumps. There was no English ale on offer, which disappointed, so he ordered what he recognised, a pint of Budweiser. As the barmaid, a thin, dark-haired, slightly harassed, but distinctly attractive woman in her thirties busily pulled his drink and called out instructions to her colleagues, he took one of the laminated menus and considered what was on offer. When she set his lager before him, he asked for fish and chips with mushy peas, paused, and ordered a side order of chips as well. You can never have too many chips when you're in the mood, he told himself. He was about to pay but the barmaid told him to take a seat. 'You can pay for the Bud and your meal when you've finished,' she said. This time she looked Perceval up and down as if seeing him for the first time. He thought her look was an appreciative one, so he smiled appreciatively in return.

'We're a bit short-staffed this evening,' she apologised, blowing a wisp of hair from her eyes. 'Your order won't be long though.' She looked him over again, and Perceval was flattered. About to say something to him, the barmaid was called upon (reluctantly, he thought) to serve one of the T-shirted youths who interrupted their exchange with a complicated order.

Perceval took a table in the annex and in that benign humour which finding favour with a woman can bring a young man, greeted the other diners, all middle-aged, and very English-looking, who nodded in return. He expected the barmaid he'd spoken to would bring his order and he set about preparing a witty remark. But it wasn't she who arrived. It was a teenage girl who didn't look twice at Perceval. In fact, she didn't look at him at all, turning her head to speak to a colleague, another teenage girl, as she set down the plates on his table. As she walked away to catch up with her friend, Perceval heard her mumble, 'Enjoy.'

The fish and chips weren't the best he'd ever eaten but they were just what he needed. When he'd finished off the remaining chip on his side dish, he sighed with satisfaction, sat back and stretched his legs languorously. It was a feeling he hadn't experienced recently and thought the appropriate expression was 'comfortable in his own skin'. It certainly made the world more inviting and fuller of possibilities, just as Jo promised it would. When the teenage waitress removed his dishes, Perceval asked for another Budweiser.

'No problem,' she replied, unenthusiastically.

'And the bill please,' he added.

'No problem,' she repeated, equally unenthusiastically.

When his next pint arrived and he'd paid the bill, Perceval wandered over to a table near the TV, checking if the barmaid was still on duty. He saw a bearded man in a white shirt behind the bar now, chatting paternally with the young waitresses hovering around the kitchen door. As Perceval took his seat, the barmaid emerged from a door near the kitchen. She shrugged on a trench coat, adjusted her shoulder bag, and hurried towards the entrance with short steps. As she passed Perceval, she waved her phone in the air and, without noticing him, called to the other staff, 'Taxi's here!' They waved and called 'See you, Ffion!' and turned back to their conversation. Perceval watched the woman go out and with her, the possibility he'd recently imagined disappeared into the night.

Chapter Fourteen

'Excuse me. Are you waiting for someone?'

A woman Perceval guessed to be in her early forties was pointing to the two empty armchairs which were placed around his table. She was of medium height and build, dressed in blue jeans, white trainers and a neat, tailored black leather jacket, partly un-zipped to reveal a soft, crew-neck cashmere sweater. The effect was casual and yet everything about this woman's clothing was stylish, considered, and probably expensive. What was most striking about her was the copper hair, bushy and curled, wild and untamed, thick and full. It framed her face in a way that seemed rebellious and constant, natural and artful.

Her expression was calmly confident, the slight smile on her closed lips suggesting warmth, the light blue eyes intelligent and affable. She exuded self-assurance and without any hint of reserve in her gaze. Perceval didn't know why exactly, but he sensed the presence of someone visionary, not visionary in the way of Jo, trailing mysteries of the esoteric, but visionary in the way of someone who was decisive, enterprising and knew what she wanted. She had the sort of charisma which commanded respect. Dynamic was the word, he decided. Perceval almost turned his head to see if she was talking to someone else rather than him. He sat up from his slumped position, stood as his mother had told him you should do if a woman comes into your company, and said, 'No. I'm not expecting anyone. I'll be going soon myself.' He pointed to his half-drunk glass of Budweiser. 'When I finish this, you can have the table to yourself.'

'Sit down, sit down,' she motioned with her hands. 'I should apologise for disturbing you. You really don't mind?' she asked, dropping into the chair opposite him, holding a large glass of white wine at shoulder height. She told him she was waiting for her husband who was on a business call. 'He's still in the car outside. Not to be disturbed … even when we're supposed to be on a short holiday from work.' Perceval noticed her Welsh accent. 'Are you on holiday too?' the woman asked him. 'I can tell you're not a local,'

He explained briefly where he was from, as well as his reason for being on the canal.

'That's very honourable *of* you,' she said, 'and very nice *for* you. Also, it's quite brave if you're in charge of a narrowboat for the first time. Is that yours tied up beside the pub?'

'No, I'm a little further down below the canal turn.'

The woman set her glass on the table, and, in her movement, Perceval detected a subtle scent of florals and spice. 'I've never been on a narrowboat,' she admitted.

'I thought if you lived here, you'd have been an expert.'

'Oh, we don't live here. We have a holiday cottage near Llangollen. That's where we're heading now. London is where our home is. Where our work is, I should say.' She brushed a few strands of wayward hair from her cheeks. 'And what do you do when you're not delivering boats?'

Perceval explained his indeterminate employment status and mentioned about settling his mother's affairs in Northern Ireland. The woman expressed her condolences, shaking her head slowly at the sadness of his words. Her hair tumbled across her face and she used both hands to push it back.

'And what is it you do in London?' he asked. 'I noticed your Welsh accent.'

'Do I sound to you like Nessa from *Gavin and Stacey?*'

Perceval was about to protest that she neither looked nor sounded at all like Nessa, but her laughter stopped him.

'I'm joking. Not that I've anything against Nessa, you

understand. It's what I get sometimes from people in London. I always assume their hearts are in the right place. And yes, I *am* a Valley Girl, Rhondda Valley in my case, not San Fernando.' She ran a hand through her hair. Coping with it seemed to be almost a full-time job. 'And what I do, what *we* do I should say, is AI. We run a start-up in freight logistics, won't bore you with specifics, but think inventory planning, supply trains, that sort of thing. We started with a small team of five. We now employ fifty engineers, analysts and designers. A big responsibility … My husband and I need to recharge our batteries. That's why we are here.' She smiled. 'As you know, recharging batteries more efficiently is the world's problem today.'

'Wow!' Perceval said, pleased that his first impression of 'dynamic' had been correct. 'I'm truly impressed!' His exuberance seemed to please the woman for she smiled, putting out her arms like a magician who has performed an amazing trick and accepting the audience's applause. Perceval didn't clap, but said, 'Unfortunately, AI came just too late for me. I'm sure my university coursework would have benefitted from an intelligence more artificial but less superficial than my own.'

She liked his line, throwing back her head and laughing loudly. Then she leaned in towards him and wagged a finger. 'That's your nineteen sixty-three.' She paused to ask his name and told him hers was Angharad. 'That's your nineteen sixty-three, Alex.' Perceval spread his hands to show he didn't understand. 'It's from that Philip Larkin poem about the year in which life was never better but which came too late for him.'

'I only know his poem about your mum and dad. Not *your* actual mum and dad, of course, but mums and dads in general.' Angharad smiled at his correction. 'But I'm too polite to mention why in the company of a lady.'

She liked that line too and laughed again. 'You are such a good-mannered young man, Alex.' She raised her glass in a toast and took a sip of wine

'I know nothing about AI, really,' Perceval admitted. 'Apart, that is, from what appears from time to time in the media, you know, all the stuff about computers taking over the world.' Angharad made a face conveying that was the sort of thing people always said and that people were always wrong. 'AI sounds like magic to me,' he persevered. 'Even my mobile phone is magic to me, everything to do with computers or the internet, too.' Angharad's expression didn't change, so he went on. 'I was talking to a woman earlier, down where I'm moored,' he gestured vaguely towards the canal, 'and she was talking about the poetry and legends of this area. She mentioned King Arthur, the Sleeping Lord, whose spirit must be roused to save the environment so we can return to simpler ways of living. I think I've got that right.' Angharad raised her eyebrows, looked interested this time, and took another sip of wine. 'Her view was that we need to get back to a more natural way of life.' He hesitated to add the woman's apocalyptic conclusion but thought he might as well. 'She told me she dreams of a world without any humans at all ...'

He was surprised that Angharad's response was a loud guffaw. Putting a hand to her lips to prevent spilling a mouthful of wine, she said, 'That's a good one.' When she'd recovered her composure, she said. 'You hear stories about how super intelligent machines will replace mankind and how robots will wipe out humanity. If true, this woman should welcome scientific progress and not deny it. What do you think? If you went back to 1963 ...' She stopped abruptly. 'Sorry, Alex, I'm being mischievous. Take no notice. Please go on.'

'This will sound silly to you, I'm sure. But when I think of AI I'm reminded of Merlin, you know, someone who could see the future, bend reality to shape destiny, that sort of thing.' He shook his head and took a gulp of lager. 'You must think

I'm a fool. I'm just trying to be clever so take no notice of *me*.'

Angharad waved away his self-deprecation and ran her fingers through her hair once more. 'Not at all. In my school we were raised on Arthurian legends. The Welsh gave the world those legends, don't forget. Merlin, yes,' she said, 'hmm, maybe you *could* think of him as the first data scientist.' She reflected for a moment. 'What do you make of this, Alex? Think of Merlin as someone who saw patterns no one else could see. Think of him not as someone casting spells but as someone interpreting the unseen forces of the world. Think of him not as a wizard of the dark arts, but someone who could read the stars, the tides, the fates of kings, you know, the pseudo-science of his time. Then think of him turning his knowledge of nature, plants, people, and alchemy into powers which enhanced human capability. I suppose you *might* say today he'd be doing what I'm doing, only this time using logic, maths, digital networks, and machine-learning to enhance human capability. For Merlin, magic was mysterious and artful. For us, AI is rational and scientific. Is that what you're getting at?'

'I really don't know what I'm getting at …'

She laughed again, not dismissively but indulgently. 'At least you are honest, Alex. I like that. Maybe if I say AI takes data, about us and our world, and reveals patterns that are normally hidden from us, does that make sense? Not magic as in a conjuring trick or an illusion but showing reality more clearly. In some ways that must seem "other-worldly" (Angharad made quotation marks with her fingers) to most people.'

'To people like me it certainly does.'

'Look, it isn't a mystery. AI doesn't do anything supernatural. It adds to our understanding by turbocharging our capacity to analyse the facts of life.'

'Do you think AI is today's quest for the Holy Grail? If you don't think that's an even sillier question.'

'You are bringing back a lot of memories, Alex. My dad was one of the last coalminers in the valleys. Mrs Thatcher had done for the mines before I was even a teen. But we had a videotape recorder if you know what that is.'

'I did see one in a museum once,' he said, making clear it was a joke, not a comment on Angharad's age, and she took it in good humour.

'Dad and I watched numerous times the old eighties film *Excalibur*. When childminding, unemployed he was …' A look of sadness briefly displaced her vitality. 'Helen Mirren's in it, and your compatriot, Liam Neeson. There was a lot about the Holy Grail in that. Have you seen it?' Perceval said he hadn't. 'Doesn't matter … if you take the Grail to mean knowledge … To answer your question, in a way, AI *is* our age's Holy Grail, a great quest to heal the land, yes. And reduce poverty, prevent diseases, avoid natural disasters, plan the future, increase wealth, save the environment, understand the universe.' She ticked off the objectives on her fingers. 'You've heard all that, I'm sure, the other side of the scare stories. But we can only do those things if we ask the right question. "Whom does the Grail serve?" That was the Arthurian question. Whom does AI serve? That is *our* question.' She took a sip of wine. Perceval expected her to leave things there, but Angharad had more to say. 'I used to listen to my grandfather talk about barges full of coal and steel going up and down the canals. That world is gone. And yet here we are, polishing its relics, telling ourselves it was a golden age. Things move faster today. We can't stop progress, despite what that woman would like. In AI, as in anything else, you need to move fast because tomorrow you could be a dinosaur … and we all know what happened to them.'

Perceval looked at Angharad. The last thing he could imagine was her becoming a dinosaur. Since he had nothing intelligent to add, he was happy for her to continue.

'You know,' she leaned towards him, 'you hear people speak of the "leisure society" as if floating along a canal on a boat is the pinnacle of human achievement. And yes, others say we should abandon the goal of progress. We should rewild the valleys and return to some imagined harmony with nature. But tell me, Alex, who honestly wants to return to nature? Do people even know what that means? Do they really want the struggle, the poverty, and the pain? I doubt it. You know very well from history what life was like. Until very recently, that is.'

'Nasty, brutish and short?'

'For the vast majority, yes. For women, even nastier and shorter.'

Angharad sipped wine quietly for a few moments as if expecting Perceval to query what she'd said. But he had no questions to ask. She set down her glass and fixed him with her eyes. 'To tell you the truth, Alex, I'm tired of this country wallowing in heritage and nostalgia. Who really wants to live in a museum? Who wants to be stuck in aspic? It's self-indulgently defeatist when what we need is *renewal*. All eras of decline become inward, obsessively subjective. Eras of progress look outward and build something substantial. These canals. These aqueducts. These tunnels. That's the creative confidence we need today, Alex, not navel-gazing over the past.' Angharad paused to judge the impact of her words. She must have thought her tone a little too preachy and changed its register. 'Remember who we were, of course we should. But let's show who we still are. And that we can do it. You know, whenever I hear people from home saying we can never compete with the Americans or the Chinese, I tell them we don't need Silicon Valley. We need the Dee Valley, we need the Rhondda Valley, wired and working. We have the talent, the roots, and the resilience. We need to believe in the future not wallow in the past.'

'That really would be magic, as in "magic" as a wonderful

thing. I feel like you've shown me the future.' In truth, he felt as if he had been given a very accomplished sales pitch by a very accomplished woman of affairs.

Angharad sat back again. 'I suppose the old Arthurian legends are about universal truths. As a historian, you'd know more about it than me.'

Perceval was flattered but not deceived, remembering the hours he should have been studying in the library he'd spent playing with bat and ball as the shadows lengthened over the playing fields of East Yorkshire.

'The old order changes, yielding place to the new,' Angharad went on. 'That's what is *natural* for us humans. It just happens increasingly quickly today. You must have faith that ... Ah, finally!'

She waved as a man her own age came into the pub. He was dressed in jeans, Barbour jacket, and checkered blue shirt. Like her, his causal dress conveyed style. Angharad's husband was tall and well-built and Perceval assumed he worked out at a gym. He'd always imagined anyone in the world of AI to be scruffy and nerdy, like characters he knew from *The Big Bang Theory*. These two weren't.

When he reached their table, Angharad indicated Perceval, who stood up to shake hands. 'Troy, this is Alex ... Alex, Troy,'
They shook hands.

'Alex saved this damsel in distress while you were otherwise engaged,' Angharad joked.

'My boat is actually called *Knight Errant*,' Perceval felt obliged to mention, hoping to deflect any suspicion on Troy's part that he'd been trying to chat up his wife.

Troy's self-assurance wasn't so easily disturbed. He patted Perceval hard on the shoulder and said with genial enthusiasm, 'Good man!' He bent over to Angharad and put his arm on her shoulder. 'That would be a new experience for you', he said, kissing her on the cheek. His accent wasn't Welsh but well-to-do Home Counties. Troy turned again to Perceval 'So, you're the skipper of a narrowboat, Alex?'

Perceval explained yet again the task his uncle had given him.

'Good man!' Troy repeated with the same genial enthusiasm. He sat down, and Perceval followed suit.

'Before you arrived,' Angharad explained, 'I was telling Alex all about AI. We were discussing whether it was like magic, the kind of power Merlin had to change reality, you know, like in the old Arthurian tales.'

Troy didn't seem to find the Arthurian analogy interesting or relevant. 'Magic you say? I wish we could raise a magic money tree' and he looked at Perceval, like he was about to make a pitch for funding. 'Never mind education, education, education. Investment, investment, investment, that's what we need.' Troy must have realised the incongruity of thinking Perceval might have access to a magic money tree for he changed tack. 'What do you do, Alex?'

Perceval told him that he was a history graduate 'in between posts at the moment'. For a split second he wondered if Troy was about to offer him a job for he paused before responding.

'I see.' Troy turned his head away as though he needed to compute this fact, then turned back to look at Perceval. 'As a historian, this may make sense. The Llangollen Canal you're on was part of the nervous system of the Industrial Revolution. It was once cutting-edge technology. Think of AI as a canal channelling vast currents of raw data, refining it into knowledge, detecting patterns, revealing hidden connections, and manufacturing opportunity. The more data that flows, the more AI can learn and transform lives. And the *faster* it flows, the better the outcomes. *Knight Errant* you say?' Perceval nodded. 'Well, Angharad and I, we have our quests. We have our dragons to slay. We have our weapons of the algorithmic age. You could say we are part of a new chivalric order in search of solutions to humanity's ills.'

Angharad clapped Troy's words. 'Bravo! Bravissimo! *Da iawn*, Troy!' she smiled. 'Alex, you've just heard the clarion call of the new Camelot.'

Perceval found it hard to imagine this new Camelot but he could imagine Angharad and Troy as successful business people. Right now, he was tired, he was slightly drunk, and in their company, thought himself profoundly out of touch with the modern world as well as out of his intellectual depth. A good night's sleep was what he needed.

'Thank you. I do see what you mean,' he lied. 'Thank you both. I must get up early to transport my little bit of metal along the Llangollen superhighway. I'd better go and leave you both in peace.' He was surprised that they found this silly rejoinder amusing.

'I think I owe you a drink, Alex, for coming to the rescue of My Lady Angharad,' Troy said, delicately touching his wife on the knee.

Perceval thanked him for the offer but excused himself, saying he hoped they would enjoy the rest of their evening. In turn, they accepted his refusal and wished him all the best for his journey. Troy shook his hand again. Angharad stood and put her arm around his shoulder. Perceval felt her copper locks on his cheek. When he got to the exit, he turned to wave but Angharad and Troy were deep in conversation, and he knew he'd passed out of their lives for good.

PART FOUR: THE PROMISE

Chapter Fifteen

Next morning Perceval boiled up a couple of fresh eggs for breakfast. The rich creamy yolk, deep orange in colour, was delicious. All that was missing was salt. He couldn't find any in the galley cupboards and hadn't thought to buy some in the little store in Whittington. He tried the honey on slices of slightly burnt toast and was surprised by its thick texture and its floral aroma. The woman from the cottage had been right. You wouldn't find anything like her eggs or her honey in supermarkets, the ones he shopped in anyway. He felt well set up for the day as he unhooked *Knight Errant* from the metal piling, cast the ropes bow and stern, and manoeuvred from the bank.

It was another dull, cloudy day, cool, but still dry, the weather remaining far from wintry, and pleasant for November. On the towpath, two women in Lycra jogged by and a man walked his dog. They greeted him good-humouredly as Perceval tried to give the impression of a seasoned boatman, waving nonchalantly in return. The white geese were foraging on the wetland meadow and in the water before him the ducks paddled reluctantly out of his way.

He cruised round a tight turn, went past some more waterside cottages as well as a couple of narrowboats which looked like they were tied up for winter. Though he was now confident enough of his abilities to travel faster, he found the engine reluctant to respond. The flow must be much stronger here, he decided, and gave *Knight Errant* a little more throttle. It made no difference. Today was going to be tougher and much slower than he'd expected.

Before long, he saw The Bridge Inn. On a grassy slope

between the pub and canal, a group of young women moved about in various stages of preparing inflatable kayaks. He remembered his uncle warning him about the kayakers and had another look at the map. Sure enough, his uncle had marked the possibility here. Perceval supposed Thursday must be kayak day.

The women were wearing waterproof leggings and bright yellow windproof jackets, some seated on the grass adjusting neoprene socks, some on their knees, packing dry bags with snacks and thermos. Others stood making final adjustments to beanies and gloves or shrugging on lightweight life jackets, some already carrying their paddles to the water's edge, flexing arms and shoulders as they walked. Most of the kayaks had been inflated already and foot pumps were set in a pile by the open door of a battered, muddy, transit van. These young women shared an enthusiastic camaraderie, eager anticipation of the challenge ahead, a lot of laughter, and a lot of teasing. They made Perceval nostalgic for the banter of the cricket team.

Before dejection at his loss possessed him, one of the young women looked up from her preparations and smiled at him. She leaned on her paddle and waved. Her greeting seemed to him more intimate than mere acknowledgement and he sensed a connection, a bond. Why this was so he couldn't explain. Intrinsicate … wasn't that the word Jo had used? Perceval smiled and waved in return. Maybe the woman sensed the effect she'd had on him and felt encouraged by it, for she called out, 'I'll catch you up in a moment, slowcoach. Bet I can overtake before you reach the aqueduct.' Her tone wasn't overtly flirtatious but Perceval couldn't help thinking (rather, wishing) they were more than merely casual remarks.

'Good luck with that! My trusty beast will have something to say about it,' he called back, patting the top of *Knight Errant* as if it were a cavalry charger, imagining she'd respect him more if he gave as good as he got.

She looked with more attention at his boat and frowned slightly. 'You really are struggling.'

Perceval assumed she was playing mind-games, the sort of sledging his teammates used to play on opposition batsmen and laughed dismissively. *Knight Errant* wasn't charging at all. She was right about that. It was labouring as if moving through treacle. Perceval could smell diesel fumes and for the first time he noticed intermittent puffs of smoke exiting from the engine, its normal steady throbbing become a shrill whine. He nudged the throttle forward even more, but instead of responding positively, the engine appeared about to stall. He started to panic. Something was wrong, he knew, and imagined the eyes of the kayakers upon him, pitying, or perhaps amused, at his discomfort. Unexpectedly, the young woman appeared jogging at the side of the boat. She'd run from the Bridge Inn, her beanie now slightly askew. She slowed to a walk and made a gesture with a finger across her throat. He didn't know what she meant, and she repeated the gesture more vigorously. 'Stop,' she shouted over the engine's whine, 'you're overheating,' and pointed to white smoke billowing from the engine compartment. Perceval pulled the throttle sharply into idle, letting *Knight Errant* drift to a halt before turning off the engine.

'I think your propeller is clogged,' she told him, looking at the stern. She put both hands on her hips, and corrected herself, 'Not think. I know. It *is* clogged. Definitely.' Perceval looked confused. He glanced first at her and then at the stern. 'From the leaves in the canal,' she explained, her tone gentle yet insistent. 'You need to reverse with short bursts on the throttle. It will clear the blockage.' She made vigorous circles with her hand as if to demonstrate water spiralling down a plughole. 'Otherwise, you risk blowing the engine completely.'

What a fool he was. Of course! The mechanic at Whittington had mentioned leaves in the canal as well as telling him about the tactic of reversing the throttle. He'd forgotten. Perceval put on his innocent look to hide his embarrassment. 'I forgot. It's my first time. I'm learning by my mistakes … how can I ever thank you? You've been immensely kind. I really am very grateful.' He wondered if he'd overdone the thanks, but she seemed to appreciate his response, smiling but hesitant, as if there was more that she wanted to say.

Glancing towards her friends already on the canal or sliding into their kayaks at the bank, she hesitated. Then she looked directly at Perceval. 'Fleur,' she said.

Perceval was enchanted by her eyes so brightly green, her expression so calm and confident. He stood transfixed by her look and realised he hadn't taken in what she'd said. 'Sorry?'

'Fleur,' she repeated. 'My name is Fleur.'

'That's a beautiful name.' He said this honestly and yet was surprised at his honesty. Shakespeare was right. Love learned in a lady's eye courses swiftly through veins and heart. It felt like he was in love. Perceval pointed to his chest and said, 'Alex.'

'Yes,' Fleur replied. 'I didn't think it could be anyone else.'

He knew he must have appeared ridiculous, and his face conveyed this fact to her. Normally, being bested like this would only have irritated him. Not in Fleur's case. Her smile broadened and Perceval heard one of her friends shouting her name.

'I'll have to go,' she said and turned away, then stopped to look back. 'It's been nice meeting you, Alex. Remember. A few sharp reverses to clear the leaves and you'll be okay. Maybe I'll see you later? We're coming back mid-afternoon.'

'I'll keep a look out. I won't forget.' He almost added 'you' and immediately regretted not doing so.

'You promise?'

'I promise!'

'You mean it?'

'Of course, I mean it,' Perceval touched his heart.

'Sure you won't forget?'

'I won't forget'

They held each other's gaze for a few seconds, as if sealing a pact.

'Okay. I'll see you later then,' she said and jogged back to her friends.

'Thank you, Fleur! I owe you,' he shouted after her.

Perceval restarted the engine and followed her instructions, idling for a moment, then reversing the throttle. He heard a brief muffled churning and, looking to the rear of the boat, saw a swirl of dead leaves loosening and spiralling away from the propeller in a frothing backwash. The kayakers began to paddle in a line on his port sicde, avoiding as best they could the disturbance he'd made in the water. The young women made encouraging and chirpy remarks when he said hello as they passed. He couldn't suppress the suspicion they thought him a simpleton.

'Better now?' Fleur asked, paddling alongside, keeping pace with *Knight Errant*.

'Yes, thanks to you. You saved me from disaster.'

'I'll still beat you across the aqueduct. See you later then?'

'Yes, later.' He wished he could think of something poetic to say, wished he had the literary depth of Jo to conjure up a memorable quote.

At their exchange, a few of Fleur's friends began to tease.

'Oh my God, Fleur, you've totally pulled,' one said loudly.

'Always the man-eater, Fleur' another called.

'We can't take you anywhere!' yet another joshed.

Fleur rolled her eyes at these words, but Perceval noticed a faint flush on her cheeks. When their eyes met again, Fleur shrugged but looked happy. She kept back from her friends for a moment. 'Remember your promise, Alex,' she spoke quietly and then paddled vigorously after the line of kayaks.

Perceval was certain the women's conversation had changed already and that he'd been only a momentary interest, quickly forgotten, and his exchange with Fleur of no lasting importance to them. And yet it had been more than that to Fleur, hadn't it? It had been more than that to him. He believed their moment had something of the eternal in it (though he was conscious of being influenced by Jo's reading of his destiny). Maybe drawing the Lover's card had been prophetic after all? He couldn't tell. But he had promised that they'd meet again. He'd given his word. And he was determined to fulfil that oath.

Knight Errant made better progress even though the contraflow was stronger than before. The kayakers in front moved with rhythmic strokes and had the edge on him. Fleur had been right to be confident of beating him.

Very soon Chirk Aqueduct came into view and the canal narrowed to a one-way channel. A sign announced that he was entering Wales. He'd heard it said that between Wales and England there was a crossing rather than a border, a connection between people and communities, rather than a division. If so, what a crossing this was! The towering stone structure arched across the valley with the Ceiriog River far below, the canal suspended in air like a primitive miracle. To his left, a railway viaduct ran parallel, another triumph of engineering. Angharad and Troy had spoken of the intelligence revolution unfolding around him, where creativity and potential had no natural limits, with mind and technology triumphantly harmonising. This aqueduct spoke to him of another time when ambition also knew no bounds, the world reshaped by nothing except Thomas Telford's genius and the labour of navvies, English, Welsh, Scottish and Irish, a physical union of peoples. No invisible data flows here, rather the visible and solid bulk of things. Perceval could only wonder how they'd managed to build it as he could only wonder at the mystery of AI. Suspended up here, past and present seemed to blur, a bridge not only between England and Wales but between what was and what is to come, a once and future kingdom. It wasn't just the aqueduct's monumental scale which impressed him but how the stonework seemed an intimate part of this landscape, as if nature had entirely embraced it. Did the woman at the cottage approve? Somehow, he thought, despite everything, she would. He remembered Angharad's words about no one wanting to live in a museum, polishing their relics, the country being stuck in aspic, and wondered if the new times she promised would also be like this when they too were old. What monuments to AI would stand like this? He didn't know.

On the pathway running alongside the aqueduct were walkers, mostly retired, dressed in hiking gear, boots, backpacks, some of them using trekking poles. A young couple stopped to take in the view and the woman turned to take a photo of *Knight Errant* crossing. A little boy waved enthusiastically at Perceval, and he waved back. Everyone appeared exhilarated by the wonder around them and possibly apprehensive about the drop below. Perceval supposed it was a privilege to be taking his boat through the sky, the sort of thing (it used to be said) he 'could tell his grandchildren' (if people of his generation ever had children, if they would ever know grandchildren). Despite the grandeur and the beauty of this place, his thoughts were elsewhere. They were on Fleur.

He could still identify her amongst the companions, paddling with an easy stroke. He willed her to look back at him. Just once would do. She was close enough for Perceval to think that he could catch up. And yet he wasn't closing the distance between them. The flow of water in the aqueduct continued to make *Knight Errant* struggle and movement was hindered even more by his periodic reversing of the throttle to clear any new accumulation of leaves. Each time he pulled back the throttle there was a falling off in momentum before the boat moved forward once more. It was clear (though it did surprise him) that Fleur and her friends, with only muscle power, were better able to traverse the aqueduct than *Knight Errant* with its diesel. Their athletic ability impressed and exasperated him in equal measure, like one of those frustration dreams in which no matter how fast you moved, you could never bridge the gap, and no matter how much you tried to shout, no words ever came. Fleur might as well have been a world away, might as well have been a dream, and he a mere spectator of his own longing. Still, he hoped. And he'd promised.

Once across the aqueduct, Perceval could see the kayaks regroup and the young women catch their breath in the large pool before the tunnel, Chirk Tunnel, all 460 yards of it. They were putting on head torches and he could hear girlish shouts of mutual encouragement. There must have been no narrow-boat coming down for they set off in file once more, Fleur still in the middle, and paddled into the mouth of the tunnel. They were swallowed by the void, their thin beams floating in the darkness. Though a distance behind, Perceval assumed he would have the advantage this time. *Knight Errant* was moving with greater ease across the pool as Perceval lined it up for the entrance. At the tunnel's edge was a large evergreen tree, the roots of which seemed to burrow deep into the underworld and its branches stretch high to the sky. He thought once more of the knot intrinsicate. He considered it his guarantee of safety. He believed it would later unite him with Fleur.

The atmosphere of the tunnel was chill, heavy with the scent of wet stone, and the walls slick with a damp which seemed to seep under his skin. For a moment at the tunnel entrance, the contraflow held up *Knight Errant* completely, its engine fighting valiantly to break free, before the current lost its grip and allowed him in. Ahead, the lights of the kayakers bobbed like will-o'-the-wisps. As Perceval bent down to flick on the headlight switch, sudden turbulence in the water made him lose grip of the tiller, pushing the boat first against the wall and then against the towpath on the other side. No matter how carefully he tried, he found it impossible to keep *Knight Errant* centred. A few hikers walking in single file appeared like phantoms and overtook him. Perceval considered their silence a sort of condemnation. *Knight Errant's* hull knocked uncomfortably through the tunnel. He even tried pushing against the wall to make progress but his hand slipped too easily. He no longer thought of Fleur, no longer thought of catching up. Perceval thought only of getting out of this tunnel as black as witches' oil. So much for his courage! This netherworld accentuated every uncertainty, every doubt, every failing, all those pitiful deficiencies he thought he'd be able to master.

Though it seemed he'd been in the tunnel forever, the exit finally loomed. Perceval could now glimpse greenery with trees lining the open canal, and at last he could breathe fresh air. His muscles, formerly tensed and tight, began to relax. After the dark nightmare, the contrast of washed-out November light was almost dreamlike. Well in front now, he saw the kayaks circling. He heard the women's laughter, their whoops of achievement, and though he had emerged from the tunnel almost spent, mentally rather than physically, their energy appeared undiminished. He saw Fleur leaning across to high-five one of her friends, but her words were lost to him. After their celebrations, the kayakers moved into line once more to paddle on. This time Fleur did look back. She held up her arm but Perceval at this distance couldn't make out whether she was waving a greeting or waving goodbye. He waved furiously for it was pointless shouting. He could push on, but right now he had lost the will to do so.

Her wave, rather than encouraging, momentarily dejected him. Was it fantasy to believe there was anything more to his brief encounter with Fleur than a passing attraction? Hadn't Fleur simply been helpful? Hadn't she just been only 'a brick'? Wasn't that the public-school term? (He didn't know why he assumed Fleur had attended a public school. Was it her name, perhaps?) Hadn't she been simply and instinctively decent in her well brought up fashion? How often in the past had he read into female friendliness a deeper attraction which had never been there? He thought of the barmaid from last night. It was hard to suppress his fatalism, that old self-protective emotional default, even though, after what Jo had told him, he could no longer be sure it *was* self-protective and not self-destructive. Then again, he wasn't always mistaken, and he didn't think he was mistaken this time either. Or so he wished to believe. Fleur had told him the kayakers would be returning. Mid-afternoon, she'd said. Hadn't she been insistent about seeing him again? On the canal, how could he possibly miss her? And he'd made that promise. His mother had told him never to break a promise. He didn't intend to do so.

Right now Perceval needed to revive. His thoughts were all over the place. He guided *Knight Errant* to the bank where mooring rings had been set for boats awaiting the exit from the tunnel of upbound traffic. Nearby was a footpath running up a steep incline towards the road which should take him to Chirk. On his map it didn't look too far, and he thought the walk would refresh him, clear his mind of negative thoughts. Lunch would give him positive energy. It wasn't yet midday. He had plenty of time before Fleur and her companions would return.

Chapter Sixteen

H E had expected a village, but discovered Chirk to be a small town, its main street at a right angle with the road to the railway station. He found a large public garden with a gated entrance and, before it, standing on a traffic island, an impressive war memorial, an obelisk of Portland stone. Perceval crossed to take a look, dodging a milk tanker turning cautiously towards the vast Cadbury's chocolate factory beside the canal. On the monument was a carving of a soldier in greatcoat, helmet, rifle and bayonet, on sentry duty it seemed, his left hand raised as if to deny passage. The inscription beneath stated the memorial was dedicated 'in righteousness' to the fallen by their fellows of the parish. Kneeling to read the dedication, Perceval discovered the source of that striking phrase. It was from the Book of Revelation: 'And in righteousness He doth judge and make war'. And he thought of the soldiers who had perished, of the father he'd never known, of the mother who'd lamented unto death, thought of his own minor worries, and considered himself a hollow man by comparison.

He crossed the road in search of something to eat and something hot to drink. The damp chill of the tunnel hadn't left his bones despite the brisk walk from the canal. He found nearby a café decorated with stuffed toys. It was somewhere he would normally avoid, expecting young mothers with babies and infants, ladies nostalgic for the dreams of childhood, perhaps an old man returning in honour of his dead wife's favourite spot. Not his thing, with all those soft fabrics, prints, the grandfather clock and Welsh dresser filled with porcelain figures. He was about to go on and find somewhere more to his taste, but decided to give it a try, not wishing to waste more time and possibly miss Fleur's return. He stepped out of the grey morning into the warmth of the café with its soft murmur of conversation, its clink of cups and cutlery, faint tick of the clock.

It was busy and, as he'd guessed, the tables were occupied by retired couples and young mothers with prams. Perceval waited awkwardly as a waitress moved between customers. He was on the point of turning to leave when she noticed him. 'There is a place free in the next room,' she said. 'Just give me a moment, will you?' The waitress disappeared and returned a few moments later. 'Do you mind sharing a table? I asked the young lady, and she says it's okay as she'll be leaving soon.'

Perceval nodded and followed her, trying not to dislodge a pot of tea from one table, jostle an arm at another. No one seemed to mind. Everyone was gracious and smiled a welcome. But he suspected that the 'young lady' probably had been too polite to say no, too willing to accept being disturbed, and just willing to be accommodating. Rather like he would do, he thought. He prepared himself to be charmingly apologetic.

At a small table in the corner by a window he saw the 'young lady'. She was in her early twenties, a notebook open on the table beside her coffee cup, a pen lying between, and a hardback book in her hands. She was very thin, a delicate almost ethereal presence, her fragility accentuated rather than diminished by the loose, heavy beige jumper she was wearing, the cuffs of which covered her hands to the fingertips. She sat with a slight hunch of her shoulders as if she felt cold, even though the room was, if anything, overheated. Her dark hair was long, natural not styled, and since her head was bent over the book, it completely covered her face from view.

The waitress stopped and looked at Perceval. It was a knowing look, the sort of look a woman might give if she were trying to matchmake. Or so he imagined. She pulled out the chair from the table and stood aside like she was unveiling a secret. The sound interrupted the young woman's concentration (or maybe it was only discomfiture she was trying to hide). When she raised her head, her face was pale, her eyes hazel, and her look bashful. She was attractive, Perceval noted that immediately. The young woman smiled wanly and returned to her book without saying a word. Perceval ordered a black coffee as the waitress handed him a laminated menu and, as she did so, made a surreptitious nod of encouragement. Curious now, Perceval waited for the waitress to go and, still standing, observed his new acquaintance.

In the second she'd looked at him, her expression had been contemplative, her eyes and mouth suggesting not only melancholy but also quiet resolve. It seemed an unusual coupling, to Perceval at least, of pained reflection and determination, her demeanour appearing to reflect either the certainty of uncertainty or the uncertainty of certainty. The subtle downturn of her mouth hinted at isolation imposed but also accepted. Her subdued mood didn't convey distress, more resignation, as if she was secure in her emotional withdrawal. Perceval recognised that inclination. He'd grown up with it, after all. Yet the young woman, rather than exuding an air of defeat, conveyed quiet strength as well as self-containment. It made her appealing to the chivalrous male desiring to ride to the rescue – irrespective of whether this woman needed to be rescued. But her disposition was also forbidding. A man, any man, whatever his intentions, should only expect rejection, which was what Perceval did expect. Anyway, he had no intention of trying to woo. But he couldn't help thinking of her as a challenge, a challenge on the cards.

'I really am sorry,' he said. 'I'm sure the last thing you need this morning is me disturbing your peace and quiet.' He nodded at her notebook and pen. 'Do you really mind if I sit with you?'

He noticed she tensed slightly at being spoken to, and he

wasn't sure if her gesture meant surprise at his question or merely irritation he should bother asking. She didn't answer when she looked up, merely blinked an acceptance. She closed her book slowly and set it beside the notebook. Perceval noticed the title – *The Oxford Book of Welsh Verse*. Thanking her, he sat, shifting the chair closer to the table. Neither of them spoke as he glanced over the menu and he had the impression she was measuring his character without looking at him directly. When the waitress returned with his coffee, Perceval ordered a sandwich. He would have been too self-conscious to eat a plate of sausages and mash in present company. And he imagined it would make his imposed-upon companion even more uncomfortable.

'Would you like another coffee?' he asked her. 'I think it's the least I can do for my intrusion.' He could tell her instinct was to refuse, but she hesitated and finally accepted his offer.

When the waitress had gone, the young woman sighed. 'You know, I'm convinced they call me the girl who never speaks. I'm sure they think I'm rather sad. It was deliberate don't you think?'

'What was?'

'Putting you at my table.'

Perceval knew she was right but couldn't possibly say for it would have put him, never mind the waitress, in an awkward position. He might be a fool, but he wasn't totally stupid. 'No one,' he replied with a straight face, 'could ever be *that* cruel.'

She pulled back her head sharply, her expression mystified, then his meaning dawned, and she laughed, putting fingers over her lips. She shook her head as if to say 'no, I didn't mean to be rude to you'.

'I'm glad you didn't confirm or deny,' Perceval said, immediately thinking his words sounded phoney. 'My name's Alex, by the way.'

'Elin,' she said hesitantly.

Perceval leaned across to shake her hand, which was cool to

the touch. Elin seemed taken aback, yet also amused, by his formality, then became flustered as the smiling waitress set her coffee on the table before her.

'Is that a Welsh name?' he asked.

'Some say it comes from Greece. But, yes, Welsh too.' Her accent was different to Angharad's, more mellifluous, more musical.

'It sounds Welsh the way you say it, anyway. I like it.' He hoped that didn't sound cheesy.

'You're from Northern Ireland, yes? What brings you to North Wales in November?' Perceval explained his presence in Chirk. 'I wouldn't have the courage to do that', she said quickly. 'I certainly couldn't do it alone. I'd much prefer to be punted down the river on a beautiful summer's day, to lie back on thick cushions, and read a book.'

'Poetry in motion … I'm sorry but I couldn't help noticing your book.'

'Oh, I see.' She acknowledged his wit with the flash of a smile. 'I do read a lot of poetry,' she said, laying her hand on the book. 'I try to write it too.' She placed her other hand on the notebook. 'Not very good poetry, though …'

'Well, I wouldn't have the courage to write poetry. Who are your favourite poets?'

'There are so many! Gillian Clarke, Gwyneth Lewis, R. S. Thomas, Rhydwen Williams …'

'The former Archbishop of Canterbury, you mean?'

Elin put fingers to her lips and flashed another smile. 'No! That's *Rowan* Williams … though he's an accomplished poet too. Recently I've been reading David Jones.'

'*The Sleeping Lord*,' Perceval said emphatically, hoping Elin would be impressed. And she was.

'You know his poetry?' Her eyes widened.

'I know him only by reputation.' Perceval told her of the

conversation yesterday with the woman from the cottage. 'I intend to read it,' he added, 'if it's not too difficult for me, that is.'

'Don't be silly. His poetry is so rich, myth, legend, culture, history, language, Welsh as well as English … sorry, I'm going on. Yes, you *should* read him. I'm certain you'd enjoy it. Oh, please do.'

Perceval observed a slight flush on Elin's cheeks. Perhaps she rarely had a chance to express enthusiasm like this. Perhaps she really didn't speak to many people, too much of a dreamer for this prosaic world. He could sympathise. He also wondered if she had a boyfriend. He told himself (and honestly believed) he had no wish to become romantically involved (as they say) with Elin. He was curious about a boyfriend because, in a very simple (or was it very masculine?) way, Perceval thought her beauty should not be wasted, like a lady in a tower or a novice in a convent. And he couldn't help but wonder if Fleur would be jealous to know of this meeting with Elin. He hoped she would be and it helped his good humour.

'What do you do, Alex?'

Her question was asked shyly. In fact, Perceval now thought that everything Elin must do or say in public would be something of a trial. He told her about being 'between jobs' and added some detail about his time as an undergraduate. 'And you?' he asked.

'I look after my mother.' It was a small confession and said uneasily. 'It's not quite a fulltime job. As you can see, I have a bit of time to myself.'

Perceval told her about how he was settling his own mother's affairs. 'I really admire you for looking after your mother. My mother dedicated her life to me. And I left. Now she's gone. And I can't help feeling guilty about not having done more, about being absent when she needed me most. What you are doing is important … you have my respect.'

'My mother has never found it *important*. Unlike you, she doesn't show much *respect* either. She thinks it's my *duty*. I suppose you probably think, to use my mother's sort of language, that I'm living a "guilt trip". It's more complicated than that.'

Since Elin didn't expand on the complications, Perceval thought he could picture the smallness of her life. The quiet house, the shadowed presence of her mother everywhere, Elin's room her only refuge, books, notebooks filled with poems perhaps begun and never finished, the predictability of days, her little escapes to this café, speaking to no one, watching other people's lives pass by, as life was passing her by. This vision made him sad and, though he did feel compassion, he questioned the reason for his compassion. Was it really self-pity, Elin a more reticent, more elusive, yet more creative female version of himself? Maybe a couple of days on *Knight Errant* had encouraged the absurd idea that his duty really *was* to rescue damsels in distress, even if the truth had so far been the opposite. Anyway, Elin didn't give the impression of being in distress. And was her existence any less pointless than his? Probably not.

'My mother lived what you might call an untamed existence,' she told him. 'You might also call it rootless, alternative, unconventional … maybe like life on a narrowboat? You'd know better than me.'

'Me?' He laughed. 'I wouldn't know. This canal trip is a once-off. That sort of life is not for me. I wouldn't make a good hippy. I don't have a pilgrim soul.'

Elin smiled at the words 'pilgrim soul' and said, 'You are poetic without knowing it, Alex. Pilgrim soul, that's from Yeats.'

'I didn't know that.'

'Actually', Elin's smile faded, 'my mother wasn't good at living alternatively either. Her pilgrim soul was always getting lost. She's not very good at living in general. She finds it hard to cope, if you understand what I mean.' She paused. 'If you appreciate ironies, she doesn't want me to live like her, even if we're stuck together, so that, in a manner of speaking, I *do* live like her. So, here I am.'

Elin took a sip of coffee and seemed about to say more but stopped abruptly as Perceval's sandwich arrived. The waitress smiled benevolently at them. The sandwich was substantial and just what Perceval needed. He examined the thick slices of bread and the sizeable chunks of cheese. He glanced at Elin and said, 'I see the Welsh like their food satisfying and simple. It's just as I like it too.' She smiled weakly and he had the impression she was about to retreat into silence again and return to her book. 'I feel bad now not only for disturbing you but for stuffing my face in front of you. Can I offer you half of this sandwich? There's such a lot.'

Elin's expression was briefly one of horror at this suggestion, but she recovered her cool quickly. 'No thank you. I think you need all the energy you can for a hard day on the canal. I can't deny you the full pleasure of our Welsh cuisine.'

Perceval thought denial something Elin was well-practised in. And he suspected that for her eating in public was uncouth, impure, too primeval, an appetite best kept private and under control. And respecting her delicacy, he didn't wolf down the food as he wished, but ate decorously, aware that she averted her eyes as he bit and chewed. He couldn't help wondering if physical intimacy of any sort might appal her as much as eating in public would. Was she denying herself relationships because of the messiness and loss of control? Maybe she didn't need anyone to love her, preferring to remain unknowable, loving instead the exquisite sorrow of being separate from the world and a life of loneliness? Such idle speculation! Who did he think he was? Sigmund Freud? He smiled at his pretentious imaginings as he sat back from the remains of his sandwich.

Elin misinterpreted his expression. 'You look as if you

enjoyed that.'

'I did. And I apologise for my vulgar appetite.' Perceval noted she accepted his apology as if 'vulgar appetite' was exactly how she did think of it.

Elin glanced at the clock and he assumed she must leave at the same time, every day. As she made motions to go, pulling out a purse from a crocheted shoulder bag hung on the back of the chair, he told her he would pay the bill together. She shook her head but he insisted. At the till, he paid by card and added a decent tip.

'Thank you,' the waitress said, 'much appreciated.' She glanced round the cash desk at Elin, who, still seated, was fussing on a winter coat over her heavy jumper, and whispered, 'I'm glad she had some company. She always seems so lonely.'

'She may not thank you for having to put up with me.'

The waitress nudged his arm and said, 'Oh, go on with you.'

Elin had remained seated, out of courtesy he thought, and thanked him again for paying. Perceval gestured that she should stay seated. 'Only for a moment,' he said. It was obvious from her look she was apprehensive about what was coming next but there was also a suggestion she was intrigued. 'It's only something I was told my first night on the canal. As a poet I thought you might find it interesting. Would you believe I'd tried to moor up but hadn't a clue about how to tie a knot.'

Elin put a hand to her lips again and her eyes widened in disbelief. 'No!'

'You may not think I could be such a fool ... no, no, please don't tell me!' She did laugh this time. 'Luckily for me, a woman, Bron was her name, saw me struggling like an idiot and came to my rescue. She showed me how to tie up properly. Then she made me do it for myself.'

'She sounds like a headmistress. Did she just happen to be passing?'

'She was on a boat nearby. She was a retired policewoman, actually. Her friend, Jo, she *was* a schoolmistress once. She gave me my first ever tarot reading.

'Really? They must have liked you a lot.'

'And they fed me well too.'

'Mothered you, maybe? In that case, you really *were* lucky.'

'Bron gave me a knot. She'd made it from a strand of rope from her own boat. She told me it was a memento not only of what I'd learned but also a symbol for living.' Perceval fished it out of his jacket pocket to show Elin.

'Was this something to do with the tarot reading?' she asked with a hint of scepticism.

Perceval wondered if her mother's alternative lifestyle had involved tarot cards, incense, chanting mantras, and that he may have touched a nerve of resentment. 'In part, yes. What the reading taught me was that everything is puzzling, everything is capable of being read in different ways, and that life is a tangle for good or ill. Bron gave me the knot to keep that truth in mind. Jo, the tarot reader, called it "the knot intrinsicate." I liked that.'

'What does intrinsicate mean?' she asked.

'Life is an intricately woven tale of complex strands … I think … for instance freedom bound up with attachment, responsibility with recklessness … paradoxical, I guess … maybe in life there are things you *shouldn't* untangle but maybe there are those which you *should* … But you're the poet. You'll know how words can have many meanings. Anyway, I thought the knot might interest you …'

Elin considered his words for a moment. She smiled. 'You've given me something to think about, maybe an idea for a poem.'

Chapter Seventeen

KNIGHT ERRANT cruised along a passage of canal overhung by trees on both sides, a rural idyll tempered only by the steam from the stainless-steel chimney of the chocolate factory rising like emissions from a power station cooling tower, a dissonance corresponding to Perceval's own conflicted thoughts after meeting Elin.

When they parted, there'd been no exchange of telephone numbers, a mutual understanding, it seemed, that the preciousness of their exchange was its transience. Perceval had walked away with a sense of satisfaction that Elin had found pleasant diversion in his company. And possibly a poem. But doubts had crept in later. What if she hadn't taken it that way? What if, in her mind, the knot he'd spoken of was something more than a universal symbol? Had he, in his ingenuous way, implied something he hadn't meant? As he kept a steady hand on the tiller, his memory of what had passed between them became uncertain.

He replayed their conversation, his words, her expressions. He'd meant well, been an agreeable companion for a while, made her smile, and he'd even made the waitress happy. But did meaning well absolve him of consequences? He pictured her at home, retreating from the mother to her room, collapsing onto the bed, sighing, thinking of him, the gallant romantic on his narrowboat. And would this brief encounter become another source of melancholy in her life? Would she return to the café, hoping he would come back to make things right in her life? Had he unintentionally made her life less, rather than more, bearable?

You really are a fool, Perceval shook his head. You're living no medieval romance. His imagination switched to Elin arriving home, dealing with the needs of a spaced-out mother talking about her Glastonbury days, uninterested in her daughter's morning, and demanding her full attention. He could see Elin sighing, responding to insistent practical demands, looking forward to peace and quiet later, undisturbed by intruders into her personal space, Perceval already forgotten, and a poem to be written. That scene eased his conscience. And there was Fleur to meet again.

He leaned forward to consult the map set on the cabin's hood. He'd be at Chirk Marina shortly. His goal was to reach the village of Froncysyllte before dusk and maybe tie up there for the night. He was expecting at some point to encounter the returning kayakers. Perceval tried to shake off the doubt which now seized him – if he could imagine already being forgotten by Elin, might the same not also be true of Fleur?

Perceval had written down his mobile number on the reverse of a grimy sheet of paper he'd found in the boat. He'd folded it, put it into the plastic bag required for toiletries at airport security, and carefully sealed it. If he saw Fleur, his intention was to slow and hand over his number. Or, if that didn't seem possible, he would throw the bag into the water as near to her kayak as he could. That plan was back-up. Better, of course, if he could stop and spend time with her. But he wasn't sure if it was possible. As he committed to fulfil his promise, a watery sun dispelled the gloom of the day, and he took this as a good omen.

At a canal bend, he got his first sighting of Chirk Marina. Rows of boats were wintering out, tightly moored in front of a large white building behind which was open farmland. What made his heart pump faster was the sight of young women on the grassy ridge before the marina, their paddles cast aside at random, lifebelts dropped wherever they'd been shrugged off, kayaks scattered along the bank. They were standing or sitting, drinking from water bottles and eating, chatting animatedly with one another, an easy solidarity binding them. He scanned the faces at a distance but couldn't see Fleur. Cutting the throttle on *Knight Errant,* he slowed, ready to wave and shout her name. But she wasn't there. Was it the same group as before? Surely it must be. Yes, it was. He recognised one of the women who'd made a saucy remark earlier. But where was Fleur? Had she spotted Knight Errant and, embarrassed, was deliberately avoiding him? He didn't want to believe that.

He could see no possibility of tying up on the marina side. The bank was in shallow water and hidden by reeds, rising gently to where the kayaks lay. Perceval prepared to move across as close as he could when another narrowboat came cautiously around the bend towards him. Port to port he remembered and adjusted his course across the canal. As they passed slowly, the man on the tiller shouted, 'Much better day now'. Perceval replied flatly that it was perfect for November.

The boat was called *Nemesis* and despite Perceval raising himself on tiptoes to look over its roof, it blocked his view until *Knight Errant* was beyond the marina's bank. There was no way back now. Another boat was approaching from the rear and Perceval couldn't do a reversing manoeuvre without drifting into its path. And as the canal narrowed approaching the tunnel ahead, Perceval couldn't stop either without blocking it and causing a jam. So, he had to go on.

The maw of Whitehouse Tunnel swallowed him into darkness. It was much shorter than the one at Chirk, but the flow of water had the same effect, pressing against the hull of *Knight Errant,* resisting its progress, giving Perceval as little control as before. It slowed him too. The atmosphere was the same, close and dank, the walls slick with moisture with drops of water dripping from the tunnel ceiling onto his forehead. Perceval had the impression of being entombed and the only sense he had of moving at all was to look backwards to the boat following behind. It seemed an age to reach the exit and when he was finally out of the tunnel, the sun had disappeared again. The clouds above were a uniform grey, the water below gun metal, and the day was drifting towards evening. He needed to tie up quickly and run back to the marina. He had made a promise.

He let the following boat overtake, the man on the tiller giving him a friendly blast on the horn to thank him. Perceval waved hastily in acknowledgement, nudging his boat towards the bank, seeing that he would have to knock in pins to tie up. More time wasted. He worked quickly, locked up the boat, and ran back as fast as he could. Reaching the tunnel, he was impeded by a group of middle-aged cyclists pushing their bikes towards him. They took up the passageway and he had to wait until they were through before he could dash on. Please Lord, if there is a Lord, he said to himself, please don't be sleeping when I need you.

When he got to the marina, the women had gone. He ran around the turn, but he couldn't see any kayaks on the canal ahead of him. With the flow in their favour this time, they'd obviously made much swifter progress. He looked at his watch. It had taken him just over half-an-hour. What a difference half-an-hour made. He wanted to shout at the sky. Or should he shout at the earth? The Sleeping Lord had betrayed him. Or had his own faint heart denied him? Why hadn't he stopped when he first saw the women on the bank? And where had Fleur been? He'd let the opportunity slip by lacking true resolve. He knew he'd betrayed himself.

And he'd broken his promise.

Chapter Eighteen

Perceval travelled on dejectedly.

In a narrow stretch of water after the tunnel and distracted by his failure, he steered *Knight Errant* precariously close to the far bank. There was an ugly noise as the hull scraped along heavy stones supporting the canal edge. He cursed this March of Wales where Offa had built his Dyke. He cursed this furrowed body of land with the hanging trees over the water, Godforsaken and threatening. He raged against the sleeping Lord. He damned the promise of the tarot cards. Despite correcting course, the scraping continued. He gritted his teeth at the sound, praying that, having got this far, he wasn't going to tear a hole in the hull, sink ignominiously, and block the Llangollen Canal. His heart was no longer in what he was doing and for the first time since childhood, he felt like weeping.

'Discipline! Steady hand on the tiller,' Perceval counselled himself. 'Steady hand on the tiller … and get Fleur out of your head, you fool. You lost her.'

Ahead was a lifting bridge, something else he'd never encountered, and beyond the village of Froncysyllte, a watering station, and then the Pontcysyllte Aqueduct. He was certain neither his discipline nor his self-talk was up to taking on another aqueduct today. Perceval looked at his watch. Only a few hours of daylight were left. He had no idea how long it would take him to lift the bridge and bring it down again. He would look for a suitable place for *Knight Errant* as close to Froncysyllte as possible. There was a pub there which his uncle had circled. That's where he would go to drown his sorrows.

The approach to the lifting bridge did require discipline.

A row of narrowboats occupied the left bank, and he slowed to a crawl as he went by. These boats looked like they were in permanent residence. Chained to the bank, not roped, their roofs were covered with supplies of wood and coal, their bows converted into additional living or storage space by cratch covers, and their sterns protected by all-weather hoods. One name struck him as he passed, *The Boar of Cornwall*, alongside which sign had been painted a fierce boar's head. Under it was written in smaller script the words 'All shall fear his courage'. Quite the statement, Perceval thought, and he felt shame at his own lack of self-belief.

Pulling over *Knight Errant* to the near side of the bridge, Perceval tied up to a ring in the concrete towpath. He took a windlass and walked quickly towards the bridge, overtaking an elderly woman hobbling along, her knees and hips giving obvious trouble, with two equally elderly Jack Russell Terriers. She asked Perceval if he could wait before lifting the bridge so she could drive her car across and pointed to a small SUV parked at the gate of field next to the canal.

'Yes, of course,' Perceval answered, glad that he had an excuse to take some time. He would need to figure out the lift mechanism. When the woman asked him to allow her car across, he'd been surprised the bridge was strong enough to take its weight. He anticipated the winding would require a lot of effort. The woman waved a thank you as she drove over, while her dogs gave him curious looks from the back window. Perceval fixed the windlass into place over the spindle and began to wind. The machinery functioned with surprising ease, though nothing happened for a time. Then he saw the heavy decking start to lift, slowly but distinctly, as the counterweight did its work.

Two cyclists, a man and a woman in their late fifties or early sixties, dressed in matching bright yellow jackets and black leggings, arrived at the far side when the bridge had risen about one foot off the bank. They spoke to one another, glared across at Perceval, spoke to one another again, looked back at him impatiently, their faces primly entitled. The man raised his voice enough so that Perceval could hear him moan about the inconvenience he was causing them. Damn them, he thought. Wasn't it the canal code that life should be taken slowly? After the blockage at Whitehouse Tunnel which had delayed him getting to the marina in time, he had, as people like to say, 'issues' with cyclists.

Out of the corner of his eye he saw the couple having another discussion. It must have dawned on them not only must they to wait for the bridge to rise. They also had to wait for Perceval to return to *Knight Errant*, take it through the pinch and tie up before it could be lowered again. An argument started between the couple, the man pointing out *Knight Errant*'s position, pointing to where it needed to be taken, jabbing his finger at Perceval, and finally spreading his arms wide in frustration. He lost patience and pushed his bike towards the pedestrian footbridge, reluctantly followed by the woman and they began to struggle up the steps. Nearing the top, the man slipped, tipped forward and lost control of his bike which ran backwards into the shins of the woman. Perceval heard a sharp female yelp, a loud male curse and glimpsed the entanglement of bodies, wheels and metal frames. A group of middle-aged walkers who'd stopped to watch Perceval at work shook their heads in disbelief at the scene on the footbridge, the men making comments out the sides of their mouths, the women turning their backs as if in contempt.

Oh sweet, sweet, *Schadenfreude,* Perceval smirked. Only bad things come to those who cannot wait. You breach the canal code at your peril. When the couple finally made it down the other side, physically bruised, their dignity lost, still arguing with each other, they cycled off along the towpath towards

Chirk, their day probably ruined. And, Perceval thought, it couldn't have happened to a nicer couple. How true were Hazlitt's words? 'To see others suffer does one good, to make others suffer even more so'. It certainly had done Perceval good.

The bridge fully raised, his spirits lifted, Perceval sauntered back to *Knight Errant,* nodding genially to the walkers, who said hello in return. After untying, he cruised carefully through the pinch, no bumping this time, and tied up on the other side. He lowered the bridge with greater facility as a pickup truck and a small van arrived at the far side of the canal. When he'd finished winding, he waved them onto the bridge, and they acknowledged Perceval as they drove over. He took the boat across the turning circle and steered past a row of narrowboats moored before the water point.

It probably wasn't necessary for him to fill up the tank but he thought it best just in case. Darkness was almost upon him. Streetlights had come on already in the village on the hill.

PART FIVE: THE FISHER QUEENS

Chapter Nineteen

A T the water point a long rubber hose stretched from the boat at the end of the row to the first tap. No one appeared to be attending to it and Perceval wasn't sure if the hose was a permanent attachment. All the other taps were free. He uncoiled his much smaller hose from where it lay in the bow, pulled it across the towpath to one of the free taps, and fixed the nozzle securely. In a reprise of his first night fiasco with the knots, when he looked for the cap of the water tank on *Knight Errant*, he couldn't find it. He searched on the bow decking. It wasn't there. He walked the length of the boat, checking along the hull for something resembling a petrol cap on a car. He couldn't find one. He swore under his breath and was about to abandon the job when a woman appeared on the transom of the boat to which the long hose was attached. She stepped onto the towpath and walked towards the taps, adjusting the lay of the hose a few times with her foot as she went.

The woman was of average height with a scrawny build, dressed in shabby blue jeans and a well-worn T-shirt, so faded Perceval couldn't decipher what was printed on its front, though it looked like the ghostly image of a heavy metal band. It was quite cold at this hour, and he was surprised that such a gaunt woman wouldn't be wearing more substantial clothing. Her cheeks were sunken, her expression was pained, not by physical ailment, Perceval thought, but by existence itself. It was hard to guess the woman's age, early fifties perhaps, though she might be younger. On her lips hung a half-smoked cigarette and she didn't speak or greet, her mission, it seemed, only to check if the water in the line was flowing properly and the nozzle secure.

Perceval stood hopelessly, ridiculously, holding the open end of his hose at his chest as if at any moment he was going to blow down it.

'Excuse me,' he said in a tone of vulnerability, expecting it to provoke sympathy. 'I know this is a silly question, but have you any idea where I can attach this hose on the boat and fill the water tank? I can't find the cap.'

She looked Perceval over, not with contempt (or he assumed not) but with irritation (he read that for sure), didn't say anything immediately, but walked past him to check her own tap. When she was satisfied everything was in order, he saw her shoulders sag and heard a heavy sigh. The woman turned and walked to *Knight Errant*, Perceval following behind with his hose like a schoolboy. On the narrow ledge which ran along its flank, she tapped a small, recessed metal disk. 'You'll need a key to open. It's usually where the windlass is kept,' she said squinting to avoid smoke from the cigarette which bobbed on the lower lip getting in her eyes. 'That's where it should be, at any rate.'

Her accent was Scouse, not strong, but recognisable. She added nothing to what she'd said and, returning to make a few finicky adjustments to her own hose, she walked back to her boat. She stubbed out the cigarette on the edge of the bank as Bron had done, not flicking it into the water or throwing onto the towpath, but dropping it into a small metal bin on the transom. This woman's behaviour had thrown Perceval. He wasn't used to women treating him so dismissively. However, he accepted that he probably deserved it for being so unobservant. And she had helped him in the end.

He searched in the locker by the cabin door and on the shelf below the windlass he found what looked like the key, a brass affair shaped like a miniature tomahawk. Sure enough, the blade of the tomahawk fitted the indentation of the cap, and he was able to screw it off easily. Perceval inserted the hose deep into the tank, went back to the tap, turned it on full, watched the hose come alive as the water flowed and heard it gush into the tank. He walked back to stand by the boat just in case the hose became dislodged. The woman's baffling coolness was immediately displaced by an image of Fleur, her intelligent eyes, her warm smile, her physical vigour, her voice … no, he couldn't quite recall the voice, and it bothered him. Perceval stared at the trees across the canal, the leaves as they fell, and tried to conjure the sound of her voice. Nothing came to him. He closed his eyes. Still nothing came. He could only hear his own voice saying 'Promise'.

'Got it, then?' It was the Liverpudlian woman back at her tap, turning it off, a fresh cigarette on her lips.

'Oh, yes, thanks, I really felt stupid for not knowing and apologies for interrupting you earlier.' His mother had taught him that civility cost nothing.

The woman waved one hand in dismissal as she unscrewed the hosepipe nozzle with her other. His civility was acknowledged with a tentative grin (though it was hard to tell. The woman's lips might only have been adjusting her cigarette).

'It's been a hard day,' she said through the tobacco smoke, and Perceval knew this was as close to an apology or explanation as he was going to get.

'I have another question, if you don't mind.'

The woman shook out some water from the nozzle and set down the hose on the towpath. 'Go on.' Her cigarette bobbed up and down as she spoke slowly, warily.

'Is it alright for me to stay tied up here for the night?'

'Normally it's not. The answer is in the name.' This wasn't said cuttingly but factually. She took the cigarette from her lips. 'Water points should be kept free for those who need water, obviously.' She looked up at the darkening sky. 'At this time of day, at this time of the year, I'd say you're the last boat coming up. Did you notice anyone behind you earlier?'

Perceval told her not since the Whitehouse Tunnel and that boat had overtaken him. No one, he added, had come through the lift-bridge.

'You can take a chance on staying where you are, then. You're not taking up every space as it is.' She put the cigarette back in her mouth and began to gather up the hose to drag it back to her boat, then hesitated. 'If you are tying up here, you'll have to be away at the crack of dawn. Sometimes boats come through early and water up before going over the aqueduct. The weekend starts tomorrow. You don't need some old Blert kicking you out of your scratcher at an ungodly hour, do you now?' Perceval said he certainly didn't need that, and laughed. 'If I were you,' she added, 'I'd pull over to the other side. Boats tie up both sides in summer, especially when there's a queue to go across the aqueduct. Canal's wide enough for anyone to pass, up or down. Then you can kip as long as you want.'

'Thank you. I think I'll take your advice about the other bank. I've had a hard day too, can't rule out sleeping in tomorrow morning.'

The woman's expression suggested Perceval didn't know the meaning of the term 'hard day' and it made him feel ashamed. Water starting to pour out of *Knight Errant's* tank (it mustn't have been even half-empty) and interrupted what might have been a difficult moment.

'I'd better not waste the water', he said and ran to turn off the tap. By the time he'd done so, the woman was gone.

When he'd stowed the hose, Perceval set about taking *Knight Errant* across the canal. He was about to untie the centre line when he saw the woman walking back towards him.

'I should have mentioned, if you're looking for anywhere to eat,' she said, 'the pub in the village is a good place. You need to be a bit of a mountain goat to get to it, up there on the hill,' and she pointed out the top of a tree-lined ridge. 'But it's worth the effort. It should be no bother for a young man like you. There's also a decent take-away a bit further along. The village store is probably closed by now.'

'Thanks so much. With the water cap and all, I don't know what I'd have done without you.'

For the first time, the woman's face lost its mark of pain, and her dull eyes lit up at his gratitude. She hesitated, as if wishing to say more, and Perceval wondered if, in her hesitation, she was about to ask him for dinner on her boat. Or was she hoping he would invite her out with him? They held each other's gaze briefly, an instant broken by a loud male voice in a thick Scouse accent.

'Steff! I need some help with this damned gas bottle.'

The woman's slight frame stiffened visibly at the words, like they were a claim on her life. A heavily built man with a shaven head, rolls of flesh bulging on his neck, face angry and flushed, a paunch straining buttons on a short sleeve checked shirt, was standing on the transom of her boat. As she turned quickly to go, Perceval thanked her again. The woman's look conveyed a habit of obedience and a sadness he could only guess at, and beyond any remedy he might have. Perceval couldn't help thinking he'd failed again.

Chapter Twenty

Perceval walked on the towpath heading to Froncysyllte. There was a gentle breeze and leaves along the canal were falling thickly. Even in the short time it had taken him to have a wash and change his shirt, the black roof of *Knight Errant* had become nature's orange and yellow. When he was parallel with the Liverpudlians' boat, the *Spirit of Mersey*, the couple appeared onto the transom. Across the canal, he waved to the woman framed in the light from the cabin. She nodded back shyly and Perceval heard the man ask, 'Who the hell is that?'

He went over the lifting bridge and walked along the path by the basin before turning onto a narrow curving road where he found a set of steep steps rising directly towards the pub. Perceval had to stop for breath a few times as he went up and decided he really must get fit again. And he thought of Fleur once more, paddling across aqueduct and through tunnel, leaving him and his boat far behind. He visualised her now in company, maybe at The Bridge Inn where he'd seen her this morning, laughing, joking, and having a good time without him. He saw her, in his absence, surrounded by other men, their eyes on her, her eyes on them. What a wretched fate, what sickness unto death! But had her eyes not chosen him? In a fit of self-pity, the regret of the afternoon returned to plague him. He needed to get a grip. Discipline, he told himself, discipline. And beer!

At the top of the steps, yellow light from the pub fell across the street. 'A good feed will always sort you out,' his mother used to tell him. What she never said was 'a drink is what you need'. She rarely touched alcohol, but not for religious or health reasons. Alcohol made her think too much about the past and what had been taken from her. 'It only makes me want to kill those who murdered your father,' she would confess. He remembered as a boy saying something like she wasn't alone in that wish. She'd hugged him and then said severely, 'Promise me never to get involved in anything like that, Alex.' And he hadn't. He wondered if alcohol would make him wish to kill those men he imagined with designs on Fleur. He didn't have to wonder. He felt that way already without alcohol. So, what did it matter?

In the whitewashed stone hallway of the inn sat a man on a wooden bench, a small dog sleeping on a blanket beside him. He was powerfully built, had a long beard as well as a full head of salt and pepper hair, and wore a grey chunky woollen jumper which, at first glance, looked to Perceval like chain mail. They greeted one another. The man's accent wasn't Welsh but sounded like West Country. He recognised Perceval's accent immediately.

'You're from Ulster, aren't you?'

It was a statement rather than a question. Perceval hadn't heard the word 'Ulster' used in years, not as a description of someone's birthplace anyway. 'That's right. I've just come up on the canal from Whittington and heading to Llangollen.'

'Hire boat, is it?'

Perceval explained the purpose of his journey and told the man about *Knight Errant*.

'Sounds like you're on a quest,' he laughed. 'You're not called Lancelot by any chance, are you?'

'No, Alex.'

'Arthur,' the man replied and held out a hand. Perceval expected his own hand to be crushed but Arthur's grasp was gentle.

'Are you from Somerset?' Perceval asked.

'Me? From Somerset? You should be grateful I'm not easily offended,' he said and laughed even louder. 'I'm Cornish, born and bred.' A young barmaid with jet black hair, a friendly face and full rosy cheeks, came into the hallway from the bar. Arthur looked at her and chuckled. 'This young man, a stranger in these parts, thinks I'm from Somerset. What do you think about that, Cerys?' Turning to Perceval, he lowered his voice and almost whispered, 'But I've been called much worse here.' To Cerys he said, 'Isn't that right, my girl?'

'What you on about now?' Cerys shook her head dismissively. 'He does talk some rubbish.' Her Welsh enunciation trilled on the 'r' of 'rubbish'.

'Alex here is from Ulster, he's on a quest, a knight errant he tells me ... and this, Alex, is Cerys, a damsel of these parts, quite often distressed ...'

'He knows my name already,' Cerys said. 'Get on with it. Some people have work to do, you know.'

'I said to Alex here I might feel insulted to be thought I hail from Somerset (he pronounced it Zomerzet) except your Welsh lot use an even worse insult. And Alex here made a genuine mistake whereas you do it deliberately.'

'It's well deserved, though,' she said.

'Do you know how they insult me here, Alex?'

'They call you English?'

It was the issue, half joke, half complaint, he knew everyone from the so-called Celtic fringe would have. And he also knew from his aunt and uncle that the Cornish cherished their own distinct identity. Arthur and Cerys laughed loudly, simultaneously putting out their hands as if warding off evil. Perceval hadn't expected quite such a brilliant success.

'An insult, my young friend,' Arthur smiled, 'which Cerys and I can share. It's about the only thing we do share.' Cerys didn't dissent. 'No, here they call me ...'

'The Bore of Cornwall, as in B-O-R-E' Cerys interrupted. 'Just happens to be true.' She trilled the 'r' once more.

'See what I mean, Alex. Just proves I'm not easily offended, doesn't it?'

'When I arrived, there was a boat tied up below called *Boar of Cornwall*,' Perceval said matter-of-factly. 'It was spelled B-O-A-R this time.'

'That's his old wreck.' Cerys pointed at Arthur. 'It's been here so long we can't get rid of it. Or of him for that matter.'

'You'd go broke in this pub if it weren't for me.'

'Huh, you wish,' Cerys said and turned to Perceval. 'Can I get you something to drink before he bores you to death?'

Perceval eyed up the three-quarters empty pint of beer sitting on the bench beside Arthur. It looked like his thing. 'I'll have what the B-O-A-R, is having,' and asked Arthur if he'd like another.

'Thank you, my chivalrous friend, but as Cerys has reminded me, I've been here too long already,' Arthur replied, glancing at his watch. 'And Hector here,' he patted his dog, 'needs his evening walk before we both turn in.'

It seemed early to be thinking of turning in for the night but then Perceval didn't know what Arthur did for a living, if anything. He remembered King Arthur as the Sleeping Lord and grinned. When Cerys returned carrying his pint, Perceval asked about the menu. She directed his attention to a blackboard chalked with a large choice of dishes.

'You're a brave man, Alex,' Arthur chuckled.

'Don't listen to the B-O-R-E,' Cerys told him.

'Believe it or not, Alex, the food is good,' Arthur said then hesitated. 'More than can be said for the service, eh Cerys?'

'Didn't you say you had to go?'

Arthur finished off his drink, roused Hector from his slumbers, then stood and stretched. 'I'll be off then,' he said to Cerys.

'Good riddance,' she replied.

'I'll see you tomorrow,' he answered.

'See you tomorrow,' she said in a comradely tone.

'Godspeed, good knight,' Arthur said to Alex, slapping him

on the back. 'Let's go Hector', and they went out into the night.

Cerys told Perceval she'd put his pint on account. 'Just give me a shout when you're ready to order,' she said and left him to contemplate the blackboard on the wall.

He dithered over what he should choose, and eventually he went for Spaghetti Bolognese, ordering extra bread. He thought a lot of carbs would do him good as well as soak up the beer he intended to drink. Cerys showed him the main dining area with its half-a-dozen polished wooden tables and chairs. He was the only person there. Sitting outside on the balcony, Perceval could see a middle-aged couple sharing a bottle of wine. Near them and leaning on the guard rail, two young men gazed onto the canal below, smoking. From across the hallway, in the public bar, intermittently he could hear muffled chatter, and every now and then a loud guffaw.

Arthur hadn't misled him. As he ate and drank, Perceval's earlier dejection about Fleur began to lift. Not entirely but sufficiently for him to enjoy his meal. He tried to concentrate on the positives of his 'quest' as Arthur called it. Hadn't he got this far without mishap? His uncle hadn't checked up constantly on his progress and hadn't that affirmed the trust he put in him? Perceval wondered if he should call him now but decided against it. What better moment to call than from Llangollen, his quest over, and to bask in his uncle's gratitude. Who was he kidding though? Even his safe arrival wouldn't compensate for breaking his promise and losing Fleur.

Suddenly, he had the idea of looking on the internet for kayak clubs in the area. Might he get Fleur's address that way? Did that sort of information even exist? He typed into his mobile the words kayak club, Shropshire, Fleur. He scrolled through a few results but couldn't find her. He typed in kayak club, Wrexham, Fleur. No luck either. He tried a few other permutations of place and substituted canoe for kayak. Still he found nothing. He tapped on images. There were plenty of photos of club members but he saw no one who looked like Fleur. Should he phone a club secretary and ask for help? But mightn't they think he was some kind of stalker and call the police? Defeated, he abandoned the idea and went to the bar, intent on settling his bill.

'Don't you want another beer?' Cerys asked. 'There's a nice fire going in the room over there. Warm you up before heading back to your boat.'

Perceval had drunk two already and, though he didn't need a third one, the prospect of a fire and warmth did appeal, and he told Cerys she'd sold him on the idea. On the off chance, he asked if she knew of a Fleur who kayaked on the canal. He described her as best he could.

'No, sorry,' she answered, drawing out and trilling the 'r' again.

'Pity,' he replied, and Cerys looked at him knowingly but didn't prompt Perceval to elaborate.

'I'll put everything on account,' Cerys told him. 'Have a seat and I'll bring your drink over. Same again?'

'Thanks,' he said.

As he strolled towards the saloon, Cerys called after him, 'I'll ask the others here if they know of a Fleur. And don't worry. The B-O-R-E won't be back in this evening.'

Chapter Twenty-One

So, this is where everyone is, Perceval said to himself. Logs burned brightly in a free-standing metal fire-basket set into the original stone. There were wooden benches with cushions along the side walls and most of the spaces were already taken. The clientele consisted of middle-aged couples like the one he'd seen earlier on the balcony. Nobody took any notice him. A smaller bench on one side of the fire was free and he took a seat, stretching out his legs towards the flames.

Cerys set his pint on the table and told him the bad news – no one knew of Fleur.

'Thanks for asking anyway,' Perceval said to her. 'It's pleasant here. But I shouldn't drink too much. I just remembered I've got all those steps to negotiate later.'

'You can always go down by the road. It's longer but safer.'

'Oh, I'll risk the short cut.'

'Famous last words,' Cerys said.

Alcohol, which could stimulate others into volubility and expressiveness (or in his mother's case, to thoughts of murder), tended to make Perceval quiet, almost somnolent (much like the Welsh people in this cosy room, he realised). Tonight, no Dylan Thomas held forth, no Rob Brydon entertained. These locals were unlikely to engage with him, he guessed, and his mind drifted, unmoored, to thoughts of Fleur, the way she'd run beside his boat to warn him of leaves in the propeller, her look when friends teased her. He replayed what might have happened later, Fleur paddling across to *Knight Errant*, their easy conversation, exchanging phone numbers, and indulging the promise of what could follow ... promise ... he'd broken his promise.

A movement beside him disturbed his reverie. A woman who appeared to be in her early forties sat down heavily beside him, trailing with her the scent of cigarette smoke, fresh about her hair, stale on her clothes. From the corner of his eye, Perceval caught the briefest glimpse of something in her expression, weariness perhaps, bitterness possibly, or even worse, the grim face of comfortless despair. He looked away quickly, sensing only tension in her presence. From the woman's loud throat-clearing hack, he suspected there was possibly aggressive shamelessness in her behaviour. There had been no introductory pleasantries, no 'do you mind' or 'is this place free'. She was no Angharad.

Perceval considered himself imposed upon and, more importantly, he felt slightly intimidated. This woman had all the no-nonsense abruptness of Bron but possessed none of Bron's finesse or civility. He saw others in the room doing their best to ignore her and considered his intuition of trouble was correct. Yet he knew he would sit on, rather than move away, as he had every right to do, accommodating himself to the world rather than imposing his will upon it. He felt resentful, not only because of the woman beside him, but also because of that acceptance he too readily indulged. It pulled him back to his lack of courage at the marina and to the image of Fleur being seduced by some other man. It was an image which made him queasy.

The woman put on the table a pint of lager and a whiskey chaser. He'd never seen a woman drink a whiskey chaser. He glanced quickly again. She was obviously strong, solid and muscular, though now tending towards overweight. Her trousers were army desert fatigues, and she wore a loose khaki T-shirt. He assumed her bulk made her oblivious to the chill of a November evening. Her face was full and round, her complexion swarthy, though the tiny red veins threaded across her cheeks and the bridge of her nose betrayed overindulgence in alcohol. The puffiness beneath her eyes appeared to confirm the toll drink had taken. By the awkward way she stretched out her right leg, Perceval was certain it was prosthetic. One of his father's former colleagues had been the victim of an IRA bomb blast, losing one lower limb and the use of an arm. Perceval was all too aware of the signs. As his neighbour adjusted the position of her prosthesis, her elbow struck Perceval hard in the ribs. There was no apology.

Why shouldn't he move to stand at the bar where maybe he could chat to Cerys? Why not? But he knew why not. Civility. He'd read in a novel once (he thought it was a Graham Greene story, but couldn't be sure) where the author says of one of the characters that he would risk death rather than breach decorum. He'd always put himself in the same category. His mother had brought him up to be 'proper' and this was one of its consequences. And since his pint was only a quarter drunk, he wouldn't have the opportunity to leave any time soon. No, he was stuck. What a bloody awful day this has turned out to be when it began with such promise, he thought. Promise …

He heard the woman sigh loudly and then grunt (it may have been a suppressed belch, he wasn't sure). Though Perceval kept his head down, literally, staring into his beer, at the edge of his vision he saw the woman's hand grab the whiskey glass, put it to her mouth, and swallow the contents in one go. The empty glass was slammed back on the table as she exhaled noisily. She then took a deep draught of lager, wiped her lips with the back of a hand, and only when she leaned back on the bench did she appear to notice Perceval's presence. She looked at him coldly. He felt obliged to be polite.

'A hard day?' he asked agreeably, nodding at the empty whiskey glass.

'A hard day? A hard life!' she replied with an edge of scorn. 'If it's any business of yours,' she added with an edge of contempt.

Perceval was tempted to put up his hands to convey, 'You

see, I tried my best' and walk away. He judged he would have the sympathy of everyone else here. Instead, he apologised. 'I'm sorry, no need to take offence. It came to mind only because someone said those words to me earlier today.'

'Yeah, I'm sure they did. "Hard day!"', she imitated a whining tone. 'Jesus Christ Almighty … hard day' Yet her eyes showed pain rather than anger. Was it her leg? If she'd walked to the pub from the canal, he could understand her being in pain.

Perceval held her glare trying to show the woman that nothing she could say would provoke him out of good manners. For the time being at least, he thought her volcanic resentment had been stilled, her rage swallowed. She inspected Perceval more closely and then her attention shifted to others in the bar. He followed her gaze and noticed that they either looked away uncomfortably or continued to ignore the woman as best they could.

'People here think I'm half-mad,' she said in a voice loud enough for more than Perceval to hear. She snorted. 'No. Forget "half". They think I'm *completely* mad.' She knocked away the empty whiskey glass with a flick of her fingers and said in a lowered voice, almost conspiratorially, 'I'm not welcome here, you know.'

Perceval thought of Cerys, her genial banter with Arthur, her friendly smile, and found it hard to think this was true. Maybe if you annoy customers the bar staff might not be too welcoming? He didn't know. It was really none of his business. Yet hadn't she involved him in her business? He decided to take a risk, even if only to forestall another rant, and reached out a hand. 'My name's Alex. Alex Perceval.'

She was genuinely surprised. Perceval noticed how her hand twitched indecisively before she extended it to grasp his. Her shake was unexpectedly firm, more powerful than Arthur's earlier, almost crushing. 'Rhiannon. But no one ever calls me that. Rhi. Rhi Fisher. Then again, hardly anyone ever speaks to me these days.' She motioned to others in the room. 'They don't want to know me. Full stop.'

Perceval didn't ask Rhi why. He was certain she was going to tell him. She leaned forward and put both hands under her right thigh and pulled up the prosthetic limb from its stretched position. 'I'm sure you noticed but were too polite to ask,' she said. 'You don't need to apologise.' Perceval was sure that if he had asked earlier, Rhi would have responded aggressively. And he didn't ask now, merely blinked to acknowledge her point.

Rhi tapped her leg. 'I lost this one below the knee serving Queen and Country in Afghanistan.' She guffawed and took another deep gulp of lager. 'They say "lost", don't they, like I mislaid it somewhere and if only I'd looked hard enough, thought more about *where* I'd left it, I could go back and find it again. Then everything would be back to before. I'd be the good soldier I am – or was. Don't you think that's funny?'

Perceval wasn't being asked to comment, for Rhi wasn't looking at him but at her glass of lager. Now she had drawn his attention to the euphemism, he did think it strange. But he considered his opinion, one way or the other, to be irrelevant.

'I was one of two hundred and fifty British amputees. We all knew what the risks were. You can't be a soldier and not know the risks, even if you don't want to dwell on them. Don't get me wrong. The training, discipline, belonging, comradeship, being part of something.' She made quotation marks with her fingers at this last term. 'I loved army life. I was proud to be one of "the professionals" as they used to call us. That was all *before*.' She tapped her thigh again. '*Before* I left my leg on Afghanistan's plains and couldn't find it again.'

Rhi snorted and turned her glass around as if inspecting her past in the light gold of what remained of her lager. For the first time Perceval saw deep scarring on her neck below the thick black hair.

'I wasn't even frontline, you know. Women weren't allowed to be in so-called close combat. We were supportive role back then … except we never knew where the frontline was. And I was supposed to be an intelligence analyst. Can you believe that?' She raised her eyes from the glass and looked directly at Perceval. 'I was close enough that day. Have you ever heard of an IED?' She didn't wait for an answer. 'It's an "improvised explosive device". Whatever bastard improvised that one did a bloody good job. From their point of view. Not mine. Our Foxhound took a direct blast. The first thing I knew was when I woke up in the field hospital at Camp Bastion. They told me I'd been lucky. My mates were killed.' The aggressive tone returned. 'Do you think I was lucky, Alex?'

What should he answer to this question? He could only stay quiet and hear her out. Rhi swore loudly and unexpectedly. A woman across from their table shook her head in disapproval while her husband glanced reproachfully, as much at Perceval as at Rhi. He got the impression he wasn't considered with sympathy any longer but with irritation. He was Rhi's opportunity to ruin their quiet evening.

'Lucky, my fat ugly arse, Alex,' she said in a lower voice. 'I really won the lottery that day, didn't I?' Rhi took another drink. 'Here's a nice bit of military banter for you. A guy in hospital who was also recovering from amputation said to me, "I see you didn't make it home in one piece either." That sort of humour was the thing that kept me going back then.'

Rhi had squeezed so close to Perceval that he could feel the trembling tension in her body. Then he sensed its slow release as she set her glass back on the table. Suddenly, her face looked younger, fresher, as if she had discovered a gentle temperament long suppressed. 'I apologise, Alex. You shouldn't have to put up with me behaving like I really *am* mad.' She picked up her glass and finished her lager in one long draft.

It felt like her words had thrown down the challenge Jo had spoken of, the challenge for connection and compassion. 'Rhi, let me buy you another drink,' he said, doing his best to remove any note of pity from his voice.

'Oh!' she said, taken by surprise. 'Ah, ah, ye … well … yes. Thanks.'

'Same again?' Perceval pointed at the two glasses. When she hesitated, he added, 'I'm on my own tonight, had a bad day,' he smiled, 'and I could do with some company.' So far, she'd shown no interest whatsoever in him or why he was here. He would only volunteer that information if she did ask. Otherwise, he'd just let her talk. 'Scotch or Irish?' he asked. She hadn't heard properly and looked confused, so he lifted the shot glass. 'Scotch or Irish?'

'Scotch,' she mumbled.

'Double or single?'

'Double.'

As he walked to the bar, he heard her add under her breath, 'Cheers.'

Chapter Twenty-Two

PERCEVAL didn't want another beer. He was tipsy enough already, and a fourth was one too many. But he couldn't return without a drink for himself, sure Rhi would take it amiss as a sign of unwelcome charity. A half pint, he thought, would only make him appear wimpish, a non-alcoholic drink even more so. So he ordered another pint for himself – which he could always leave unfinished – along with the lager and whiskey for Rhi. He settled this dinner bill at the same time.

Cerys eyed up his order, reached beneath the bar, and pulled out a round plastic tray. She set the glasses on it. 'There,' she said, 'a bit easier for you now.' As Perceval prepared to go, she leaned across the counter, and lowering her voice, said, 'Thanks for keeping an eye on Rhi. But please don't let her drink too much. She's on meds, they're quite strong, so ...' and her voice trailed off.

For a short, befuddled moment, Perceval believed Cerys was warning him not to take sexual advantage of Rhi, an idea which had never, and would never, cross his mind. Even the suspicion of the accusation unsettled him. He could imagine the looks, the outrage, if, innocently, he were to leave the pub with her. Somehow, he must avoid that. Lifting the tray with both hands, he nodded to his own pint and explained, 'This is my last of the evening. After that ...' and shrugged his shoulders to indicate Rhi would no longer be his responsibility.

'Okay, fair enough,' Cerys said. 'Then I can keep an eye on her. And thanks again. You're being very good as it is.'

When he returned to their table, Perceval motioned for Rhi to take her drinks off the tray. He put the new pint beside his half empty glass and set the tray at the table leg. He shrugged off the critical looks of those around him.

'Cheers!' Rhi said once more as he sat beside her. She seemed more at ease with his presence if not with her life. She narrowed her eyes, pushed in further towards him, moving her head slightly to indicate everyone else in the room. 'Look at them. You've annoyed them no end.'

Her words provoked in Perceval's mind scenes from old films where a stranger arrives in some small town in Louisiana or maybe some village in Yorkshire, and quite innocently provokes the wrath of locals by poking into secrets they wish to keep hidden or by befriending the ostracised loner who embodies their guilt and shame. Why should it be any different in a Welsh village like this one? The thought made him uneasy. But those strangers in the films usually outstayed their welcome and asked uncomfortable questions, whereas he was going in the morning, leaving their secrets (if they had any) undisturbed. 'You know something, Rhi? That must be the first thing I've done right all day.'

Her eyes brightened but she didn't laugh. He wondered if she was capable of laughter anymore. 'You know something, Alex? You're not a bad sort.'

'Correction. Not *too* bad, you mean.'

'Okay. I'll give you that. Not *too* bad.' She raised her whiskey glass and swallowed the double in one. She shook her head at the effect of the Scotch then said, 'If only they were all like you.'

'Hold on, now. Hold on. Not so fast. The world would go to hell in a handcart if everyone really *was* like me.'

'I like you, Alex. You sound like my old army mates. Never accept praise. Just get on with things.'

'Unfortunately, getting on with things, even small things, that's my problem.'

She didn't take him up on this confession. And for all his

'being very good' as Cerys had put it, Perceval knew he hadn't deflected Rhi from the dark place in which she was confined.

'What was it for?' She slapped her thigh noisily. 'What was it all for?'

One couple left, looking over at them, the woman taking the man's arm and whispering something in his ear.

'I was wounded in 2016. That's almost ten years ago. Hard to believe. I'm not complaining about my treatment. They looked after me well, in Afghanistan and here. The medics, nurses, physios, therapists, they were first rate. They made me feel like a hero, you know, a warrior returned from battle, a good soldier who did her duty, carried home not on her shield but on an evacuee's trolley. It didn't last. It's an old, old story. You go home, are notable for a moment, an interest for a time, an object of pity for a while. Then you become someone to avoid because they don't want to be reminded *too* often, for they know you'll be a burden forever.' She shook her head. 'You're a nice boy, Alex, and all this is new to you. You're hearing me for the first time. But given time, *you'd* be like the rest of them. You'd cross the street to avoid me. You'd look on me as an embarrassment too. You'd think I should just get over it and get on with life as normal. But I don't really know normal any longer.

How could he respond without sounding either defensive or obsequious or challenging? He kept his mouth shut.

'Did you see on TV how they scuttled out of Afghanistan? The Americans pulled the plug, and our mission went down the drain. We abandoned everything, all the military hardware we dumped when we cut and ran. The ones who nearly killed me took over, they're probably still laughing at us. I was so ashamed. And I thought, Jesus Christ, what a complete and utter waste. It is a wound much deeper and more painful than this.' Rhi slapped her thigh. 'I can walk, just about. But the wound of betrayal, I don't think that will ever heal.'

Perceval was quite drunk now, thinking of his mother, of his father, and Northern Ireland, not of Rhi and Afghanistan.

'Like I said to you ...' Rhi's words were becoming slurred, 'nobody wants to know any longer. My presence here makes them feel uncomfortable.' She coughed a smoker's cough. 'Do you know *Fawlty Towers?* Do you know the sketch about the Germans? "Don't mention the war". Yeah, don't mention the bastard, pissing war!'

Her voice was raised again and another couple stood, shaking their heads. As they did, Rhi slammed a fist to her chest. 'Don't mention the bastard war because you'll have to mention me.' Rhi watched them leave, before turning back to Perceval. 'The real wound is here, Alex,' she repeated, pointing to her forehead. 'The real wound is that the country I served doesn't care. It's that the politicians who sent me there don't give a damn. They've all moved on. So why can't I? It's like *I'm* the problem and not them.'

A group of young men could be heard on the balcony being laddish. Rhi looked towards the sound as if it reminded her of army days. 'But it's not *me* that's sick. It's the nation that's sick. You put your life on the line to protect people from terrorists and later you're abandoned to lawyers representing those terrorists. Government washes its hands of responsibility, puts you at the mercy of human rights lawyers. Human rights, bollocks. In the future, who would be stupid enough to risk their lives? And who could blame them?' Rhi slumped back as if exhausted. She grabbed her lager and took another drink and exhaled slowly. 'You're young, Alex I'm sure all of this is ancient history for you.' She paused as if suddenly struck by something. 'You don't ask many questions, do you?'

'What you have to say is more important than any questions I may have.'

'You are such a nice boy, Alex,' she repeated, her words slurred even more. But they weren't said lasciviously or suggestively. Rhi, Perceval was sure, was no sexual predator of young men. 'Can you understand what I'm saying?' she asked.

Now was his time. So, he told Rhi about the murder of his father before he was born. He told her how that murder had deprived him of a parent and how it was a wound that would never heal. He told her about the effect the murder had upon his mother, how she had retreated from life, from her old home, her friends and relations. He told her how she'd given up the chance of romance, pleasure, and companionship. He didn't use the word 'defeated'. But that's how he'd always thought of his mother. He told Rhi that whatever words of comfort had come from clergy, whatever support his mother had been given by public agencies, whatever sympathy had been shown by his father's colleagues, none of it could compensate for her loss. And as the years went by, and those who had ordered his father's murder became lauded as peacemakers without showing any remorse, her cynicism about and detachment from society had become complete. And he reminded her, if she'd forgotten, of roadside bombs in Northern Ireland, the deaths, the mutilations, the agonies still suffered. And he asked the question, now that terrorists had escaped justice through secret deals with those same politicians who'd sent Rhi to Afghanistan, if it had all been worth it?

'Who do you serve now, Rhi?' He asked. 'You must serve your own life and live it as best you can.'

When he finished, Rhi reached out to touch his hand, perhaps the deepest expression of sympathy she could show. Perceval's confession couldn't fix her. That resurrection from despair into meaning was for her alone to make.

Chapter Twenty-Three

Perceval did make it down the steps without mishap. And despite staggering once or twice, he avoided falling in the canal. By the time he'd said farewell to Rhi, they'd become sufficiently at ease with each other for him to wag a finger jokingly and say, 'Don't be drinking too much without me now, comrade.'

Awkwardly, they'd embraced, he bent over, she still sat, prosthetic leg stretched. She'd nodded and said, 'Go on, Alex. I'm fine now. No more booze.'

As Perceval had walked towards the exit, Cerys followed after him and asked how Rhi was doing.

'She promised me no more booze tonight,' he told her.

'You're a star,' Cerys said, rolling the 'r' like it was a fine wine.

That night Perceval dreamed he stood on the deck of a sailboat on a wide river. Floating towards him, he saw a young woman lying in a punt which was draped in black cloth. It drifted slowly for there was no oarsman. Perceval recognised the body. It was Elin, pale with hands folded across her chest, clutching a single wilted lily, her hair spilling over the punt's edge and trailing in the water. In death she was equally beautiful as in life, equally tragic, and just as untouchable. Her face was serene yet haunting, her lips parted slightly as if about to whisper a secret. Perceval felt the weight of this death like an accusation.

He woke up with a start, his mouth sticky from the beer he'd drunk and his mind woozy. He sensed the beginning of a headache. Dehydration, he told himself. He swung his legs onto the floor, shivered, put on the cabin light, and made his way haltingly to the galley. He stubbed his toe on the edge of the table. 'That really hurt,' he howled and hopped the final few steps to the sink. He had run out of bottled water and wondered if the reserve in the tank he'd filled earlier was fit to drink. He had no alternative, bent down, put his lips under the tap and took a long draught. Had he remembered to bring some paracetamol tablets? He thought he had and rummaged in his rucksack but couldn't find the packet. He took another drink of water and limped back to bed, hoping he hadn't broken his toe.

This time, Perceval dreamed he was in a vast desert landscape, scarred with stony ridges and dry riverbeds. Suddenly, Rhi appeared on the crest of a ridge, dressed not in military fatigues but in silver armour. She wore no helmet, her eyes were sharp and clear, gazing intently across the desert like a warrior queen. She held before her a heavy broadsword, its tip planted firmly in the sand, as though drawing strength directly from the land beneath. Around her, the desert began to flourish, tender shoots of green pushing up from beneath the sand, along with wildflowers and heather. A stream trickled into life nearby and Perceval heard birdsong. At that moment, she turned to Perceval, didn't speak but looked at him as if to say the old Rhi had returned, strong and self-confident. He'd stirred from sleep again and once more needed water. He checked his toe. It was bruised and painful, but he believed, from cricketing experience, there was no break. When he got back to bed, he tried to conjure Fleur in his dreams. He failed.

When he awoke fully in the morning, he heard walkers chatting as they went along the towpath. Sitting up to peep through the bedroom curtains, he saw a middle-aged jogger trot slowly by, her expression one of duty rather than enjoyment. It was nine thirty. Perceval was glad he'd taken *Knight Errant* across from the water point and not felt obliged to rise at dawn. His hangover still hovered but hadn't developed into a throbbing pain. He examined his toe. There was no purplish swelling to indicate a break, but it remained painful. He'd survive.

Remembering the fallen leaves, Perceval went on deck and saw the roof was covered entirely, this thick abundance of natural decay overwhelming. From one of the cupboards, he retrieved a yard brush and set about dragging the leaves onto the towpath. He made a mental note to give the engine a fierce reverse thrust and it brought back the memory of Fleur. He put pressure on his painful toe to distract the memory of his failure, too much in fact, and he yelped automatically.

A woman walking her dog looked up from her mobile in surprise. 'A difficult job?' she asked him.

'I stubbed my toe,' he answered.

'Housework is never easy, even on a boat,' she said. 'Are you about to go over the aqueduct?'

'That's my intention, yes.'

'I've just walked across. It's clear right now.'

Perceval thanked her and the woman walked on, turning her attention once more to her mobile.

When he'd cleared the leaves as best he could, Perceval untied *Knight Errant* and stepped gingerly back onboard. He gave the engine a long reverse thrust, which churned up leaves and water in a bubbling wake, making him drift across the canal towards the *Spirit of Mersey*. He didn't relish a confrontation with a bull-necked Scouser this morning. Luckily, there was no sign of him or his long-suffering partner. Irrationally, he considered that woman's fate another of his failures.

As he travelled towards the aqueduct, a low winter's sun threatened to force its way through the clouds. It failed and, in the greyness, he felt spots of rain. He'd watched the videos about this 18th-century engineering marvel running high above the River Dee. He'd read how it was essentially a ribbon of water suspended in the sky. And here it was before him, an iron trough not much wider than *Knight Errant* itself. The woman had been right. There was no boat coming over towards Froncyscllte. Perceval took a deep breath.

Around him was a panorama of Welsh hills, thick woods and green fields. Below, the river ran fast and white over mid-stream rocks. On his right was a railed pathway busy with hikers and a few dismounted cyclists. On the other side was the edge of the trough and a sheer drop. It had always irritated Perceval when the only word commentators on TV could think of to describe something remarkably beautiful, strange, or dramatic was 'amazing'. They were paid good money and should be more articulate or poetic, he thought. Yet the only word which came to his mind right now was 'amazing'. It did seem amazing that he should be way up here, defying gravity in this narrowboat of twelve tons. So strong was the current against *Knight Errant* that a corpulent old man, walking with a crutch, overtook him. Observing the look of determined concentration on Perceval's face as he worked the tiller to keep the boat in line, the man stopped. 'There's no need for you to steer,' he said. 'The trough is narrow enough to keep you straight.' Perceval didn't bother to reply, and the man hobbled on. When he was out of ear-shot – which was soon enough for the wind on the aqueduct was noisier even than *Knight Errant's* struggling engine – he muttered, 'Stupid old bugger.'

When he'd made it across, Perceval was euphoric. The feat was done. No trumpet sounded, no cheer was raised, but he knew he'd achieved something special. Did he really do that? Or had it been a fantasy? He remembered a phrase of his German teacher – *einmal ist keinmal* – as she had interpreted it, 'to do something once is like you've never done it all.' Perceval, still young enough that most things were indeed for the first time (like learning German), hadn't grasped the significance of those words. Until now, that is. The euphoria vanished, replaced by the uncanny idea that the crossing hadn't happened at all.

The canal led directly into Trevor Basin. He could see boats tied up on both sides, leaving only a gap between them not much wider than the aqueduct trough. Perceval needed to buy groceries and wondered if he could find a place to tie up close to the town. He was about to try his luck when he heard someone calling across to him from a grassy slope. It was a stocky woman dressed in waterproof trousers, Wellington boots, a very old and shabby Barbour jacket, and on her head a floppy bush hat. She was sitting on a little folding canvas chair, a large tackle box beside her, an umbrella planted in the earth behind, a fishing rod in hand, its line in the water. Perceval hadn't heard the fisherwoman properly above the sound of his engine. He cupped his hand to his ear inviting her to say it again. She pointed with her free hand towards the basin. 'All the moorings are taken. It's a dead end. Don't try to go up there.' She indicated the bridge over the canal at a right angle to the position of *Knight Errant*. 'You need to go this way. It will take you away a piece, but you can tie up further along and walk back.'

'Thank you,' Perceval waved to her. 'You've rescued me! I would have got stuck for sure.'

The woman looked at Perceval's position in the turning pool and advised, 'You'll probably have to reverse up some, then turn sharpish and line up with the bridge.'

'You must have seen a lot of clumsy efforts,' Perceval laughed.

'You could say that, and you'd be right,' she replied, keeping an eye on *Knight Errant* as he did what she recommended. The bridge was narrow and angled but he made it through comfortably. The fisherwoman waved farewell and Perceval thanked her once more.

The canal narrowed, the banks on either side solid concrete, and he was glad there was no oncoming traffic. He passed under two metal bridges which, he assumed, provided pedestrian access to Trevor, but could see no suitable point to tie up without being a nuisance at best, an obstacle at worst, for other boats. The foliage, despite the season, remained full, trees overshadowing the waterway, thick bushes between them. The towpath was well-maintained, hobby cyclists and walkers, a husband and wife with a pram, were taking this opportunity to enjoy the mild temperature, despite the hint of rain. Their mood was cheery, the cyclists waving as they passed, the walkers and the couple greeting him with friendly hellos.

Perceval kept an eye out for a place to stop, not wishing to get too far away from Trevor. Around a turning was a wider stretch of water. On his left the trees had thinned, permitting a view of hills in the near distance and, in the valley, the River Dee. On the right stretched open farmland. Along the towpath bank was a mooring rail, wooden this time, not metal. Perceval angled *Knight Errant* towards it, slowed and stopped. He jumped off with the centre line, wincing at the pain in his toe, and looked at the condition of the rail. He judged it too degraded to be safe, the wood having either rotted in places or become partially detached from the bank. There was nothing for it but to hammer in stakes. It took some effort but eventually, after a couple of tries, he considered the boat was stable. In everything he'd read about canal boating, he'd never come across the one thing which caused him concern. What was to stop some vandal, just for fun, or some malicious passerby, just for the hell of it, undoing the knots and pushing a boat into the middle of the water? So far, he'd been able to tie up in company which had provided some security but there was no one out here. He was compelled to rely on the kindness of strangers.

Perceval got back on board and emptied the remaining fresh clothes from his rucksack. It was too big really for the things he needed to buy, but it was all he had. On his mobile, he checked Google Maps for the nearest supermarket. He found a Tesco, not in Trevor but in a place called Cefn-Mawr which adjoined it. If nothing else, he needed some exercise. He might even walk off the pain in his toe.

On deck again, he saw a line of kayaks coming from the direction of Trevor. His heart leapt up. Was it Fleur? Was this a day to be blessed by good fortune? Had compassion for Rhi brought him good luck after all? Had the fisherwoman's advice been a sign? Perceval shrugged off the rucksack and watched as the kayakers neared, but quickly realised it wasn't Fleur's group. They looked like weekenders who'd hired their kayaks for the day. There was no rhythm to their strokes and they paddled erratically, as much side to side as forward. At the end of their line was a seasoned guide calling out instructions now and then in a bored voice. Leading in a double kayak were two Muslim girls in headscarves who appeared to be having a great time, laughing, sometimes shrieking. They lost control as they neared *Knight Errant* and accidentally knocked into its side.

'We're so sorry!' they twittered simultaneously.

'There's no damage,' Perceval told them. 'Are both of you alright?'

'Yes,' they said together. The girl at the back added, 'No damage to us either.' They each raised a hand to wave him a gracious farewell and lost control once more.

As Perceval shrugged on his rucksack again, the leader of the group passed by. 'Apologies,' he said sheepishly.

'None needed,' Perceval replied. 'They seem to be having a good time.'

There was another shriek of laughter ahead.

'It would appear so,' the instructor smiled. 'Now all I have to do is get them back to Trevor.'

PART SIX: THE REDEMPTION

Chapter Twenty-Four

DESPITE the ache in his toe, it didn't take Perceval long to make it to Trevor and he found himself near the Anglo-Welsh Wharf. The fisherwoman had been right. All possible moorings had been taken. He consulted Google Maps again and keyed in directions. Avoiding busy roads, the App estimated a walk of twenty-one minutes to the Tesco store. At his normal pace, he reckoned, it should take him only fifteen.

He went along a path on the edge of a park where dogs ran off the leash, following an elderly man walking at a sedate pace. The man exited at an iron gate at the end of the path and, noticing Perceval for the first time, raised his walking stick in greeting. Perceval called to him, 'Excuse me. Sorry for disturbing your walk. I'm looking for the Tesco store.' The old man was hard of hearing and asked him to repeat his question, so he rephrased it. 'Do you know the way to Tesco?'

'Yes,' he said, 'Yes, I do know. If you turn right down here,' he waved his stick towards the bridge, 'and walk along the river path. You'll find steps up by a few cottages. It's pretty steep, mind. You'll come out opposite the Queen's Hotel. Turn right along Queen Street, go further up the hill and then bear left. You'll see the Holly Bush Inn. Tesco is on your right.' The old man made a dipping movement with his hand as if the supermarket was at the bottom of a slope.

Perceval was impressed for he was hopeless at giving such precise directions, his visualisation never as clear as this old man's, whose body might be failing but whose mind was still sharp. He went as advised, leaving the man to his own thoughts. He discovered the steps soon enough and, turning a corner, encountered a short, middle-aged man with a goatee beard. He was chatting to a woman kneeling at a tidy rock garden in front of their cottage and attending to some plants. Perceval worried he may have wandered onto private property. He stopped, about to retrace his steps. The man saw him and said, 'Up that way,' nodding to a path around the garden.

Perceval mustn't have been the first to stand here indecisively. Maybe in the tourist season hordes of hikers came tramping up this way, asking directions. If so, he was struck by the man's genuine helpfulness, his lack of suspicion, the absence of irritation at the intrusion, and the warmth of his gesture. 'Thank you,' Perceval said, and then sheepishly. 'I'm looking for the Tesco store.'

'Ah,' replied the man, chuckling, 'many like you come to these parts seeking glory or fair maidens.'

His wife (Perceval assumed that's who she was) dusted some soil from her hands, looked up and said, 'Others come seeking the Holy Grail.'

'But mostly,' the man chuckled, 'they come seeking Tesco.' He looked at his wife and they smiled at each other. Perceval, in another mood, might have found this couple's intimacy grating but there was something sweet in their affinity and nothing mocking in their words.

'You're on the right track,' the woman told him, repeating the directions he'd been given by the old man earlier.

'Thanks again,' Perceval said to them both.

They wished him good luck and returned to their conversation that his sudden appearance had interrupted.

This part of Cefn Mawr sat on a ridge above the Dee valley. The place had a different feel to Trevor which had adapted – at his first impression – to the new world of leisure-as-business, the economy Angharad and Troy had spoken of dismissively. Cefn Mawr, by contrast, retained the character of its heavy industrial past and its working-class appearance yet, when he paused at the top of the road, Perceval could see no evidence of such industry. If there was little sign of activity or busyness – he was the only person on the street and no cars passed – and if he couldn't describe the village as prosperous, there did appear to be community spirit and resilience. Beyond the Holly Bush Inn, Perceval saw the sign for Tesco, its bright red letters and blue under dashes. And the old man's description had been accurate. The supermarket did lie in a hollow where the road curved down to a large car park. Now Perceval could have been anywhere in the country. The store was the universally brash, functional, no-nonsense, single-story, rectangular building of metal and glass, designed for consumption and not for production. This was no dark satanic mill. It was bright and welcoming, familiar and reassuring, convenient and comforting. As far as Perceval could judge, those collecting trolleys and preparing to enter, those emptying their trolleys having left, all looked to be in good humour.

He bought some cans of beer, half-a-dozen eggs, a small loaf, milk, a large bottle of water, some apples, one tin of corned beef, one of beef casserole, one of baked beans, and a large bar of chocolate. It was hardly what his mother would have recommended, but then he'd eaten less well sometimes, not only as a student but also as a very minor university administrator. He wouldn't be aboard *Knight Errant* for much longer and he considered the food would be more than enough.

The walk back to Trevor seemed to take no time at all. The early afternoon had become much cooler and the clouds darker, but they weren't yet rainclouds. When he reached the wharf, at the corner of yet another hilly street he discovered a tea room, a large redbrick building which must once have been a church filled with worshippers. If leisure had replaced industry in Trevor, it seemed to have replaced religion as well. Perceval decided to try it.

He almost expected to meet a churchwarden in the narrow hallway and be handed a prayer book and hymnal. Inside he encountered a buzz of conversation and the noise of cutlery on plates, cups on saucers. He almost tripped over a black Labrador sitting patiently begging at table. Perceval's first thought was of Toby from *The Flower Maidens* and hoped he might find Jo and Bron once again. But it wasn't Toby. And there was no Jo and Bron either. The Labrador belonged to a young family, the mother and father drinking coffee, proudly watching over their toddlers, a boy and girl, eating ice cream sundaes. Every table was taken, like the one at which this family sat as well as the long benches at which sat groups of hikers and cyclists. A high ceiling delivered an airy yet grounded ambiance – Perceval thought of Bron's knot – a former place for worship, now a place for eating, hearts once reaching for Heaven, hands now reaching for food. The tall arched windows of plain, not stained, glass let in a soft light. A magnificent polished wooden staircase rose to a glass-fronted mezzanine which once was the chapel's gallery. The tearoom was simple yet elegant and characterful without being twee. A waitress told him there might be a table free upstairs. He lumbered up the steps past a large bible set on the old pulpit just as a young couple had vacated their table. Perceval set his rucksack on one chair and sat on the other. He scanned the menu and decided on egg, beans and chips and looked over the bannister to catch the eye of a waitress.

'You need to go down to the desk and place your order.'

Perceval turned his head. It was a slim woman, mid-thirties, bob-cut black hair, dressed in a dark blue trouser suit, white blouse and high-heel shoes. She was sitting on a small vintage leather couch, a MacBook on her lap.

'Thank you,' he said and, as he stood, his chair screeching on the parquet flooring as it moved back. Perceval made a face. 'Sorry.'

She raised one hand slightly in acknowledgement of his apology, her attention fixed on the MacBook screen. When he returned from placing his order, the woman didn't look up but asked, 'Get it sorted?'

'I did,' he replied. 'Thanks.'

As he waited, Perceval looked at his mobile. There was no message from his uncle. There was no message from anyone. He put the mobile away, feeling a sad loner. He recalled his encounter with Tristan but had no time to wallow in self-pity as his food arrived. 'There you go,' the waitress said, setting his plate on the table. 'Enjoy!'

A few moments later the well-dressed woman walked by, laptop bag over her shoulder. '*Bon appetit*,' she said, stopping on the second step. 'Or *Mwynhewch eich bwyd* as we say in Wales.' Perceval repeated the phrase, and said he'd try to remember it. The woman went cautiously down the stairs in her high heels. He continued to eat intently, a focus maintained, not disturbed, by the noise of conversations below. When he'd finished, he sighed with satisfaction and sat back relaxed.

'Finally!'

Startled, he looked up. 'Fleur!'

'Alex!'

Chapter Twenty-Five

FLEUR'S eyes were wide and bright, her face beaming with obvious delight at finding him. Perceval shook his head slowly in disbelief, unable to move. Sometimes he would see someone briefly, retain an image of their features idealised into dreamlike loveliness but, when they met again, he would notice only blemishes and imperfections. Not in Fleur's case. He scarce could take it in.

Fleur's cheeks were slightly flushed and there was the faintest sheen of perspiration on her upper lip. She had cycled here, that was clear. Dangling from one hand was a matte-finished, vented helmet, and in it, Perceval noticed short-fingered cycling gloves as well as a pair of amber-tinted protective glasses. A black headband still covered her ears and forehead. She was wearing a windproof cycling jacket in bright yellow, unzipped to the waist, revealing a tight-fitting blue, turtleneck underlayer. Charcoal cycle leggings, with reflective strips, showed off her toned thighs. This stylish gear, which looked to him expensive, confirmed that Fleur wasn't only an accomplished kayaker.

It seemed she realised from Perceval's initial movement as he stood that he was about to do something ludicrous, like extending a hand to shake hers. She put her helmet on the table, stretched out her arms, inviting him to hug her. They embraced and Perceval calculated the pressure of his squeeze in response to Fleur's. Hers wasn't tight, but gentle, though she held him longer than expected, even laying her head on his chest. For a second, he thought she might cry. This experience was entirely new to him. Pulling away, she said, 'I thought I'd missed you for all time, you know.' He removed his rucksack from the chair and she sat down. 'I couldn't think where you'd got to. It was as if you'd vanished into thin air. I almost believed I had imagined seeing you.'

'If you can believe it,' he said, 'I thought exactly the same thing.' He shook his head and exhaled heavily. They held each other's gaze as if fearing either would vanish. 'Yet here we are,' he said.

'Yes, here we are.' Fleur whipped off the headband and her shoulder-length, auburn hair fell loose. She brushed it back from her forehead and tucked loose strands behind both ears. She put the headband in her helmet on top of gloves and cycling glasses. Perceval observed her closely as she did this, her skin soft, her complexion clear and natural without makeup, her high, rounded, cheekbones subtly pronounced. The light green eyes were almond-shaped, with a gentle upward tilt at the corners, striking but above all, intelligent. Her lashes were slightly curled, eyebrows arched, but not artificially sculpted, giving her face an open, lively expression. Things in her helmet properly arranged, Fleur set it beside the chair, unzipped her jacket fully, and looked at him once more. 'You promised, remember?'

'I know. I did promise. But you must believe me, Fleur. I tried my damnedest. After the tunnel I tied up and walked to Chirk for lunch. You told me you'd be returning mid-afternoon and I did see your friends at the marina later. But I didn't see you. To get a place to tie up, I had to go through the Whitehouse Tunnel and run back. You see, I *didn't* forget my promise. But when I got to the marina, you'd all disappeared. It was a nightmare, truly a nightmare. But I'm so glad you *are* here.'

'That explains it then,' she said matter-of-factly, as if this was yesterday's news, delivered and to be forgotten. 'I do believe you. I tracked down *Knight Errant* this morning. I left my mobile number in the door hatch. Just in case. Then I came looking for you. And here *you* are. Here *I* am. Here *we* are.'

'Sorry about yesterday …'

'Apology accepted. And don't look so sad. You should be delighted *I* keep *your* promises.'

'I couldn't be more delighted.' He paused. 'At the marina, I looked but didn't see you. Where were you exactly?'

'Alex, there are some questions you shouldn't ask a lady,' Fleur looked at him mischievously. 'And there are some answers which a lady can't give without destroying the romantic mood. So, out of delicacy, it's best that I say nothing.' Perceval shifted uncomfortably in his chair and reddened slightly. Fleur smiled and touched his arm indulgently, then noticed his empty plate. 'You've eaten?'

About to say sorry again, he stopped himself and asked, 'Are you hungry, Fleur?' He enjoyed saying her name.

'I'm famished.'

'Let me get you lunch.' He passed her the menu, and she glanced at it quickly.

'Egg, beans, and chips, for me,' she said with relish and he couldn't but be charmed.

'Good choice,' he said. 'I have to go down and order.' He made to stand but she put up a hand.

'Oh no, Alex, stay right here. I don't want you to go missing again.'

Perceval pointed to his rucksack. 'I won't be going anywhere without this. So, as Arnie Schwarzenegger says, "I'll be back". Anyway, what would you think if I let you buy your own lunch on our first …'

'Date?'

'Yes, why not! Few better places, don't you think? It's like our time together is blessed.'

'I see what you mean,' Fleur replied, gazing around the former church. 'Well then, thank you. How could I not accept?'

'Coffee or tea or …?'

'Tea for me … and tea for you?' Fleur sang the words to the tune of the familiar song.

'I will order with that song in my heart.' He glanced at the counter below. 'There's only a small queue at the till. So don't *you* be disappearing … wherever it is a lady disappears to.'

'Oh no, not this time,' she laughed self-consciously.

As Perceval stood in line to order, he was astonished how this meeting with Fleur, bizarre and unlikely as it was, felt exactly as it should be. Her vivacity lifted his spirits. That she had put herself to such trouble, searching for *him*, finding *him* … then, suddenly uneasy, he began to doubt his own worth. For God's sake, he told himself, don't be so bloody dim. Don't mess this up. Again. Fleur was a confident, strong-minded, smart young woman who knew what she wanted. And it seemed she wanted him. What more could he ask for? It must truly have been on the cards, he smiled.

He returned with a large pot of tea, set it on the table and arranged the cups, telling Fleur her lunch would follow. 'Just tea for two and two for tea,' he sang softly.

'Just me for you, and you for me,' she sang, paused, and added, 'alone.'

The song had been another of his mother's favourites, on a good day that was. Perceval knew the lyrics, and was about to continue with, 'I can picture you upon my knee', but considered it going a little too far – for now, anyway. Instead, he asked, 'Shall I be mother?'

'You know, you're the first man ever to ask me that question,' she said coyly. Perceval poured Fleur a cup, added a little milk, and did the same for himself. 'Mmmm,' she said after taking a sip. 'Exactly what the doctor ordered.' Her face became serious, lips tightening in a frown. 'When you were gone just now, I was thinking all this must appear completely over the top to you, bizarre in fact, me turning up here out of the blue, following you like some demented stalker, acting on a whim and assuming you'll put up with it. With me, rather.'

Perceval watched her lips as she spoke, following the cadence of her voice, mesmerised by the rhythmic poise of her educated middle-class English accent. Only when he heard her ask, 'Do you understand?' did he snap out of the spell her words had cast. His expression must have signalled he wasn't sure what her question meant.

'I was saying you must think it quite bizarre for me to track you down like this. We've hardly been introduced ... oh, that sounds so silly, doesn't it? Like something out of Jane Austen. But really, what must you think? That I do this all the time? Meet someone once, exchange a few words, and then expect ... well, tea for two?' she said, raising her cup. 'Okay, I can be a little forward at times, can be pushy if I need to be. How can you not be when you've two older brothers? But I just want to assure you, *this* isn't like me at all.'

Fleur didn't define what she meant by 'this', assuming it was self-evident, and took another sip of tea. In the order of human time, Perceval didn't know her at all but felt he knew her intimately outside of it. He could hear his mother sing a song from Disney's *Sleeping Beauty* with the line 'I know you. I walked with you once upon a dream'. He remembered it because it was the only line she sang, humming the rest of the melody. He considered saying those words but knew they would sound wrong.

'You must think it presumptuous of me too,' she continued. 'You may have a girlfriend.' He shook his head. 'A wife even.' He looked taken aback and guffawed. 'No matter,' and having suggested these possibilities and seeming happy with his responses, Fleur returned to the point. 'Here am I. I wander in, making claims on you, even if it is only for a plate of egg, beans, and chips.'

'And tea for two … too,' he added matter-of-factly.

They burst out laughing simultaneously at the delicious absurdity of it all.

Fleur sat back as a waitress slipped her lunch plate in front of her and set knife and fork beside it. The waitress removed Perceval's plate and asked if there was anything else they needed for now. They both said no. When the waitress had gone, Perceval said to Fleur, '*Mwynhewch eich bwyd.*'

She was astonished. 'You can speak Welsh?'

'No. A woman said it to me a while ago.'

'My dad is English but mum's Welsh. She really doesn't speak it either, fluently I mean. I picked up a few phrases from her, but that's about it.'

'We embody the whole of Britain, then. My mother was proud of being an Ulster Scot, though we hadn't any Scottish relatives that I knew of. My dad was classic Northern Irish, maybe with a bit of Norman heritage.'

'There's a coincidence. My dad claims Norman heritage too. He's a Stephens … like me, I suppose,' she grinned.

'Fleur Stephens. Lovely name.'

'It might have been Blanche Stephens. Blanche and Fleur are my forenames. I'm glad my parents only ever used Fleur.'

'Fleur by any other name would sound sweet to me.'

'Ha!' she said. 'I should hope so too. And …?' Perceval looked confused. 'Your surname is?'

'Oh Perceval. No other forename, just plain Alex.'

'Alex Perceval. Lovely name … and this looks lovely too,' Fleur said, cutting up the egg so that the yolk ran and then spearing a chip to dip. Before putting the food in her mouth, she faltered as if her action was somehow ill-mannered. 'You don't mind me eating in front of you, do you?'

'Of course not. Why should I mind?' He thought of his encounter with Elin, and how grounded Fleur's character was compared with her ethereal personality.

'Well … okay, then,' and she ate the eggy chip with obvious pleasure. She was about to repeat the action but set down her knife and fork on her plate. 'Look, about my intrusion, I'm going to blame my brother Jacob.' Perceval raised his eyebrows. 'When he stole my chocolate, or sneaked into the bathroom before me, or snatched something I wanted from under my nose, he used to say to me "snooze, you lose". I hated him for it, of course. So, you see, my motto is the woman who hesitates is lost. And I didn't want to snooze and lose this time. I didn't want you to get away so easily.' She frowned as if that explanation wasn't exact enough. 'No, that's not quite right. I *slept* on it and decided I should take the risk. When I spoke to you yesterday … I know this probably sounds like girlish fantasy stuff to you … but I wanted to find out more. Didn't you?' Before he could answer, Fleur added, 'It does seem weird, as though I'm here by some magical power, and yet it seems totally natural too.' She picked up knife and fork again and began eating, but her eyes remained fixed on his.

'I was thinking the same thing earlier when queuing up at the till,' he said. 'Those two words, bizarre and natural, came to my mind as well. Things destined in life often seem bizarrely natural. I think so anyway. Like me on this canal in November, leaves in the boat's propeller, you in a kayak, and we meet again in a former chapel. What were the odds?'

Of course, it suited Perceval to accept that fate was involved, that their paths were always meant to cross, and that they were bound to meet again. He knew it was fantasy, conscious that none of it would have happened, not before the aqueduct at Chirk and certainly not in this tearoom at Trevor, if it hadn't been for Fleur. He thought he should admit that truth. 'For the rest of my life, I would have regretted missing you … through my own fault and inaction. If our meeting was made into a film,

Fleur, you'd have the leading role. *You* made the story happen.'

'I can see it now. 'Not *When Harry met Sally*. Instead, *When Alex met Fleur*. No, it should be *When Fleur met Alex*. I love that film. And do you remember the famous line at the end?'

'I don't,' Perceval said, not wishing to admit he'd never seen *When Harry met Sally.*

'I don't think men do remember, even though the words are spoken by Harry and not by Sally. Maybe they think they're too feminine. The line, Alex, and it comes with the loud sounding klaxon of a cliché alert, is, "I came here because when you realise you want to spend the rest of your life with somebody, you want the rest of your life to start as soon as possible". So, what do you think of that?' Fleur tilted her head in expectation of an immediate answer.

'Is this the end we start from? If it is, I love it.'

'It's a good place to begin, Alex,' she laughed. 'At least you're asking the right question.' Fleur cut up more of her food. 'When I saw you on your boat and all alone, I felt drawn to you. I can't explain why. As I said, it's not like me at all. And it wasn't only because I thought you needed help and looked so vulnerable. I don't know what else. I wanted to get close to you, I suppose. Alright, alright … I thought you were cute.' A slight blush accompanied her admission, though she didn't seem self-conscious about this confession.

'Your wish is mutual. So too is your thought. I couldn't stop thinking about you.' Perceval's confession, however, did make him self-conscious.

'So, I was right all along. It *was* worth finding you again.'

There was a silence which wasn't awkward but confirming, an acceptance which didn't need words.

'If you don't mind me asking, what *are* you doing alone on the canal, especially at this time of year?'

While she ate, Perceval related the story of his aunt's

illness, his uncle's request, and the challenge he'd accepted. He mentioned his failings as a novice boatman. The story of his struggle to tie a knot and moor up the first night on the canal made her chuckle. 'I arrived on *Knight Errant*,' he said, 'and it was a damsel who rescued me in my distress.'

'Yeaah!' Fleur waved her knife in the air. 'I like the sound of that.'

'You could say, I've been serially reliant on damsels rescuing me. And then, of course, there's you. My engine would have blown if you hadn't been kind enough to warn me.'

She accepted his gratitude with a playful nod. In fact, her playfulness was part of the joy of being in her company. At the same time, Fleur wasn't frivolous, for sincerity underpinned her humour, her lightness complementing, he suspected, deeper emotions. They were emotions he believed he could trust, sensing she was free spirited but not reckless, independent but not irresponsible, determined but not stubborn, teasing but not insensitive. He smiled, thinking these paradoxes would match a Jo Tarot reading, their entanglement a Bron knot. Of course, he couldn't be certain. How can you ever know anyone, and not just *at first*? Perceval liked to think he would have lots of time with Fleur to find out.

'And is kayaking your sport?' he asked.

'I enjoy it, yes, but I wouldn't call it my sport. I don't compete if that's what you mean.'

'But you're part of a club? Like yesterday's group?'

'Oh, that group. They're old schoolfriends, mostly. We did some kayaking together when younger and meet up when we can. Most of us are at university. At the end of the half-term break, it seemed like a good idea to do the two aqueducts. It was a bit of a challenge, but worth it.'

'Pity about the tunnels in between. I had a dark night of the soul getting through the big one at Chirk.'

'Really?'

'I finally saw the light, though.'

'That's terrible!' Fleur shook her head at his poor wit.

'You must think I'm a wimp struggling on a diesel-engine beast like *Knight Errant* when you had to paddle. It felt like that tunnel was never going to end.'

'Let me tell you it *was* tough enough. The flow was strong yesterday. My arms and shoulders ached this morning … they still do.'

'If you don't mind me asking where did you come from today?'

'Chester.'

'All the way from Chester?' Perceval knew from his uncle's map that Chester was quite a distance, twenty miles or more.

'Not all the way by bike, of course. My parents live near Chester. I drove to Llangollen, parked the car, and cycled down from there. It's not that far.'

'How did you know I'd be here?'

'In the tearoom? I didn't. I knew you hadn't turned after the Chirk Aqueduct. Some holiday boaters do that because they don't fancy the tunnel. I could see your headlight behind us and there's no turning circle until Fron. So, I guessed by the time you got there it would be too late for you to turn back. And if you crossed the Pontcysyllte Aqueduct this morning you couldn't be much further beyond Trevor.'

'I'm impressed, Sherlock.' Fleur chuckled at the reference. 'You guessed right. And I forgot to say, another damsel, a fisherwoman on the bank before the canal turn, stopped me from getting stuck in the boats moored at Trevor. I can't believe I thought that was an option.'

'Oh dear, you might have been really stuck in there. As it turned out, *Knight Errant* was easy to find. You were a bit more of a problem.'

'Sorry about that.'

'No need to be sorry, Alex. You didn't know I was looking for you. I went to the aqueduct in case you'd gone back there to take some photos. No sign. Then I thought you might have gone sightseeing in Trevor – still no sign. Maybe shopping, so I cycled to the Tesco in Cefn Mawr.'

'I was in Tesco.' Perceval pointed to his bulging rucksack. 'This is beginning to sound like a French farce, you go in one door, and I go out another. And what made you try here?'

'You weren't in the pub across the road. This place was my last throw of the dice. I put my head round the door and saw you straightaway.'

'A tale of the last chance saloon.'

'If you hadn't been here, I would have gone back to your boat and waited. I'd have made sure you found my mobile number. You can see I'm persistent.'

'I'm glad you are.'

Fleur had finished her lunch. In the tearoom there was a slow turnover of customers from lunch to afternoon tea, and in the lull the waitress came to clear Fleur's dish and cutlery.

'Would you like something else?' Perceval asked Fleur. 'Their cakes look excellent.'

'I can't ask you to pay for anything more.'

'At university, I had a history tutor who was a bit of an old style socialist. He used to have tea and biscuits now and then in tutorials. If there was one biscuit left on the plate and we were too polite to snatch it, he would say, "For God's sake you lot, don't be so *bourgeois*". So, Fleur, don't be so *bourgeois*. I know you would like a piece of cake.'

'Well, if you put it that way … and did you?'

'Did I what?

'Take the last biscuit?'

'Me? Of course not. I'm more *bourgeois* than I look.'

'That's too funny.'

She came down with him to choose her cake and Perceval ordered another pot of tea. Back at their table, Fleur asked, 'Sure you wouldn't like to try some of this cake?' Her fork hovered over a slice of Vanilla layer cake with rich buttercream icing.

Perceval didn't have cake, not for reasons of diet but because he hadn't a sweet tooth which, his mother had told him, was one thing he shared with his father. This wasn't what Perceval would have expected, given the cliché of cops and doughnuts. Or was that only an American thing? He didn't know.

'I feel bad to keep eating while you're not,' she said.

'You know what I'm going to say now, don't you?'

'You're really funny, Alex.' She took a small mouthful, ate slowly, and said, 'Mmmm … this is to die for.'

'Too soon,' he said, 'I'm only getting my head around that Harry and Sally "rest of your life" thing.'

Fleur pointed her fork at him and corrected, 'Fleur and Alex thing. Does that thought frighten you?'

He pretended to give her question serious consideration and replied, 'It seems to me like the sort of life sentence that would do me a world of good.'

'Too funny.'

'You said you are at university? Which one?'

'Oxford. I'm studying medicine. Third year of five now,' Fleur said casually.

'I am honoured.'

Fleur accepted that he was being sincere and not sarcastic. 'Thank you. But it's not such a big deal.'

'Oh yes, it is. I worked in university admissions for a while after graduation. I know how prestigious the medical school is at Oxford. I also know how good you need to be to get in. So, I say again, I *am* honoured.'

'I feel I should offer my hand to be kissed when you say those words.'

'I am honoured,' he repeated.

Fleur proffered the back of her hand. Perceval leaned over and brushed it with his lips. 'Another first for me,' she grinned. 'If you're curious about why medicine, my parents are both doctors from long lines of doctors on both sides, so I'm following in the family tradition.'

'And your brothers? Are they doctors too?'

'No. Hywel is in the Royal Navy, somewhere in the Far East. Or so I understand. He would have you think what he's up to is very hush hush, like he's James Bond. Jacob, the one I told you about, the snooze and you lose, I'll take what I like, brother?'

'Yes?'

'Jacob's training to be an Anglican priest. He got religion at Oxford, all the bell, book and candle, John Betjeman, stuff. I still find it hard to believe, pardon the pun, but we're all so proud of him, proud of both of them, of course. And your family? I couldn't help noticing you used the past tense when speaking of your parents.'

Perceval told her both parents were dead. He tried to talk matter-of-factly, not mentioning his father's murder or his mother's retreat from life. He didn't want Fleur to think he was fishing for sympathy. 'So, I've recently become an orphan. That's the long and the short of it.'

She set down the fork beside her half-eaten cake and stretched out her hand to touch his arm. 'That is so sad,' she said. 'I don't know what to say.'

There was a short silence and she pushed away the remains of her cake as if she had lost all appetite. She changed subject and asked him what he did. Perceval mentioned his former part-time post. 'It wasn't the most exciting job in the world, but I was in the running for a full-time position. I suppose it would have allowed me to work my way up. Deputy-Director told me my prospects were good.'

When these last words were out of his mouth, Perceval knew they sounded old-fashioned. It was the sort of thing a young suitor in a Victorian drama would say to the father of the woman he wished to marry. He'd only said them to let Fleur know he wasn't a complete loser. To cover his tracks, he thought he should add something. 'I got on well with the women in the office. When I look back on it, they were very good to me.'

'All sorts and conditions of women seem attracted to you, Alex.' For the first time, Fleur seemed slightly disconcerted.

'I think it's my innocence. They must feel safe with me.'

'And tell me, are you innocent? And are you safe?'

'I can't possibly say. You must be the judge of that. And I trust your judgement.'

'Hmmm,' Fleur teased, 'neatly evasive but at least not self-endorsement, Alex Perceval.'

'That's good enough for me, Fleur Stephens. You have the rest of your life to put me to the test.' He couldn't believe he was saying things like that.

'I like the sound of that,' she said, then hesitated. 'Look, Alex, I may appear very self-confident and pushy but I'm not really. Being open with you today makes me quite vulnerable. Do you understand?'

'I do understand. You can trust me ... even if I'm not a doctor.'

Fleur found that amusing and relaxed again. She glanced at her watch. 'Goodness,' she said. 'Look at the time. I can't believe it. I'd better get going. My brother needs the car this evening. And I don't want to cycle along the canal in the dark.'

'Yes, of course,' Perceval said.

'We can walk together to your boat.'

As they came down the stairs, Fleur stopped at the large King James Bible which lay open on the pulpit. 'I wonder if it has a message for us?' she asked.

They stood in front of the Bible for a moment. Perceval put a finger on some lines from Proverbs and read, 'Let not mercy and truth forsake thee; bind them around thy neck, write them in the tablet of thine heart.'

He looked at her and softly, Fleur put a hand on his shoulder. 'I don't need my brother to make sense of that for me,' she said.

Chapter Twenty-Six

As they strolled together to *Knight Errant*, Perceval thought of that Fool card he'd drawn in Jo's reading and how, not knowing what he was looking for, he'd discovered Fleur. But his joy was haunted by his familiar uncertainty, as if he was still in the circle of the Eight of Swords. Could it be true that someone like Fleur had chosen to be with him? He did find it difficult to accept. Yet hadn't she gone out of her way to find him? And here she was, walking beside him, pushing her bike, her conversation animated like she too was possessed by an exhilarating spirit.

Along the towpath, they talked about their first encounter, going over the details of what they'd said and their smile, surprise, attraction, small things which now had, as Perceval joked, almost world-historical significance. Fleur looked at him thoughtfully and replied that yes, it did seem that way now. And when he saw how she looked when she said it, heard the conviction in her words, he was ashamed of his doubts and uncertainties. In this extraordinary moment, shouldn't he act the 'fool' as Jo advised, and be open to her unreservedly, trust his own intuitions, take the risk, and make happen what he most desired? Fleur's presence, he thought, had overcome his old network of emotional deflections. They appeared worthless in the face of the gift she was offering. Why not believe in miracles?

Another group of kayakers went by heading towards Trevor, kept in line by the same instructor Perceval had spoken to earlier that morning. Two women in multi-coloured wetsuits followed behind on paddle boards, chatting casually. Fleur waved enthusiastically and the women waved back.

'Do you know them?' Perceval asked.

'No,' she answered, 'but it looks like they're having fun.'

'That's the first time I've ever seen anyone on a paddle board. It looks quite difficult.'

'Really? They're common along the canal. Have you ever been in a kayak before?'

'Never.'

'In that case, I will have to take you one day.'

'I'd love that,' he said, though it wasn't the idea of paddling a kayak he loved but the future together her words implied. 'Since I stopped playing cricket, I'm not as fit as I was.'

'You look in good shape to me,' she said.

It was darkening when they reached *Knight Errant* and looked ever more like rain.

'Are you going to stay tied up here?' Fleur asked.

'I'd rather find another spot. I prefer being close to other boats if possible. The loneliness of the canal is more of a challenge at night.'

'Are you afraid of ghosts, Alex?' She teased and tickled his chest.

Perceval snorted at the idea, singing the line from *Ghostbusters*, 'I'm afraid of no ghosts', as if what she'd asked was entirely fanciful. In fact, if *believing* in ghosts was going too far, he did not dismiss the possibility of their existence. 'We are haunted, Alex, by what we've seen,' his mother told him. 'But we are haunted also by what we can't see and never saw'. He thought her words summed up his view on ghosts.

'I'm only joking,' Fleur said. 'I did see a boat on the way down from Llangollen tied up at the Bryn Howell Bridge. It's close so you'll make it before the light goes.'

'Great. I'll seek it out. You can travel along with me for a bit, if you like.'

'I'd love to. We did some canal boating with mum and dad

when we were kids. That's how I knew about the leaves. But it's much quicker for me to cycle and I'm kind of pushed for time,' she said, looking at her watch.

'Okay.' Perceval swallowed his disappointment.

'Number?' she asked.

He didn't understand.

'Your mobile number?'

'Of course, sorry.' He struggled to extricate his phone from his trouser pocket. 'I can never remember it offhand.'

'You don't do this too often, I'm happy to see,' she smiled. 'I told you I left my number with a note for you.' Fleur pointed to the door of the cabin and Perceval noticed a folded page lodged between the locked doors. He was about to fetch it when Fleur put her hand on his arm. 'Don't read the note until after I'm gone.' She took her mobile from a pouch in the thigh of her leggings. 'Right. Read out your number to me.' Fleur typed it into her phone which she then raised to her ear. Perceval's mobile began to ring. 'Hello, woman of mystery to dark handsome stranger,' she said, and they both laughed. 'Alex don't lose that number, you don't want to call nobody else,' she sang to the tune of the old Steely Dan hit and ended the call.

He told her he liked that song and she said that was something else they had in common.

'Did your uncle tell you there are sections of the canal between here and Llangollen which are only one-way?'

If he had, Perceval hadn't remembered. His uncertain glance convinced her he had no idea.

'Tomorrow's Saturday. On any other day, especially in November, you could have taken a chance to go through on your own. But there may be some hire boats out for the day, especially since the weather forecast is good. I can meet you at Bryn Howell and you can give me a lift to Llangollen. When we reach the narrows, I can go ahead on my bike, stop someone coming down, and call to give you the green light. Only if you want me to, that is.'

He would like nothing more in the world, but his old instinct surfaced unbidden. 'Are you sure?'

Fleur shook her head. 'Your history tutor would give you a slap for being so bourgeois, Alex. It's your call. You must ask.' She spoke the words sweetly, and he heard the voice of the mysterious woman from his dream that first night on the canal. He was stunned momentarily. 'You must ask, Alex,' she repeated.

'Can you come tomorrow, Fleur? Please?'

'Of course I'll come!'

'Thank you.'

Perceval heaved his rucksack with its Tesco-bought provisions onto the deck and turned back to her. They embraced, holding each other tighter and longer this time. As they parted, Fleur brushed her lips against his cheek and whispered into his ear, 'Call me.'

'I will. Take care,' he told her. 'Let me know when you're home safely.'

'I will.' She pedalled down the towpath a short way, stopped, turned to look back, and blew him a kiss. Before he could reciprocate, she had cycled off energetically as if in a race and was gone.

Perceval closed his eyes, drained of the euphoria he'd felt so recently. On board *Knight Errant*, he pulled out her note from the cabin hatch.

> *Hi, Alex, it's me, Fleur. The girl in the kayak, remember? The one who warned you about leaves in your propeller? The one you promised to meet again but didn't. I don't know how we missed each other! Here's my number. Please give me a call. Love to talk or meet up xx.*

When he'd read her note he felt elated once more. What was the traditional rhyme they'd learnt at school in music class? It was something like 'a lady sweet and kind, I saw her passing by and I will love her till I die'. The words didn't sound quite right but the sentiment surely did. Tomorrow couldn't come soon enough.

First, he needed to get to Bryn Howell which – he checked on the map – was four bridges further up the canal. There was a hotel too marked with a beer symbol. Perceval calculated it would take him about half an hour. There should be no problem reaching it before nightfall. He put away the groceries he'd bought, untethered *Knight Errant*, and set off.

PART SEVEN: THE CONSUMMATION

Chapter Twenty-Seven

THE River Dee wound below the canal, the valley slopes steep, the hills in the distance brushed with low cloud. On his way to Bryn Howell, Perceval encountered two boats heading towards Trevor. On the first, a woman in the bow sipped from a tall glass while a man at the tiller held a can of beer, and both waved greetings. On the second, a small, sturdy, middle-aged woman was tilling and as her boat passed, she raised a martini glass and shouted 'Ta, bab!' in a rich Brummie accent. Her boat, he noticed, was called *Kingstanding Queen*.

At Bryn Howell, another boat was tied up between two bridges opposite the hotel. It was smaller than his, shabbier too, its roof covered with the usual paraphernalia of boating life, logs, coal bags, old ropes, and a bicycle. Wood smoke rose from the chimney and drifted languidly across the towpath. The bow entrance was fully opened, revealing shelves of green foliage. At the sound of *Knight Errant's* engine, a man's head appeared above the parapet. Perceval thought he must be attending to the plants for in his hand was what looked like a green plastic watering can.

'Is it alright if I tie up here?' Perceval called to him.

'*I* have,' he shrugged.

Perceval thought he'd better double-check. He wasn't sure if that answer was a yes or a no.

'Mind if I slot in behind you?'

'Be my guest. Glad to have a neighbour.'

That was more like it, Perceval thought. 'Thanks,' he called back. The name of the man's boat was *The Lady Julian*.

Perceval took *Knight Errant* towards the bank too sharply

and the bow was at the wrong angle to tie up. His intention was to avoid the far bridge and be near *The Lady Julian*, yet not so close to be intrusive. Unfortunately, he made a mess of it. Reversing up, his stern drifted out too far. Three times he tried to get the positioning right and three times he failed.

'Throw me your centre line,' the man shouted from the tow-path. 'I'll help pull you in.'

Humiliated though grateful, Perceval cast the rope towards the bank as accurately as he could. At least his cricketing skill remained true for the throw was accurate and the man caught the end of the rope

'Push the tiller all the way towards the bank,' he instructed Perceval, tugging *Knight Errant* towards him. Sure enough, the flank of the boat moved towards the towpath and gently nudged its side.

The man was dressed in a grubby denim shirt, his sleeves rolled up, black workingman's trousers spotted with engine oil, knee pads made from what looked like an old car tyre, and a pair of heavy boots, their laces undone. He must have put them on in a hurry for my sake, Perceval thought. The man had a full head of hair, completely grey, though he must only have been in his early forties. His face appeared too pale for someone who lived an outdoor life. But the most striking thing about his features was the teeth. A couple were missing at the front and the others looked widely spaced and precarious, as if only tenuously set in his gums.

'Need help tying up?'

Perceval felt mortified enough without appearing even more pathetic. 'That's okay, I can do that at least. Thanks a lot for pulling me in. I don't know what happened just now.'

'You're between two bridges here. The current can be a bit of a problem … sometimes. It can happen to the best of us … sometimes.'

Perceval noted the use of 'sometimes', as if the man had provided him with an excuse for his incompetence while remaining honest to himself.

'Right then. I'll leave you to it,' the man said and made to return to his boat. He'd gone a few steps, then turned back and held out his hand. 'Since we *are* neighbours now, I'd better introduce myself. My name is Bors.'

It sounded like 'Bors', but Perceval assumed the man's voice had swallowed the final syllable. He knew the name Boris, of course, but he'd never heard of anyone called Bors. The man's accent, to his ear, could have been either English with a hint of Welsh or Welsh with a hint of English. These were borderlands after all, so he decided to tread carefully on the matter of name as well as national identity.

'Alex', he said, reaching out his hand. 'Pleased to meet you Bors.' The man didn't correct him. Bors's handshake was remarkably tender, almost apologetic. He turned and left without saying more.

Perceval secured *Knight Errant*. Back on board he cracked open a can of lager. He was glad Fleur hadn't been here to witness his latest embarrassment. He pulled out his mobile phone but thought there was no point in calling for she was probably still on the road to Chester. And he disliked leaving voice messages, the tone and content of which always made him feel absurd. He thought it better to text. He could choose his words carefully if he texted and could edit if necessary.

> *Fleur, I'm thinking of you and hope you got back home safely. The boat is tied up at Bryn Howell Bridge. The other boat you mentioned was still here though I'm sure you saw it as you cycled by. Of course, I'm not texting you about such mundane detail. I'm texting to say how wonderful it was to share tea for two today and how*

much I look forward to seeing you. And I'm preparing for our great Titanic moment tomorrow (you can't get more Belfast than that). No, Fleur, we do NOT sink without trace on the Llangollen Canal. That's a promise which I will keep. See you soon Alex xx.

He read the message over a few times and thought it would do. He hoped she would find it suitably tender (though not presumptuously so) but also amusing and intriguing. He pressed send.

There was still some light left in the day and Perceval decided to walk across the bridge to the hotel, whose mock Tudor frontage, its roof and chimneys, he could see behind the perimeter wall and flanking trees. Bors was still at work with his plants as he passed. They seemed to be a lot of trouble, at least as far as Perceval could judge. But then he didn't have any interest in indoor gardening, or any sort of gardening for that matter.

'Taking the air before nightfall?' Bors asked.

'I'm going to have a look at the hotel, see what's happening,' Perceval replied casually.

'I'll tell you what's happening,' Bors chuckled. 'Nothing's happening. It's been closed for some time.'

Perceval felt a complete idiot. His uncle hadn't struck out the pint symbol by the hotel on the map. Had Fleur mentioned it? But why would she? She probably assumed he knew.

'If you're looking for a pint or something to eat, the Sun Trevor is up that way.' Bors pointed along the canal and paused to look at the sky. 'Be dark soon. It's about a fifteen-minute walk.'

'Thanks. I've got a few cans of beer on the boat. Think I'll just have a wee nosey around.'

'Right you are. Just don't make your *wee nosey around* a break-in,' he laughed. 'We are law-abiding citizens on the canal, my friend.'

As he stood next to Bors's boat, Perceval became aware of the unmistakable spicy aroma of marijuana and wondered about those plants he was tending to.

The old hotel looked sad and shabby, its grounds cluttered with dirty grey portacabins, which Perceval considered an insult to the place's memory. Fleur had joshed him about ghosts but he could picture ghosts in this hotel, perhaps in an abandoned parlour, or on an empty staircase, or along a deserted corridor. He was even more relieved to have *The Lady Julian* nearby. As he walked towards the main entrance, an old man in an ankle-length trench coat and flat cap emerged from a corrugated metal barn on the other side of the road. Perceval was startled by this unexpected appearance. His imagination conjured phantoms and tortured spirits roaming the North Wales countryside. The man didn't move, didn't speak, just stared, and Perceval turned back to the canal immediately, determined he wouldn't mention anything of his cowardly retreat to Fleur tomorrow.

He found a flat stone bench below the bridge and decided to sit there for a while, not wishing to return so soon, possibly to some mocking remark by Bors. He knew he should be more self-confident, but his botched mooring and his ignorance of the hotel's closure had dented his earlier poise. The time was spent staring at the water and anticipating Saturday. Thinking he'd waited long enough, he stood up just as his mobile dinged. He sat again. It was a text from Fleur.

Hi, Alex. I had a quick run to Chester. Not much traffic. Glad you made it to Bryn Howell without hitting an iceberg on the way. And I will treasure our forthcoming Titanic moment (whatever it may be). I love your own Van Morrison (his music that is!). He sings about there being days like this. And it is a day I (and let me be confident), we, will never forget. We can think of it as the beginning of our story and one without any need for cliché alerts. How does that sound? Look forward to seeing you, Love Fleur xx.

He replied, '*And the title of our story will be Crazy Love? Alex xx*'

She texted immediately '*That makes me mellow, deep down in my soul, Fleur xx*'

Chapter Twenty-Eight

B ORS was sawing branches on a trestle and stopped his work to greet Perceval. 'Fallen branches,' he told him. 'From this side of the hedgerow and not from the farmer's land,' he explained. 'It's not trespass and it's not theft. I might as well make use of nature's bounty, don't you agree? Law-abiding to a fault, that's me these days.'

Smoke from the chimney of *The Lady Julian* continued to waft across the towpath and Perceval thought of Bors's marijuana which didn't seem to bother his sense of law-abidingness. 'You've got a good fire going,' he said. 'My boat doesn't have a stove.'

'Essential if you live on your boat, Alex. Or if you intend to spend any time on it, especially in winter. Or at any time of year, really. You know what our weather is like.'

'Do you live permanently on the canal?'

'Have done for some years, yes. I got this boat for a good price. Mind you, it took all the money I had to buy it. And it takes most of my time to repair it and keep it going, to be honest.' Bors spoke as softly as he shook hands and though he had the appearance of a working man, his voice was educated. Though toughly built and it was possible to sense a hardness (he was, Perceval judged, someone who 'could look after himself'), Bors conveyed only gentleness of manner.

'Do you stay all the time on the Llangollen?'

'Recently, yes. But in the past, I've been south as far as London, west as far as Bristol, and east as far as Leeds.'

'That's just about everywhere,' Perceval said with genuine admiration. 'I've struggled up from Whittington, with difficulty as you've seen already. I couldn't imagine doing what you've done.' He could have added 'nor would I ever wish to', but that would have spoilt the compliment.

Bors looked pleased by the praise and, in turn, asked Perceval what had brought him here. He told Bors his story, mentioning the name of the boat and joking that it had been something of a challenging quest. 'There have been a few dragons to slay along the way, the Chirk Tunnel being the biggest one. I discovered the kindness of strangers too, and I've heard many interesting stories.' He would have liked to add, 'I found love too' but was superstitious about putting his good fortune into words. To speak of it now, he feared, might be to see it disappear like the wood smoke from *The Lady Julian's* chimney.

Bors didn't make any comment, only nodded, bending over to resume sawing the branches he'd found. He changed his mind, straightened and let the saw hang by his side. 'I have a story if you want to hear it. I was going to take a break anyway. There's water on the stove. It won't take a minute to brew up a cup of tea. And the boat is warm.'

Normally, Perceval's caution would have led him to decline. But hadn't he laid claim to the honour of the questing knight able to confront every challenge? Well, up to a point and apart from apparitions near the Bryn Howell Hotel. Anyway, he didn't think Bors was a maniacal serial killer. At the same time, he imagined his mother shaking her head and advising caution and, in honour of her memory, Perceval decided to provide himself with some cover.

'That's very kind of you. It is getting quite chilly,' he said rubbing his arms. 'Someone is coming from Llangollen to scout for me on the canal tomorrow, you know the one-way sections.' He glanced at his watch. 'But I've got some time. Thank you.' Perceval felt guilty about dissembling, even though he'd crafted his words carefully to avoid any outright falsehood.

The living space of *The Lady Julian* was, as Perceval expected, untidy and slightly chaotic, but it wasn't without charm nor was it without comfort. It was certainly more homely and comfortable than the evacuated state of poor old *Knight Errant*. Opposite the wood-burning stove, its chimney pipe running up through the ceiling, was a battered leather sofa which Bors had somehow managed to manhandle on board. Its torn back was partly covered by a green, textured blanket. Beside it stood a small wooden table on which sat a reading lamp and a rickety-looking wooden chair with a cushioned seat. The floor, whether original or not, was bare wood, dark-stained with varnish. Beyond the stove was another small table which Bors may have used for his meals, for a folded canvas chair was set beside it. This living space was also filled with plants, a tall one in a large ceramic pot, smaller ones stacked on orange boxes turned into cabinets. Various items, an old pair of boots, a coil of rope, some tins of what looked like paint or creosote, a toolbox, had been left lying about. On the walls, Perceval could see colourful religious icons which he found odd, for Bors didn't strike him as being pious. He thought they were possibly images of the Virgin Mary. The interior was warm, and the aroma of tobacco and marijuana permeated, but not unpleasantly. Bors switched on the desk lamp, but its light did little to dispel the gloom.

'Have a seat,' he told Perceval, who made for the wooden chair.

'No, I'll take that,' Bors said. 'It's a bit unstable. I must get rid of it at some stage. You sit on the sofa, Alex. It's more comfortable.' The kettle boiled and Bors grabbed the handle with a cloth. 'Is a mug with teabag okay for you?'

'It's what I usually have,' Perceval replied.

As the tea was brewing, Bors fussed about shifting jars on a shelf. 'Sugar?' he asked.

'No thanks.'

'Milk?'

'Just a wee taste,' Perceval replied instinctively, quickly correcting to, 'just a little, please'. He preferred his tea strong and not weak, another taste he'd inherited from his mother.

Bors handed Perceval his tea, shifted the wooden chair across to the stove, and sat heavily. The chair legs moved and squeaked. He took a sip from his own mug and then held it in both hands. 'This is a story of bad news and good news,' he said. 'To begin with, the good news was the bad news. And here's the thing. What I thought was the bad news was really the beginning of the good news.'

Perceval narrowed his eyes, trying to follow Bors' meaning and failing. He blew on the surface of his tea and took a sip and waited for him to explain.

'I know that must sound strange to you. Let me put it this way. For most of my life, I was what the cops would call a "bad un". From an early age I took easily to lying, cheating, stealing, drugs, what sociologists, I've learnt, call transgressive acts, though in mitigation, I did nothing violent. I enjoyed it. I had a gift for it. Not only had I a gift for it, I was also clever enough to get away with it. I can't call in my defence lack of parental guidance or anything else on the side of nurture over nature. My parents were loving, kind, supportive, understanding, every positive you could imagine in a progressive childcare manual. They were also, I suppose, too trusting, and I learned very quickly how simple it was to pull the wool over their eyes. They made financial sacrifices to send me to good schools, to cater to whatever whims I had. For you see I was their only child, a surviving twin. My brother died in childbirth, and I wasn't expected to survive either.'

Bors looked at Perceval to calculate what effect his story was having so far. Since Perceval was used to keeping his own counsel, he looked interested but remained silent. Anyway, he thought there was no purpose asking anything at this point.

'I've always wondered if the Lord in his wisdom had given to my brother everything that was virtuous and to me everything that was wicked. But I had no time for the Lord back then, possessed as I was by my own devilment. Doing wrong was my vocation, I believed, what I was called to do. And I did it with relish,' he went on, taking another mouthful of tea. 'I never did the right thing. I only ever did the wrong thing. And if I *couldn't* do wrong, I felt it wasn't worth doing. And if I thought that I *had* done a good deed by accident, I would repent of it with my very soul.' Bors coughed violently for a few seconds, hacked and apologised. 'I had the courage of my vices and only contempt for those who didn't.' Bors leaned from his chair towards Perceval. It creaked in protest, so he resumed his previous position. 'I felt uncomfortable when I told the truth. Anyway, so much of life seemed a fake and a sham to me, why wouldn't it? Can you see my point?'

Perceval did see his point. His words captured how his mother had talked about politics and society in Northern Ireland, denouncing the bad faith that had tormented and scarred her life. Bors set his mug on the floor, stood and took a tin from a shelf near the stove. He opened it and took out a long spliff. He sat again, lit it, took a deep drag and exhaled luxuriously. He took another drag and held out the joint for Perceval. He put up his hand to refuse and was about to say 'my body is a temple of the Lord' but thought, in the circumstances of Bors's tale, that old line would only sound too clever by half.

Bors took another drag and coughed less violently this time. 'And badness makes friends, Alex. It attracts like to like. I was part of a gang of fraudsters. I provided the brains and the smooth talk when necessary.' He paused to examine the end of his spliff and squeezed tobacco along the paper as though dissatisfied with its quality. 'We began with email scams and then moved on to more sophisticated phishing of banking details, cold calling on disposable phones. Primitive by today's standards but back then people weren't so alert to scammers. So, I prospered being bad to the bone. Not mega-rich, but it was the evil of deception which drove me. Hubris before the fall, you may be thinking? It wasn't hubris. It was human sympathy and compassion … if you can believe that.'

Perceval remained as impassive as he could. He didn't know why, but he had expected something like this. Bors nicked the end of his spliff and put it on the edge of the large plant pot next to him. He finished his tea and put the mug on the floor. As he did so, the wooden chair creaked loudly, and its legs splayed slightly as Bors's weight shifted.

'I phoned my parents one evening. I rarely did. They never had my number. I was always changing it anyway, always on the move. I can't explain it, but some instinct directed me. I found my mother in tears. My dad, who'd just retired, had dropped down dead from a heart attack. He was gardening, pulling the resistant starting cord of his lawnmower.' Bors shook his head. 'I can still hear my mother's voice, trying to be brave, asking me to be brave. Me? Brave?' He snorted. 'You may ask: Did I have an immediate change of heart? No, I didn't. But, like a virus, something must have got into my system. It was my undoing *and* my salvation. Because later, for the first time in my life, I did do something right.'

He asked Perceval if he wanted another tea. Perceval declined the offer. Bors made to get up but changed his mind and sat back, the chair creaking again.

'I was in Norwich at the time, thinking I was the master of my fate. One day I cold called an old geezer we'd targeted for a pension scam. A little financial jargon, a little bureaucratic nonsense, a little genial encouragement, a big emphasis on citizen rights, and an official prompt to "do things over the phone, quick note of bank details, and avoid all the paperwork".

Doesn't always work but you'd be surprised …'

Perceval responded with a small twist of his head, a gesture denoting he had a good idea of exactly how it might work as well as how accomplished Bors would be.

'Anyway, in the old man's voice, I heard my father speaking. I heard a cat meowing which he shushed away, just like my father used to do with our cat. And I could picture the house, the furniture, the wallpaper, the carpet. It was a punch to my black heart. And I had this crazy idea that I had to see this man for myself. I told him I would drop over with the paperwork, go out of my way to assist. He thanked me. I got the address. I went. It was as if I'd returned to my old home, gone back to my childhood. It *almost* broke my heart – almost but not quite. For the man looked nothing like my father. Having satisfied my curiosity, I decided not to steal his savings.' He paused and sighed. 'I'm sure you've guessed it, Alex. At the door were the cops. His son was a detective. The old bugger had called him up to check if it was okay for me to visit. The son had come over right away with uniformed. I'd walked into a trap of my own making.'

This time Bors did get up to make another tea. As the kettle boiled, he asked Perceval if he'd like something stronger, a whiskey perhaps? Perceval refused. This time Bors didn't add milk to his mug. Instead he tossed in a shot of Bushmills whiskey.

'I was sent down for three years in Norwich Prison. Was prison going to reform me? Not a chance. I'd serve my sentence quietly, secure remission, get out, and return to doing what I did best. So I planned.' He pointed to his front teeth. 'I lost these in a brawl not of my own making. But I kept out of trouble as far as possible. Stoical and resilient, that was me, a fortress unto myself. I got friendly with one of the prison chaplains. I thought helping in the chaplaincy, exhibiting some Christian piety, could work to my advantage. It was a fine line though. You don't want to get the reputation of a being creeping Jesus.'

Perceval laughed at those words. 'My mother used the same expression for do-gooders at home.' Bors smiled briefly but he had no interest in Perceval's mother, only his story.

'One May there was an ecumenical service for Julian of Norwich. She was a fourteenth-century anchoress. The chaplain asked me to get him the copy of her book *Revelations of Divine Love* from the library – oh, I forgot to say, I'd talked my way into a library job in the prison. Religious girlie stuff, I thought. But when I sat through the service … I don't know. All I can say is that something stirred in my soul. Afterwards, I asked if I could take the book to read. I didn't understand much to begin with. I went back to it after a few days and suddenly it made sense.'

'What did it say?'

'It told me that despite all my sins I wasn't without hope of redemption, that sin is sometimes what God uses to bring people closer to Him.'

'You mean that your former wrongdoing doesn't matter?' Perceval tried not to sound too judgemental, but he couldn't help thinking of those who'd murdered his father, destroyed his mother's happiness and had such bitter effect on his life. He couldn't help thinking it was Bors's metaphorical 'get out of jail free card', literally for terrorists in Northern Ireland.

'Oh, it matters alright. But Lady Julian helped me understand that out of bad can come forth good.'

'And what effect did it have on you?'

'"All shall be well, and all shall be well, and all manner of things shall be well", she'd written. When I asked the chaplain what that meant, he told me it didn't mean fairy tale endings for everyone. It meant that we are all capable of grace, if only we can accept it.'

'And has accepting grace changed you?'

'Here's the point of my tale, Alex. That one good deed I did? It got me a prison sentence. What's the result? I found real freedom, thanks to Lady Julian.' He spread his arms wide to encompass the boat. 'I don't have much. And yet I have everything.' He slapped his chest. 'Grace doesn't mean I'm unable to do wrong. It means I *won't* do wrong.'

Perceval didn't know if he was persuaded but he had no intention of questioning what he'd heard. Moreover, he suspected this confession revealed not so much Bors's faith in God, as God's faith in Bors. He stood, thanked Bors for his hospitality, looked at his watch and told him he'd better check on his helper for tomorrow. Again, he chose his words to avoid an outright lie but he was curious if Bors, the confessed conman, had been taken in by any of it. Perceval thanked him for his hospitality, shook hands and they wished each other well.

Chapter Twenty-Nine

As soon as he was back on *Knight Errant,* Perceval checked his mobile. There were two missed calls from Fleur and a voice message. He'd felt the mobile vibrating in his pocket when Bors was making his confession but had considered it impolite to interrupt. He listened to the voice message.

> '*Hi Alex. I called a couple of times. Wondering what you are up to in the wilds of the Llangollen Canal after dark. Is there an illegal rave going on in the abandoned Bryn Howell? Have you been partying to Techno with all the local girls? Then again, perhaps not. I picture you more as the mysterious type with a hint of melancholy beneath the good manners, like someone you might come across in a Parisian café. Or maybe in a tearoom at Trevor? Yes, I think that's more likely.*'

Fleur laughed at this point. Her tone was light, her voice lively, and he could picture her bright, intelligent green eyes. There was a momentary pause and Fleur's tone changed. Was it self-doubt, he detected, insecurity, or uncertainty about his good faith?

> '*So, are we still on for tomorrow? I can be there for about nine-ish now, if that suits? But if you've changed your mind, can you let me know? Don't worry if you have. It's okay. I'm sure you can get along very well without me.*'

The last two sentences were said quickly, almost swallowed. Perceval was innocent of most female emotions, but he wasn't stupid. He could hear Fleur take a deep breath.

> '*So, if you can get in touch … And thanks again for a wonderful day today. That lunch was a lifesaver too.*' (She laughed again and hesitated) '*That's about all. If you can, give me a call or text … I'm repeating myself.* (Another hesitation*) Hope you're alright.* (A pause) *I miss you.*'

The voice message ended abruptly.

Those last three words. Perceval's thoughts lingered on them, savoured them. No woman had ever said those words to him with Fleur's affecting resonance. That was wrong, he corrected himself. No woman had ever said those words to him, full stop. Her words were real, they were direct. They weren't open to doubt. Fleur hadn't been evasive. She hadn't tried to keep him at a distance. She hadn't used light-heartedness or humour as a way to deny or evade her emotions. He recognised that behaviour well enough because that was his style.

If he had been ungallant by nature, Perceval would have delayed responding and let Fleur wait a little longer. He was hungry. He could make himself dinner, have another can of lager and keep her dangling. He recalled one of their cricket team, a rather boorish sociology student whose lack of good looks (lack of sporting skills too) were complemented by exasperating bravado. There had been no evidence to support his claim to have 'a way with women' – not that Perceval knew of anyway. His wisdom, especially when drinking a post-match pint, consisted in repeating the line 'treat them mean and keep them keen'.

Perceval had no intention of treating Fleur mean. It wouldn't be thoughtless. It would be much worse than thoughtless. It would be a matter of dishonour, or so he believed. He'd accepted an obligation to be worthy of Fleur because he'd failed her once already. The games people played in relationships he could understand, but only intellectually, not instinctively. Did they not assume a lack of genuineness? He knew his feelings for Fleur were genuine and dialled her number immediately.

Fleur picked up on the second ring. 'Alex!'

'Your Bryn Howell raver is taking a break from … raving.'

She laughed. 'There was a rave! I knew it!'

'If there was, it was in a rather dubious looking corrugated iron shed near the hotel. And if it was there, I saw the DJ. He didn't look like he'd flown in from Ibiza. He was an old guy in a trench coat and flat cap. He may have been wearing Wellington boots too.' She laughed as he spoke. 'Does that sound about right for a rave in the Welsh hills?' Perceval asked.

'As a proper young woman, I couldn't possibly say.'

'Actually, I walked about looking for a Parisian-style café where I could sit and be moody in an existential sort of way. There was no sign of one anywhere.' He could hear Fleur laughing still. 'When I came back, I got talking to the owner of the boat tied up near mine who invited me onto *The Lady Julian* … that's the boat's name, if you're wondering. I'll tell you about it tomorrow, an interesting tale. So, that's where I was. Until now, that is.'

'Oh,' she said, 'sounds rather mysterious. I notice, Alex, you didn't tell me if it was a woman or a man on *The Lady Julian* … well?'

'It was most definitely a man, Fleur. The closest I came to a drug-fuelled party was a cup of tea. My neighbour does like his marijuana. And I came away with a definite attack of the munchies.'

'Too funny, Alex, I leave you for a few hours and you get yourself into such a lot of mischief.'

'You may very well say that. And to give a direct answer to

your voicemail, no, I don't get along without you very well.' He felt exhilarated saying those words. 'It's the reason I miss you too.' Was he being soppy? Foolish? What he said was without a flippant context to provide him an easy escape. For once, he didn't care.

'Thank you, Alex. I feared you might think my message too … how shall I say … needy, clingy? I didn't want you to think I was prying. Even if I was,' she laughed. 'You are turning out to be an exception for me in every way.'

'Tell me what you've got up to since I last saw you, what, about four hours ago?'

'It seems longer. Not much, really. I drove back to Chester. I handed back my brother's car, stowed away my bike, checked out my timetable for next week which, apart from Monday, is full on. My fourth year means hospital and general practice experience, as well as normal academic work. You know that song "when the going gets tough, the tough get going". Well, I know what that's like.'

'When you talk that way it makes me feel guilty about my own time at university.'

'It's my choice, Alex. I think I'm tough enough … on most things, anyway.'

Perceval wondered if he was tough in any way. What he said was, 'You can't really go up in my estimation, Fleur, for you already *are* the top. Like the old song "you're the smile on the Mona Lisa" (he sang the line).' It was another of his mother's housework songs.

'No one has ever likened my smile to the Mona Lisa's before,' she replied. 'You are racking up a lot of firsts, Alex, and in a good way I hasten to add. I'm hoping there's more to come.'

'Memo to self: start as you mean to go on.' Perceval heard her chuckling. 'And what are you up to right now?'

'I've just had dinner. Not that I was all that hungry after

lunch. Just relaxing before psyching myself up for tomorrow's big adventure, of course.

'*Canal of No Return*, starring Alex Perceval and Fleur Stephens …'

'Hey, wait a minute – starring Fleur Stephens, with a guest appearance by Alex Perceval.'

'Okay, that sounds about right. Smart woman saves useless man from disaster.'

'I'm really looking forward to playing that part. It comes naturally. And when you trip over the rope and bang your head, I can practise my BLS skills.'

'What're they?'

'Basic Life Support, and afterwards I can do some practical wound care.'

'That sounds like the perfect opportunity for me to speak my immortal line.'

'Oh, and what would that be?'

'Cue me sitting on the deck, head bandaged, looking up at you, my eyes brimming with gratitude but also with a sudden comprehension of destiny, and I'll say, "Where have you been all my life?" How does that sound?'

'I'm sorry, Alex. It sounds like a cliché from a Channel Five afternoon movie. And we agreed no more cliché alerts, remember?'

'I see,' he said with mock disappointment, though not entirely mock, for he'd expected a little more appreciation of his joke.

'That's the bad news,' Fleur continued. 'Here's the good news. I love it. And it's another first. And maybe you should get a job as a scriptwriter. You have an obvious talent for it.' Fleur paused. 'It is of course the question I've been asking myself since yesterday.'

'What question's that?'

'Don't be silly, Alex. *Where have you been all my life?*'

'As I keep telling the Hollywood producers, all the best lines are clichés. I know because I write them.'

'Too funny … sorry, mum's calling … what is it, mum?'

Perceval heard a woman's indistinct voice in the background and Fleur responding with 'okay' and 'will do' and 'yes, in a moment'. His stomach rumbled. He thought of food and drink and how basic needs can trump even true romance.

'You probably gathered I'm on parental call, Alex. I've got to help shift some stuff, now that my brother has conveniently disappeared off somewhere. I can't complain about him too much. He's loaned me his car for the weekend, good Christian that he's become. See you tomorrow? About nine? And I'm expecting breakfast.'

'Fleur, I shall make you a breakfast such as you've never had before. And you can take that either as a promise or as a threat.'

'Another first, Alex, no one has made me laugh so much, ever.'

'In a good way, I hope.'

'Of course in a good way. Better go. See you in the morning. Love you.'

'Love you.'

When the call ended, Perceval realised that was a first for him. He'd never said those two words before, not even to his mother, and his elation was tinged with guilt.

After he'd eaten a meal of corned beef and baked beans and washed it down with more lager, he wanted to send Fleur a text message before bed. In his head were her words – 'I'm sure you can get along very well without me'. There was another song his mother used to play, deeply melancholic, which had that line, or one like it, and it always brought a tear to her eye. Music was her daily means of coping, her way of smiling through tears, the pain ever-present, yet mostly suppressed beneath thick veils of resilience, her misfortune borne but rarely revealed. Once

Perceval had asked her why this song made her cry. She'd told him, 'It makes me think of your father. It makes me think of you too.' He'd understood the first part of her reply but not the second part. When he left for university in England many years later, he finally understood her anticipation of loss.

On his mobile, he Googled the words as a possible title (he knew the version his mother played was sung by Frank Sinatra). He found it immediately. The song was 'I get along without you very well'. He accessed the YouTube video and played it. It was the tune he wanted. But Sinatra wasn't right for Fleur. He looked for other versions and found one by Chet Baker. The wistful pitch of Baker's voice was perfect, he thought. He copied and pasted the link to a brief text.

> *You said in your voice message that you're sure I can get along very well without you. Here is my answer, Alex xx.*

He put down his phone, set about washing the dishes, and tidying up *Knight Errant*. Not that it required much tidying and thankfully no cleaning. About half an hour later, his mobile dinged the arrival of a text from Fleur.

> *Alex, thank you so much! Yet more firsts. First time I've heard that song. First time I've heard Chet Baker. Isn't it shameful? I've been listening to the song and to him repeatedly since you texted. I've had to wipe away a tear at the thought. So, never try to get along without me and I'll never try to get along without you. Fleur xx*

Before he went to bed, he decided to check his mooring. Outside was pitch-black. There was no light from *Lady Julian* though Perceval could still smell wood smoke. His ropes were secure, the knots firm. As he stepped onto the deck again, he glanced in the direction of the Bryn Howell Hotel and froze.

There seemed to be a light shining, faintly but unmistakeably, in one of the rooms. He looked again from another angle. He could still see it. Was it a ghost? Or was it merely an emergency light? He got inside the cabin as fast as he could and locked the doors, knowing this reaction to be irrational.

It would be a long, long night of waiting. However, he fell asleep almost immediately.

Chapter Thirty

WHEN the melodic alarm on his mobile went off, the sun hadn't risen. Perceval fumbled for his phone, checked that it was indeed seven o'clock, pressed the snooze button, and lay back again. In the night he'd had a curious dream. Not a dream about finding Fleur or an anxiety dream about losing Fleur. Not a dream about being locked in a Norwich prison cell or a dream about an anchorite. Not even a dream about spending the night in a haunted hotel. One or all he might have expected, but it had been none of these.

Knight Errant had been tied up in the middle of a bustling medieval street, like The Shambles in York. When Perceval stepped off, he was greeted by his old university cricket team, not in armour but in knightly attire, colourful tunics, flamboyant cloaks, tight leggings and, incongruously, cricket pads and batting gloves. Jenny, his ideal woman of university days, was with them, in silken gown and mantle, a diamond tiara in her long flowing tresses. Everyone had embraced him like a returning hero, Jenny kissing him on the cheek. He'd been led to a banquet in a great hall with minstrels, jugglers, and a jester who presented Perceval with a portrait of himself as The Fool. Yet what appeared outwardly to be a time of celebration and joyous renewal, of acclamation and welcome, had felt like a sorrowful ending, a time of farewell and exclusion. At the feasting table, everyone had been seated at a distance and Perceval could detect no warmth in the expression on their faces.

After a lukewarm shower, Perceval got himself ready for Fleur's arrival. There was nothing he could do about his stubble, though he supposed, or rather hoped, it made him appear manly and less boyish. For the first time in days, he combed his hair (though he did wonder if Fleur appreciated his unaffected dishevelment). He lingered over his reflection in the mirror, turning his face this way and that. What did Fleur see in him? He wasn't thinking of his looks, not entirely, but of Alex Perceval with all his paradoxes, his insubstantiality. What did Fleur, with her Oxford life, her vocation, her friends, her family, and – he couldn't avoid thinking of it – her secure English middle-class life, see in him, this superfluous guy from Northern Ireland?

Perceval didn't think he was vain. That required a self-belief, an egocentric disposition, which he didn't have. Or if he did, it wasn't the sort of vanity to impose himself on others. He shrugged at the notion that his ego was so inward no one could ever find it. Maybe not even him. Yet hadn't Fleur given him permission to set aside his self-doubts and open himself to her? Wasn't this the augury of Jo's reading? Didn't love entail risk, a leap of faith, having courage, like the Fool in the card he'd drawn, stepping forward without the baggage of timidity? Wasn't this him, now? He wanted to believe it was and, for now, he believed that was enough. When he thought about all that had happened in the last few days, his experience seemed miraculous. 'Ha!' he said out loud. If Fleur judged him worthy, who was he to argue?

The next hour dragged as he fussed around the boat. In that time, he imagined all sorts of possibilities – her brother withdrawing his offer of the car, Fleur having second thoughts about this stranger befriended on a whim and, on another whim, deciding he wasn't worth any more of her time. Or her parents, having been told what she intended to do today, advising that Perceval might be some kind of confidence trickster, having in mind, perhaps, someone exactly like Bors. Was he to be one of love's April fools, or in his case, one of love's November Fools? What he needed was faith.

His mobile dinged. *Put the kettle on. I'm on my way from Llangollen, and getting along without you very well xx*

When Fleur arrived, Perceval had just finished setting the table. Out of the small galley window, he saw her laying her mountain bike on the grass verge of the towpath, taking off her helmet, strapping it onto the handlebars, shaking free her hair, and adjusting a rucksack. Perceval turned off the gas under the whistling kettle and bounded up the steps onto the transom. When he was on the towpath, she walked towards him as she'd done in the tearoom in Trevor, her arms outstretched, her face radiant. Unlike that first time, their embrace was tight, and they kissed each other gently, full on the lips for the first time. They looked at each other, not quite sure if everything was real. Then they both laughed, having intuited what the other was thinking.

'It is real,' Fleur said. 'Especially the thrill of being sheltered in your arms ... I'll not forget that song you sent.'

Perceval put his arm around her shoulder and walked her to the boat. As they were about to board, Bors came on the deck of *The Lady Julian*, coughing loudly, running his hand through his hair. He had the appearance of someone who'd just awakened from a deep sleep. When he saw them, he waved hospitably then leaned against the taff rail, taking a deep breath.

Perceval called, 'Good morning. Nice day.' Though it was cool, the clouds were thin, and there was a promise of sunshine. Bors merely nodded, as if he had other things on his mind.

Perceval gave Fleur the choice of how she wanted her eggs (she chose scrambled) and as he was cooking up breakfast, careful not to burn the toast, she told him about how her father had taken the family on weekend trips in summer along the Llangollen Canal, how she and her two brothers used to pester him to get their hands on the tiller, and how thrilled she'd been as a child to feel the power of engine in her tiny hand. 'You've learnt quickly, Alex,' she told him. 'You should be proud of that.'

'If you'd witnessed me yesterday trying to bring the boat into the bank here, you'd have had the laugh of your life,' he said setting a plate of eggs on toast and a cup of tea before her. 'If Bors hadn't pulled me in, I'd still be trying.'

'That's the man we saw just now?'

'Yes.' Perceval sat down with his own scrambled eggs. He'd given Fleur noticeably more than he'd given himself as a mark of his gentlemanly manners. And she noticed.

'Alex, you've given me far too much,' she said, pointing at the portions.

'You've cycled here to help me and it's the least I can do.'

She didn't protest, and he supposed her own good manners forbade denying his gesture, never mind the awkward act of pushing egg from her plate onto his. Fleur ate with relish, and it made him feel good to see. 'Mmm, this is delicious,' she told him. 'It was worth cycling here in itself. As you may have gathered, the way to this woman's heart is though her stomach … though of course, only in moderation, and as part of a balanced diet. That's my professional, bedside manner, speaking.'

'I like the idea of your bedside manner.'

'Now, now, Alex, that's *not* what the doctor ordered.'

Fleur lifted her mug of tea, as Perceval did his, and they knocked them together in a toast. They ate silently for a while and Perceval had to admit he'd done a good job with breakfast.

'You said last night your neighbour has an interesting story?'

Perceval recounted what he could remember of the tale told by Bors, from criminality to conscience, from corruption to redemption, from the Devil to Julian of Norwich. Fleur listened closely and without interruption. 'That's about it. I suppose life on the canal is a bit like living a reclusive life. It's probably why he named his boat *The Lady Julian*. Well, in part, I suppose.'

Fleur said nothing for a while then asked, 'And do you believe him?'

Perceval was speechless for a second. 'You know, I never thought to question his sincerity.' He looked searchingly at Fleur. 'Do you think he might have been making it all up?'

'Well, with all that talk about being a confidence trickster …' She reached to grasp Perceval's hand. 'Alex, I'm sure he *was* being truthful. Who on earth would dream of telling lies to you? That *would* be a sin. Which, I suppose, is a roundabout way of saying you can trust me.'

'I trust you implicitly. You're a doctor, after all.'

'Very good, Alex. Not yet a doctor, but I'm getting there. But there is a doctor we can both trust … my dad. He gave me some info about the canal between here and Llangollen. He says there'll be quite a current downstream which will slow you up. He estimates the journey will take an hour and a half to two hours. That includes his estimate of waiting at the one-way sections. As promised, I'll cycle on and let you know if the canal is free. Hopefully, it will be. Though it is Saturday and decent enough weather, so there may be day-trippers.' Fleur looked at her watch. 'It's a little early for them yet, who knows? We should be in Llangollen by lunchtime if all goes well. About those one-way sections … do you have a map?'

Perceval fetched his uncle's map from the shelf by the cabin stairway. He pushed the dishes aside and spread it on the table. Fleur put her finger on the location of Bryn Howell and ran it up to the Sun Trevor pub.

'The first "pinch point" as dad calls it, is at Sun Trevor here. And the second is here, not much further, a little beyond bridge 44W. And the final one is just as you enter Llangollen basin. Dad says the last bit before the wharf is very tight. There's also a blind bend which can be dodgy. But I'll be on the lookout for you.'

'The Lone Boater and Tonto.'

Fleur slapped him gently on the arm. 'We better get going,' she said.

When Perceval had lifted Fleur's bike safely onto the transom and untied the ropes, he reversed *Knight Errant* a little way out into the centre of the canal to get the right run at the angled bridge just ahead. They saw Bors mounting his own bike, an empty rucksack on his back.

'Maybe see you in Llangollen,' he greeted them with a salute. 'I'm off to do the shopping.' He hesitated for a second before adding. 'And don't forget, Alex, all shall be well.' He pedalled off whistling.

'He seems harmless enough, a bit of a character,' Fleur said. 'What did he mean by "all shall be well"?'

'It's a line of Julian of Norwich.'

'I like it.'

Perceval managed to thread through the awkward narrow of the bridge without mishap, and they entered a long straight towards Sun Trevor. He reduced speed until the engine was merely ticking over. 'Okay,' he told her. 'Let's do it.'

She was taken by surprise. 'Do what?'

'The *Titanic* scene! Quick, let's do it.'

He took Fleur by the shoulders and guided her down the steps into the boat. She giggled with excitement as he pushed her through the galley, salon, bedroom, and onto the bow. *Knight Errant* kept a remarkably steady course in the middle of the canal and didn't veer towards either bank. He marshalled her to the fore and held her firmly by the waist, encouraging her to stand on the wooden guard-rail. 'You can trust *me* this time,' he told her. Perceval lifted his hands from her waist, stretched out her arms, and held them tight.

Fleur stopped laughing and shouted, 'I'm flying, Alex!' They held the pose for a few moments and then Fleur said, 'I don't want to alarm you but there's a boat coming towards us.'

Perceval lifted Fleur down and looked over her shoulder. 'Pray like you've never prayed before. Pray that all shall be well,' he said in her ear, turned and dashed back to the tiller.

Knight Errant had begun to drift to port and was now, albeit very slowly, heading directly for the oncoming boat. Perceval pushed the tiller fiercely while increasing speed to give the rudder more purchase. It worked and he got properly 'port-to-port' just in time. He pulled back the throttle to pass with as little disturbance as possible. This time there was no pleasant greeting from the other boater, a tall, bald-headed man in a brash Hawaiian shirt, who studiously ignored Perceval as if he'd received a grievous insult. Fleur climbed up the steps to the deck slowly, sheepishly, and wiped an imaginary bead of sweat off her forehead.

'We missed the iceberg this time,' Perceval said in a deadpan voice.

She laughed uncontrollably, laid her head on his shoulder, and Perceval put his arm around her, joining in her laughter. They weren't *enfants terribles*, playing with fire, far from it, but they thrilled at the joy of their silliness.

'Never let go, Alex,' she told him, squeezing him tightly around the waist. 'Never let go.'

Presently they reached the Sun Trevor which sat at the foot of a hill and across the main road from the canal. 'This is where I jump ship,' Fleur said.

Perceval took *Knight Errant* to the towpath and Fleur stepped off. He quickly handed the bike over the side, jumped down, and held the boat steady with the centre line.

'I'll call you in a mo,' she said, slipping on her helmet and pedalling away at speed. Very soon, his mobile rang. 'All clear,' Fleur told him. 'It's safe to come up.'

Her father had been right. In the narrow passage, the boat struggled against the current, *Knight Errant's* speed dropping well below average walking pace. On his left, the land descended to the River Dee, which wound its way across the valley, the far slopes thickly wooded in places. Along the canal, the trees cast long shadows as sunlight broke through the clouds, a gentle breeze stirring branches, golden leaves floating down serenely into the water. Perceval thought once more of Fleur appearing beside him for the first time to warn about the propellor. And the idea came to him that, though he was alone on the boat, he was *differently* alone. He was *together* alone. Or maybe alone *together* was a better way of putting it? It felt good whichever way he described it.

Round a blind bend under another tight bridge, the canal widened, the strong contraflow relented, and he saw Fleur sitting on a wooden bench, bike beside her, head leaning back to catch the sun. She sat up straight hearing the throb of the engine and gave him a quick celebratory clap as he brought *Knight Errant* to a halt at the towpath.

'Sorry for taking so long,' he apologised. 'The current was strong like your father warned.'

'No need to apologise,' she replied, wheeling her bike across to *Knight Errant*. 'Opportunity for me to get some vitamin D.'

'Hop on and I'll lift your bike.'

'Bend from the knees and lift, Alex,' she told him. 'Be careful of your back … sorry, that's the medical student speaking.'

'It was also the advice of our cricket coach. I believed him and I believe you too.'

'I'm in good company, then?'

'Nothing but the best.'

'I'll not argue.'

He asked Fleur if she'd like to take over the tiller.

'I thought you'd never ask,' she laughed. 'Seriously though, do you think I might? I'd love to. Just to the next one way?'

'I wouldn't ask if I didn't mean it.'

'It will bring back good memories!'

Perceval stepped aside and Fleur took the tiller from him.

Her manner was one of nervous concentration and yet childish delight, not only the look of the learner driver challenged by a new sequence of manoeuvres, but also, ironically given the speed of *Knight Errrant,* the exhilarated expression of someone speeding down a ski slope on a taboggan. He reminded her of basic boat craft which he'd mastered just about and did his best not to interfere, standing by the throttle, adjusting the speed now and then. When they turned the first bend without any trouble, Fleur glanced at him with a look of joy. She had more difficulty managing her first bridge, cutting the corner too sharply and overcorrecting, but the collision with the wall was only glancing. This time her look was one of disappointment and she shrugged her shoulders in apology.

'Welcome to my world,' Perceval said. 'There isn't a bridge I haven't hit.'

'You are too kind ...'

The canal was quiet at this time. On the towpath, a couple of cyclists passed them heading towards Llangollen. Since Fleur appeared more relaxed and comfortable, Perceval asked if she fancied a tea.

'I'd love a cup,' she said, and made to hand over the tiller.

'No, you're master and commander,' he saluted. 'I'll get the kettle on.'

Perceval grabbed the top of the cabin entrance and swung himself down the steps into the galley. He filled the kettle, set it on the gas ring, and got the mugs and teabags ready. He had taken out the milk from the fridge when Fleur shouted to him in panic. 'Alex! Quick!'

When he got back up, he understood the cause of her alarm. Coming towards them on the wrong side of the canal was another boat. Sitting in the foredeck he could see what appeared to be a terrified grandmother and mother with two young children. At the tiller was a young man, frantically pushing it this way and that, beside him an older man, possibly his father, gesticulating towards the approaching *Knight Errant.*

'It's okay,' Perceval reassured Fleur. 'We've got this.' He pulled the throttle into neutral and then pushed it into full reverse. It seemed to take an age before the engine responded, and it appeared there was no way to avoid the boat bearing down on them. As *Knight Errant* pulled back, the bow nosed towards the centre of the canal. Perceval thrust the lever into forward with full throttle. 'Hard right on the tiller, Fleur,' he said calmly. She did so, and the boat went sharply towards the towpath, the oncoming boat almost upon them. 'Now hard left!' With both hands Fleur pushed as hard and as far as she could. *Knight Errant* straightened up along the far bank and Perceval pulled back the throttle as the oncoming boat passed within half an inch.

The faces of the children, mother and grandmother on the bow deck were frozen in disbelief, jaws dropped. It was almost comical. The young man at the tiller pretended nothing was amiss, but the older man raised both hands like he was surrendering to the enemy. 'My lad here needs driving lessons,' he called. Then, possibly sensing he might have humiliated his son, added, 'The boat hire people said there might be a problem with the brake, but they didn't tell us it would be this bad.'

'These things happen,' Perceval shouted. To Fleur he said softly, 'There isn't a brake on the boat.'

Fleur laughed with relief and, Perceval thought, a sense of achievement. And the kettle boiled and whistled right on cue. 'There's another boat coming behind,' she said, a hint of panic returning to her voice, for now *Knight Errant* was out of position.

'Push a bit to the left, Fleur ... that's perfect. Now straighten up ... perfect.'

The middle-aged woman at the tiller, wearing a hippie-style boho bandana, said, 'I saw that.' She pointed to the hire boat weaving along in front and shook her head. 'That lot are a menace. Good job, you two!'

'Thank you,' they said together.

Perceval put his arm around Fleur's shoulder. 'Did you hear that? You, Fleur, really are master and commander.'

'And you, sir, are a *canmolwr bach*.'

'What's that?'

'It's Welsh for a little flatterer. Mum uses it when dad tries to wangle out of something by praising her too much. Affectionately, though.'

'Oh, I see.'

'But I quite like it … the praise that is.'

'Good to know. Still want a tea?'

'Yes please.'

Perceval went into the galley and came back on deck while teabags brewed in the mugs. There was a lift bridge ahead, already open, and the gap was narrow. 'Let's see how good you really are,' he said. 'Take us through on your own.'

'No problem.'

Fleur squinted as if preparing to thread the eye of a needle, pursed her lips, stood on tiptoes to judge the precise angle of the bow, and lined up *Knight Errant* as carefully as she could. From where Perceval was positioned, it looked like she'd got it exactly right. Sure enough, they went through without touching the concrete sills. 'Okay,' Perceval nodded. '*Canmolwr bach* or not, you really are good. Tea?'

They pulled over to the towpath a little further on and Perceval tied up with the centre line. They drank their tea on deck and enjoyed the view of rolling green hills on either side of the canal.

'Look! Fleur exclaimed. 'There's a heron.' Ignoring hikers on the towpath, even when they stopped to take photographs, the heron stood sentinel at the water's edge.

'I've never seen a heron before,' Perceval admitted.

'Yet another first! I wonder what others lie ahead of us?'

Since the next narrows was close, Fleur said she'd cash in her success and cycle ahead to check for other boats. When she called the all-clear, Perceval went on. Once more, the engine struggled against the current but soon enough the canal widened out and he saw Fleur leaning against her bike. As he made to steer *Knight Errant* towards her, she waved for him to go on.

'No need to stop, Alex. It's a very short distance to the wharf. I'll go on and give you another call,' she said, waving an imaginary phone by her ear. 'Then I'll bike it over to the basin and meet you there.'

'Okay. Thanks.'

Suddenly Llangollen came into view, and from the elevation of the canal he was able to look over slate-roofed houses and busy streets. His mobile rang. 'Everything is fine. Come straight through. Final stretch and then you can celebrate.'

The final stretch was a narrow concrete channel flanked by stone walls. Perceval headed into the wharf under a tricky bridge. When he was through, he saw Bors standing on the towpath with his bike and a rucksack filled with groceries.

'Good man, Alex!' he shouted over the heads of a group of people at the wharf. 'What did I tell you? All shall be well!' He got set on his bike and rode off along the canal towards Bryn Howell. His attention distracted, albeit fleetingly, Perceval almost sideswiped a long, but mercifully empty, glass-windowed narrowboat tied up beside a tearoom and tourist office. 'Bloody hell, Bors, you and your all shall be well!' Perceval swore to himself. 'That could have been a disaster.' He swung around into the basin, guided *Knight Errant* carefully towards an unoccupied pontoon. As he cut the engine, he saw Fleur cycling along the path towards him, one fist in the air.

She shouted, 'Woohoo! Alex, you've made it!'

Chapter Thirty-One

'It's Alex here, uncle.'

'Well?' It was a typically Uncle Frank response, a variation perhaps on a policeman's scepticism, not so much an invitation for others to explain themselves as a requirement for them to do so.

'I'm here, not only speaking to you on the phone, but also *here*, as in speaking to you from Llangollen.'

'Good lad! I knew I could rely on you. If there is anyone near you, take a bow.'

Perceval bowed low to Fleur who was standing close to him on the pontoon and she tilted her head questioningly.

'If you were wondering why I wasn't in touch the last few days,' his uncle said, 'I didn't want you to think I was checking up on you. I'd asked you to do the job and knew you would do it. Anyway, I expected if you did have problems, you'd get in touch with me. And you got there ahead of time too. Must have picked things up very quickly, I take it. Didn't I tell you canal boating was nothing more than informed common sense.' Perceval didn't tell his uncle that common sense had been his problem. 'No mishaps at all, then?'

'No, not really. I discovered very quickly that "keeping a steady hand on the tiller" and "going with the flow" aren't mere figures of speech.' He noticed Fleur smiling at his words.

'You've probably guessed the other reason for radio silence my end,' his uncle added, 'is I've been busy with your Auntie Jean. She goes in for her operation on Monday morning. We've been in London the last few days. She's resting right now. Jean's enormously grateful to you for helping us out, you know that.

I told you about the cost of a professional canal boat delivery, didn't I? You've saved us the best part of a grand. That'll pay for the tea and biscuits at this private clinic.' He snorted. 'Tell you something for nothing, Alex, you're treated like royalty here. Unfortunately, *nothing* is for nothing. I'm sure they'll bill me regally, even for the nurse's smile.' There was a pause. 'But if Jean comes out of it all with a better quality of life for what's left of our time together, it will be worth it.'

'Glad I could help. And Auntie Jean, she's bearing up okay, is she?'

'She's a bit apprehensive. But that's understandable. She'll probably want to take up horse riding after the op. You know what she's like.'

'Yes, I can just see it.'

'So, you'll be seeing Emrys tomorrow to hand over the key. He should be there early like the good soldier he is or was. Can you keep me right by getting an overnight permit at the tearoom at the wharf? Don't want him to begin his possession of *Knight Errant* with a fine. Think it's about thirteen quid … or it was. I'll see you right on that later.' Perceval protested that he'd money enough from expenses and his uncle didn't object. There was a silence. 'I'm going to miss that old boat, you know,' his uncle said eventually.

'I never thought you were sentimental. But I understand about *Knight Errant*. In only a few days, I've became quite attached too, like he was my trusty steed.'

'What a couple of softies,' his uncle laughed.

Perceval looked directly at Fleur, who had been waiting patiently. 'I'm off to celebrate, uncle. I don't need to worry any longer about being drunk in charge of a canal boat.'

'Have one on me. And thanks again, Alex. And I'll let you know asap how the op went.'

When Perceval had finished the call, Fleur came beside him

and held his arm. 'Has your aunt had her surgery yet?'

'Monday morning my uncle says.'

'It's heart surgery, right? Do you know which kind?'

'I'm not sure. I know it's not a transplant. She suffered from lack of energy and everyday activity exhausted her. She's always been active, sailing, walking, gardening, but these things became more difficult, then next to impossible. The private operation, you might say, is an investment in their future.'

'Absolutely,' she said. 'Sounds like TAVR.' Perceval looked at her quizzically. 'Sorry. Medic-speak for heart valve replacement. Prognosis is good. Your aunt should see her energy return quite quickly. After six months, I'd say she'll be back to her old self. No doubt about it. And if you're worried, don't be. It's a common procedure and very safe ... and now, about that celebration I overheard you mention. I'll just get myself ready.'

'Yes of course. You go ahead and I'll get your bike stowed.'

Perceval thought of Fleur, her presence in his life right now – he could hear her humming a tune in the bedroom – but also anticipated her departure from his life quite soon. Could he get along without her very well? He didn't think so. It amazed him how quickly his own life had become tangled up with hers. He had to face the possibility that today would be an end and not a beginning, and become yet another 'before', another lost idyll. He didn't have time to dwell on self-pity, for Fleur returned transformed. She'd changed from her cycling gear and now wore a deep burgundy thermal top, neatly shaped to her body, and certainly flattering. Over it was an open, chunky-knit, oatmeal cardigan. Neat high-waisted denim jeans had replaced her cycle leggings, and a pair of dark suede ankle boots her trainers.

'What do you think?' she asked, left hand in her jeans' pocket, the right hand loosely by her side. 'Meet with your approval?'

'You look stunning ...' That she was here, with him – that he found the most stunning thing of all.

'You *canmolwr bach,* you,' she said, but looked pleased with his response.

'*Canmolwr bach* nothing. It just happens to be true. But look at me.' He made a swift flourish with both hands to indicate his jacket, woollen jumper, cargo pants and scuffed Chelsea boots. 'You make me look like I've been dragged through a hedge backwards.'

Fleur smiled and came over to him. Lightly, she ran the back of her hands over the stubble on his chin, her palms over his chest, and then touched the thighs of his pants as Perceval inhaled deeply. 'I find it all in the best of taste,' she said, and pecked him lightly on the lips.

Perceval swallowed and said in a voice slightly higher than normal, 'That's good enough for me.'

'Good. I hope you'll always think so. Shall we go?'

The sun was bright, the sky blue, and the air was mild as they walked around the basin and over the canal bridge to the wharf. At the tearoom, Perceval paid for the overnight mooring, and they descended arm in arm the steep path to the town. Llangollen was busy. They met hikers in brightly coloured gear with trekking poles, some carrying heavily laden rucksacks, others with only small backpacks. Day-trippers like themselves, with their tourist gaze, they wandered slowly and hesitantly. Locals with shopping bags proved adept at slaloming around those who stopped to appreciate views of wooded hills or to discuss tentatively what they should do next. Fleur and Perceval stood in one of the V-shaped recesses on the bridge over the Dee. Beneath, the river was white-watered as it tumbled over rocks and around small lozenge-shaped ridges topped with stunted trees and bushes. On the far bank, the Dee eddied languidly in shallows as if gathering strength to journey on.

'Have you ever kayaked over these rapids?' Perceval asked.

'I have, actually,' Fleur said proudly.

'Hard not to do without screaming, I imagine.'

She nudged into his side, 'Only if you're a man.'

'If you mean *me*, Fleur, I have to agree with you.'

'I find that hard to believe. You're the quiet, undemonstrative type. No, I can't imagine you screaming at all.' They listened to the roar of the water as it tumbled under the bridge. 'We should do it together one day,' she said, more to herself than to him, like she was daydreaming for, when he replied maybe they should, Fleur didn't answer immediately. Then she said, 'Yes, we must. I'll be well-used, when you've gone under and I have to drag you to the bank, giving you mouth-to-mouth resuscitation.'

'I think that's what's called, first the bad news, then the good news.'

'I've got some good news for you now,' she said and kissed him on the lips.

'That's the best news I've ever had,' he said.

'Perceval in Welsh must be *Canmolwr*,' she smiled.

Fleur took him to a restaurant overlooking the river. It was just after one o'clock and the place was still very busy.

'Do you think we'll find a table?' Perceval asked.

'A-ha!' Fleur touched the side of her nose. 'Just you watch and learn.' She went across to a young waiter standing at the bar, had a word with him, and he picked up a couple of menus. As they walked past, Fleur motioned Perceval to follow. They were given a free table near the window. The waiter asked what they would like to drink and Fleur ordered a glass of white wine, Perceval, a pint of bitter.

When he'd left, Perceval leaned across the table and, glancing around at the other tables fully occupied, asked in a low voice, 'I'm impressed. How did you manage that?'

'Do you really want to know my secret?'

'Wait,' Perceval held up a hand. 'You pick out the virtuous

young man, turn on the charm, smile, and your wish is his command?'

'That's *exactly* how it works, Alex. And it works *every* time.'

'Really?' he asked sincerely, naively.

'No, not *really*. Didn't I say it would be a sin to tell you a lie?' Fleur held up her mobile, adopting a look implying the mystery was laughably obvious. 'When I was waiting for you at the basin, I called up and booked a table for two.'

'Oh, I see,' he said, sitting back as the waiter set their drinks on the table. When he'd gone, Perceval leaned over to her and said, 'There's so much I don't know about you, Fleur.'

'And I can say the same. I suppose we can never know one another fully. That's also because we cannot know ourselves fully.' When she saw the expression on Perceval's face, Fleur added, 'And no, that's not regurgitated Psychology 101, if you're wondering. Getting to know someone is an act of faith. And how wonderful is that. Don't you think so?'

'Then I look forward to finding out as much about you as I can,' Perceval replied,

'Quite right too,' Fleur answered, and turned her attention to the menu.

After some discussion and deliberation, they both ordered fish and chips. From their table they could glimpse the Dee and the old steam railway station on its far bank. Though there was a bustling Saturday crowd, families having lunch, couples taking tea, young men and women drinking and smoking on the wooden deck over the river, the restaurant felt relaxed and unhurried.

'This place is great,' Perceval said as he ate.

'Glad you like it.'

'Even if it was the biggest tip imaginable, it would still be great because you are here.'

'How many times do I have to warn you about flattery, Alex?'

Though they spoke with the sweet interchange of euphoric recognition, the thought of their parting, possibly in a few hours, still haunted Perceval and nothing in the pleasant ambiance, nothing in his blissful mood, could fight off successfully his anticipated sadness. He looked at Fleur as she ate and talked. Unlike him, he detected no hint of melancholy. She seemed happy in the present (as the mindfulness people kept advising people to be and as he kept finding impossible). And it was for this moment that he had brought along a strand of tarred rope he'd cut from the bow fender of *Knight Errant,* hoping Emrys wouldn't notice in the morning.

When they'd finished lunch and the attentive waiter had cleared away their plates, he took the piece of rope from his parka pocket and held it under the table. 'I've got something for you,' he said.

'That sounds nice,' she said expectantly, folding her hands on the tabletop.

'Don't get your hopes up. It's nothing really. But if it's the thought that counts, then it is everything.'

'I *am* intrigued.' She tilted her head and waited.

He delayed slightly before whisking up the piece of rope.

'Oh!' she said, looking puzzled.

'Remember I told you about my first night on the canal? And not being able to tie up because I didn't know how to knot the rope?'

'You did, and some mysterious damsel showed you how? Are you reminding me to make me jealous?'

'I wouldn't call her a damsel. And jealousy you needn't bother with, I assure you. Bron, that's her name, and Jo, her companion … I can't imagine I could ever come between them.'

'Oh, I see,' she laughed. 'I'll take your word for it. Go on.'

'As a memento, Bron gave me a piece of knotted rope,' he told her, tying the same knot he'd been shown. 'She'd tied it with care and told me it was a symbol of how I need to be grounded to be truly free. Happiness means being threaded through the life of another. Now, with you, I tie this same knot. For you and me together, let it be a bond that lets us be freely ourselves while also holding us close.' He paused to look into her eyes. 'It's my simple gift to you, my way of saying I want us to remain together, like we have been these two days. The knot intrinsicate it's called, meaning a deep-working fate, entwining and binding. So, I want you to have this, a memory, a wish, and a *promise*, one I will always keep.' He took her hand, placed the knot in her palm, and closed her fingers over it.

Fleur slowly opened her hand again and looked down at this simple knot. She examined it reverently, almost afraid, it seemed, that the knot might vanish. 'You ... you don't know what this means to me,' she said. 'Yesterday ... yes it was only yesterday but it seems a long time ago, yesterday I came barging into your life and expected you to accept me. And you did. You never questioned it. You never questioned me. I could have come after you as a dare.' Perceval looked doubting. 'Yes, Alex, don't be naïve, girls do those things too, just like boys. Or I could have done it on impulse, out of boredom from being away from college. And I could have been some sort of egomaniac or even a mad woman ... but I don't *think* I'm egotistical, or mad for that matter.'

Fleur closed her eyes, like she was ashamed even to mention those possibilities, like they were wicked, foul, and she wished to conjure them out of existence. She opened them again and said, 'Then you give me this little knot ...' she folded it into her palm again, 'and it says everything I wanted to say, what I felt when I first spoke to you, what I felt when I found you again. Being threaded through each other's lives, to be part of each other's stories. That's exactly what I want ... to stay entwined.' She cradled the knot like something fragile. 'Physiology, etiology, pathology, diagnosis, prognosis, my world of medical studies … it's about healing, of course, but you discover how fragile the mind and body can be, how easy it is for things to go wrong, for lives to fall apart.' Fleur caressed the knot, contemplating it, and didn't say anything for a moment. Then she looked up at Perceval. 'This will symbolise the suture which binds us. Let it tighten and not loosen. Let it hold and not pull apart.'

'What purpose does the knot serve?' Perceval asked. 'Let it bind us, never to let us slip apart.'

Their still calm was suddenly shattered by the clatter of crockery and exclamations at a nearby table. A woman had spilled her drink and, in standing from the table to wipe her skirt, knocked plates and cutlery onto the floor. A little dog under their table started yapping, adding to the commotion of concerned diners and solicitous waiters.

When things settled down, Fleur looked at Perceval playfully. 'So, we've tied the knot. Rather, you've tied the knot for me. But it isn't *tying the knot* as we know it? Is that right?'

Her question caught him off guard. Of course, he knew what the phrase traditionally meant but no one he knew had ever used it, not even ironically. It wasn't the usage today, was it? Hadn't it become like a wife 'obeying' her husband? He was about to stammer out some feeble response, but she'd read his hesitation exactly.

'Alex, I'm only having a bit of fun, trying to be clever. And I do know what you mean. It's the most beautiful thing anyone could ever think of doing, saying or giving. It is so you. And nothing could have made me happier.'

'I meant every word,' he said, serious now. 'I can't forget that you'll probably have to leave soon, return home, and then go back to Oxford. And I will have to go home too, though where home now is, I'm not sure. The world is going to pull us in different directions, and I can't prevent that. I wanted to let this little amulet or talisman, or whatever you want to call it, remind you of this time together. Soon we will be separated and alone, but let it be alone together … if you see what I mean?'

'I do see what you mean. But I'm not leaving today. I'm staying tonight,' she said matter-of-factly. 'If that's okay with you, that is?'

'Seriously?'

'Seriously.'

'Of course it's okay with me!'

'And tomorrow … you are invited to meet my parents.'

'In Chester?'

'Where else would they be? Only if you want to …'

'Of course I want to. That's very kind of them to invite me. I'm delighted to accept.'

Fleur laughed.

'What did I say?' he asked.

'What you said to me yesterday.'

'What did I say yesterday?'

'You said "don't be so bourgeois". Remember?'

'Anyway, tell them I am touched by their invitation.'

'I'll let them know. And my big snooze or you lose brother will be there too.'

There was a moment of silence then Perceval said, 'On Sunday, I'm coming to meet your parents … but it isn't *meeting the parents* as we understand it? Have I got that right?'

Chapter Thirty-Two

AFTER lunch, wandering around Llangollen arm in arm – 'intrinsicately' Fleur described it – they were wrapped up in each other as the town leaned toward evening. Though the rest of the world was blurred to him, Perceval felt benignly at peace and in harmony with everyone and everything, as if his obvious joy created its own gravity field, attracting to him and to Fleur, kindly, knowing, and indulgent glances. Their presence here, he sensed, was simply more urgent, more real than anything else in the world, the alchemy of their bond more vivid, inviting admiration but denying intrusion. The simple and significant matter was their togetherness, even if Perceval remained astonished by the fact of it.

Had he ever felt this way before? He'd been attracted to women, of course, and they'd been attracted to him. Perceval might be innocent, but he wasn't virginal. But there'd always been a disconnection between the safe, untouchable allure of the abstractly desirable (Jenny, married, unobtainable) and the messiness of being with someone real (as he'd experienced, several unfortunate times). He rarely, if ever, chose to psychoanalyse this behaviour. But not with Fleur. Fleur was different. How happy this difference made him, how insufficient his previous emotional existence now seemed, and how desperately he wanted this new life to continue.

'You know something, Fleur? I always thought a woman as beautiful and intelligent as you was beyond my reach, untouchable.' The moment he spoke he regretted the words, fearing he sounded pathetic, even contemptible. He had cast the shadow of his old insecurity across their present happiness.

Fleur stopped and looked serious, as she considered the words she'd heard. Then she let go of Perceval's arm, kissed his lips, hugged him tightly, and took his arm again.

'Untouchable? Untouchable is overrated. Love needs a touch of the earth, don't you think?' she asked. 'Idealised romance is all against it, but healthy instinct is all for it. Life's too short for untouchable. Touchable is much better. And it's also more fun. Well, it is if you find the right person to touch.' He turned to her and was about to reply but she put a finger to his lips. 'Anyway, what business is it of yours that I love you? Sorry, Alex, that came out all wrong. What I mean is this. If I love you, it's not something in your gift. It's my gift to you. Whether you accept it or not, it makes no difference, if that love is true. Do you see what I mean? So, no more talk about thinking me being beyond your reach. I'm here, aren't I? For couldn't I say the same about you, being here and with me? In the same way, what business is it of mine whether you love me or not? That is your gift to me. Remember the knot intrinsicate. It doesn't lie.'

'I was only going to say how right you are,' Perceval said.

'Okay, you're allowed to say that.'

The late afternoon became much cooler, and they decided to turn back to town. They found a pub with an attractive red brick façade and timed it just right. The place wasn't busy and they managed to get a table in the front bar. When he brought his pint and Fleur's white wine to the table, he remembered his dream.

'Last night,' he said, 'when I should have been dreaming about you, I had this strange vision of *Knight Errant* arriving at Llangollen and being welcomed by my old cricket teammates.' He didn't mention Jenny.

'What else can I say, Alex. You *should* have been dreaming about me. I'm going to put my foot down and insist from now on. Okay, what happened? Did they arrange a banquet for you?'

'That's exactly what they did arrange. It was one of those grand medieval banquets in a large hall, you know, long benches, jesters, musicians with flutes and hurdy-gurdies. There were goblets, flagons of wine, great roasts on spits. I don't know how I was dressed, but everyone else was in knightly attire.'

'A sort of Arthurian Round Table thing, you mean?'

'Yes. It was like I had returned from some difficult quest, to be honoured and celebrated.'

'My parents would like that. I don't know if there's such a word as Arthuriana?'

'Sounds like there should be.'

'That's their thing. They adore all the old legends. Well, it's mum's thing to be precise. Dad sort of follows along. Mum would love to find the Sleeping Lord, you know, the myth that Arthur never died but only fell into an enchanted slumber. She thinks he's in a hidden chamber somewhere in North Wales and not too far from Chester. You know, Chester with its Roman connections and all that. Can you guess what our house is called?'

'Camelot?'

'No. Avalon, of course. Appropriate, don't you think? Avalon is where wounds can be healed and where women reign. It sounds just right for a family of doctors and a wannabe doctor like me. The woman reigning thing is accurate enough for mum. Wasn't like that for me with my brothers – unfortunately.'

'You seem knowledgeable enough yourself about King Arthur.'

'I couldn't help picking up some of it.'

'Over the last few days, I've heard a lot about the Sleeping Lord.'

'You have? From whom, exactly?'

Perceval told her of the woman who'd helped him tie up near the pub his second night and her sorrows for the maimed land, of Angharad who had a vision of AI restoring the economic health of the country, of Elin in Chirk who suffered loneliness and isolation, and of Rhi who was truly wounded, physically and mentally.

'Hmm,' Fleur said. 'You're confirming to me you *have* spent your time in the company of women. I'm only the latest in a long line, then?'

She pouted, making as if to cry. Perceval, like the fool, thought he should have kept his mouth shut (his mother had been right). But Fleur couldn't keep her face straight. 'Don't look so worried.'

'My Lady Fleur of the Fallen Leaves,' he said, taking her hand and kissing it. 'I honour all women but will love only you.'

'I should think so too.' Fleur caressed her cheek with the back of the kissed hand and sighed. It was so falsely dramatic that they both started laughing. 'Sorry Alex, I deflected you from the meaning of your dream …'

Perceval told her about the loss of fellowship when he'd left university and the emptiness which he'd struggled to fill. Putting his troubles into words for Fleur made him feel he was a boy, speaking like a boy, understanding life as a boy, and that it was time he put away such boyish things. 'My interpretation sounds immature doesn't it,' he finished, 'romanticised, of course, mythical too. Does it make sense to you?'

'I was at an all-girls public school, Alex. Of course it makes sense.'

'You see, the mood in the dream wasn't one of celebration. There was no warmth or togetherness. There was only coolness and distance.'

'And that saddens you?'

'It did.'

'It doesn't now?'

'What's the meaning of the dream? I think it was telling me

something I knew all along. The Lord, in my case the good fellowship I once knew, isn't sleeping. It's dead. *Before* isn't returning. There's no way back to that idyll. Dreaming of *before* was a refuge, a way to avoid making any choice. The dream, I think, was telling me not to look for an answer *there* but to look for it *here*.'

'Oh, that is quite a diagnostic odyssey, Alex.'

'If I'm being honest, Fleur, my default mode is to be fatalistic, irresponsible, and passive. Just so you know. Whether I will become, or have become, more positive and more responsible, I'm not sure … I suppose that's for me to show and for others to judge.' Perceval gave his forehead a gentle slap. 'Sorry, Fleur, talking about myself is such a bore. You've been patiently listening to this … *patient* self-analysing. And here you are on a break from medical school. Look, what I want to say is simple. *You* are the damsel who saved me in my distress at Chirk. *You* are the damsel I made a promise to and failed to honour. *You* are the damsel who found me at Trevor and redeemed my failure. *You* are the damsel who came to help me through the narrows to Llangollen. Frankly, you are the Arthurian hero of my tale, not me.'

Fleur laughed as though this idea was bizarre and shook her head. She put her hand in her cardigan pocket and pulled out the knot he'd tied for her. She held it up as though for public inspection and spoke in the voice of a pompous defence barrister. 'Ladies and gentlemen of the jury, I show you Exhibit A. This knot intrinsicate was given by the defendant in good faith to a young lady as a sign of love, commitment, and support. The lady has accepted it in good faith. It is irrefutable evidence and good reason, I'm sure you'll agree, for acquittal of all suspicion of his being a wimp.' Perceval put his hands up in acceptance of her judgement. 'Alex, you're not a problem to be solved, you're not a puzzle to be explained and you're certainly not a suitable case for treatment. Stop thinking you are. I'm not either. You're just you. And I'm just me. That's the deal we seem to agree on. It's good enough, don't you think? Whatever about your past or my past?'

'Yes. Yes, I do. I only wanted to tell you of my shortcomings. My charms are self-evident, I assume.'

'I wouldn't go that far ...' Fleur took a sip of wine and then ran her fingers around the rim of her glass. 'When I asked you if you had a girlfriend or even a wife? You never asked *me* if I was "in a relationship" as people say on Facebook. Remember?'

Perceval suddenly feared the worst, and his look must have been obvious to her.

'Don't be alarmed, Alex. Being honest? Okay. I'm going to be honest as well. I never had a boyfriend – well, a serious boyfriend – during my school years. At boarding school I wasn't a jolly hockey stick girl full stop. I was good at sports, yes, but I was also bookish and arty too. All-girl schools allow you such luxury without competition over boyfriends. There isn't the pressure to be "attractive" or even "available". You can really be yourself. Being myself was about being the best at everything, though of course I *wasn't* the best at everything. But I was the best at enough things to be happy and satisfied, but not, I hope, self-satisfied. I got to Oxford. It was hard work to get there and harder work when I did get there. But I was in a completely different social world from school. I'm not being vain when I tell you male students found me attractive. What's more they let me know it. And I enjoyed going out to parties and going on dates. It was a novel feeling, as well as totally natural, to know you *are* desirable. Yet for some reason, it never seemed real. Maybe that's because Oxford never seems real, socially I mean, if not academically. Having given that social life an excited fling, become a bit of a goodtime butterfly, if not quite the *Ab Fab* type, I got tired of it. Like Shakespeare's Prince Hal,

I began to find it as tedious as work, though in truth, I *never* do find work tedious. So, it wasn't a sad case of all play and no work and then all work and no play. I didn't feel dull and I don't believe anyone thought me dull.'

Perceval momentarily recovered his emotional balance. 'I'll see your Shakespeare and raise you a Wordsworth. Dull would he be of soul, who could pass by a Fleur so touching in her majesty. Sorry, I interrupted you. And that's about the extent of my poetic references, you'll be glad to hear.'

She smiled at his jest, but her face became troubled. 'Evelyn Waugh said, "You spend the first term at Oxford meeting interesting and exciting people and the rest of your time there avoiding them." That is funny. But in my case, it wasn't funny. It was threatening. It was oppressive. I think the best way to describe what happened is that someone laid siege to me. That sounds weirdly old-fashioned. But for me it certainly felt like a siege. The man was a mature student, alpha-male I suppose you'd say. He was superficially pleasant, but there was a menacing subtext to everything he said and did. I *knew* there was. I sensed it straight away. He seemed to believe the old saying "faint heart never won fair maiden" and took it to mean insisting that *I* really wanted what *he* wanted. He wanted me. It was oppressive. I can tell you, Alex, there was nothing sweet about his approaches, you know, the shyly devotional type, always attentive, always trying to please.'

Perceval imagined the shyly devotional type might describe him. Was that his attraction for her? But he said nothing to interrupt her story.

'No, he was nothing like that. Behind every gesture and word, I detected the hint of entitlement. I should desire him because he wanted me. It wasn't only entitlement only but also a demand. He wanted me in relation to himself, not for my sake. I was his "thing", and nothing other than that. Probably as a man, Alex, you can't grasp how cheapening that can make a woman feel. Because he had picked me out, I was being obtuse not to accept the privilege of being his possession. When he pressed attention on me, first I was non-committal, then creatively evasive, and finally, but politely, I just said no. It meant absolutely nothing to him. He was clever enough not to stalk me openly, not to inundate me with messages, but, you know, he always just happened to be where I was, would come over to talk about lectures, events, parties, or whatever, very up close and personal, his words insistent and suggestive. It was intrusive, upsetting, but never to the point where I could complain without appearing to be – sorry, another cliché alert – a hysterical woman. My days became filled with stratagems of avoidance. There was relief when I didn't see him hovering, and despair when I did.'

Perceval hadn't expected Fleur's tale. Certainly, he'd heard stories like this before, he'd certainly read about them, but it was behaviour beyond his experience and the man's wilfulness was beyond his comprehension.

'He was an imposing man, big, powerful, dominating, and knew the effect he had on me and on others. What he succeeded in doing was to crowd out everything in my life and to diminish it. You may ask, how can this sort of bullying happen today? All I can say is that it did. It probably happens more than we imagine. So, I retreated behind my own walls … but not by choice, not like Julian of Norwich you told me about, but out of despair.'

'How did it end? Or has it not ended?'

'It did end. One day the siege lifted. He must have become obsessed by some other poor woman. I still saw him about, of course. And he would cut me dead. You would imagine this would bring me overwhelming relief, wouldn't you? In fact, I'd become so used to adjusting my behaviour to protective mode that I'd become the warden of my own emotional prison.' Fleur made a circle with her hands and Perceval had a vision of the Eight of Swords. 'I stayed firmly enclosed. You know the song "Bulletproof" by La Roux?'

'Yes, I do,' Perceval nodded.

'The words aren't a perfect fit, but I'd made myself bulletproof to my besieger. The effect was that no other man could get through and at the same time, I couldn't get out. Thing was, I didn't want any man to get through and I was convinced I shouldn't let one in.' She took a sip of her wine and slowly put the glass back on the table. 'That was until I saw you. Fate, destiny, chemistry, meeting of souls, immediate connection … it was just like that, every one of these emotions with a cliché alert attached. Explain it as you will, it was how I saw you. And, as you would know better than me, the rest is history. And here I am. And here you are. And here we are. Together.' She took a deep breath and leaned across the table towards him. 'Maybe I can put it this way. Your story is that I rescued you. My story is that you rescued me. Our story should be that we found each other. I have to say, it feels good to put it that way.'

'Amen,' Perceval said. 'Here's to the future.'

'To *our* future,' Fleur insisted.

'Here's to *our* future,' Perceval corrected.

'To our future *intrinsicate*,' she said, holding up the knot again.

Chapter Thirty-Three

IT was getting on for eight o'clock when they decided to have dinner and one more drink. The pub had become crowded and noisier, but they were content to stay on rather than search for somewhere else. Fleur objected to Perceval's paying again but he told her his mother, God rest her soul, would be ashamed of him if he expected a lady to pay. She asked if everyone from Northern Ireland was as gentlemanly as he was.

'Up to a point, Lord Copper,' he answered. 'And that's my only Waugh reference too, you'll also be glad to hear.'

Halfway through their meal, and maybe because he was on his third pint of the day, Perceval's mind conjured up a conundrum one which, without alcohol, he would have kept to himself. 'You know when I meet your parents tomorrow?' he asked.

'Yes?'

'How do I address them properly?'

'What do you mean?'

'Well, it seems a bit strange to address them both as "Dr Stephens". It also seems a bit discourteous to say "Mr Stephens" and "Mrs Stephens". And I wouldn't dream of using their first names, for that *would* be disrespectful. I've been considering saying "sir" to your father and "ma'am" to your mother. What do you think?'

Fleur looked at him to check if he was in earnest and, judging he was, put down her knife and fork and burst out laughing, a hand over her mouth. She tried to speak but couldn't stop, tears rolling down her cheeks. When she'd recovered sufficiently to talk, she wiped her eyes with a napkin.

'I may have had a few glasses of wine, Alex, and my apologies for laughing, but that is the sweetest question I've ever been asked – sweet, but hilarious. My dad would probably think he was a sergeant major if you called him "sir." Mum would probably think she was a Chief Constable if you called her "ma'am". They'd think it was such a hoot, too funny for words, just like me. What an introduction that would be.' She shook her head playfully. 'Now that I think about it, it would be a wonderful moment. How could they not love you to bits after that … but they'll love you to bits anyway.'

'Yes, I suppose it would sound silly. I'm still not sure what I should say.'

'You are right about one thing. They don't even let us, their children, use first names. They are old school enough to consider that presumptuous. Since you'll be with their darling daughter, it's a family occasion, why not use Mr and Mrs? You won't be meeting them for a consultation.'

'You're probably right.'

'I know I'm right,' Fleur said. 'All you need to do is get onto the topic of cricket with dad, somehow slip King Arthur into conversation with mum, and you'll be the hit of the day.' Taking out her phone, Fleur shifted from her chair to kneel beside him. 'I hope you don't mind but I promised mum I'd send her a photo of the two of us.'

'No wait!' Perceval said. 'That's not right.'

'Oh, what do you mean?' She looked perplexed.

'It won't look good if you are kneeling and I'm sitting. Your mother will think I'm unchivalrous.'

'No, she won't,' Fleur said, but Perceval could see she appreciated his tact, and they reversed positions. 'Smile like you did when you first met me,' she told him. 'That will melt her heart.'

She took four selfies, each from a slightly different angle, and showed them to Perceval. He thought his clothes appeared shabby, his hair untidy, and that the stubble on his upper lip and chin made him look less well-groomed than Fleur's mother might expect. On the other hand, his eyes were clear and bright, his smile genuine, and, even if he did think so himself, he appeared a worthy companion for her daughter. At least, he hoped so. Fleur typed a message to send along with the photographs.

'There! Done!' she said and took another sip of wine. 'Our first selfies.'

Perceval's mobile dinged with the photos. 'Thank you,' he said.

'So you never forget me.'

Fleur's phone dinged soon after. 'It's from *ma'am*,' she smiled. 'Lovely photos, she says, and she can't wait to meet you tomorrow.'

'Both of your parents sound very nice. And you seem to have a good relationship with them.'

'Yes, you could say that. And you'd be right.' Fleur swirled what remained of her wine. 'They've had a long and harmonious marriage, met when they were young. Been together ever since. Brought up three children, a positive and healthy relationship with us kids.' Her eyes narrowed slightly and her brow furrowed for a second. 'I suppose parents give you an index for your own expectations, big or small. And perhaps you can't help taking some of them on board.' Perceval understood all too well. 'Do you remember the girlie banter after I'd spoken to you before the Chirk Aqueduct? You know the "you've pulled", "can't take you anywhere", "maneater", all that joshing?'

'I was too absorbed with leaves in my propeller. And with you of course,' he lied, tactfully he judged.

'Hmmm ... well, it was nothing but girlie banter. You see, one of the things I take from mum and dad is loyalty and commitment, at least the desire for it. Quite a few of my friends at Oxford, their parents have split up. They seem to find it hard to settle with anyone for long. I'm not saying they're unhappy. Passing relationships seem to suit them, some of them anyway. I'm only saying it's not for me. I'm not like that at all. If you were wondering …'

'I'm glad. It's not like me either … if you were wondering.' At least, he thought that was true. Or was he fooling himself? Hadn't he wished to keep his distance from any serious commitment? Yet it felt true now. He had no desire to keep his distance from Fleur. 'My mother was loyal and committed too, even beyond the marriage vow "till death do us part"' Perceval hesitated. 'I don't know if they still say that. Do you?'

'We must ask Jacob tomorrow.'

'My mother remained loyal and committed even after my father's death.'

Fleur asked him to tell her about his mother. As faithfully as he could, Perceval told her of his childhood. He described how his mother, though still relatively young and attractive, had no desire to be with anyone else after his father's murder, how she'd been entirely devoted to his memory and to Perceval's well-being. He confessed to the ungrateful term 'smotherly love' but also admitted her unselfishness by encouraging him go to university in England, aware that he'd probably never return and he'd be the second great loss in her life.

Fleur's eyes welled up at his story. 'I'm so sorry, Alex. So much sadness. How did she bear it? How did *you* bear it? I want to cry my heart out now.'

'No, Fleur, don't cry. My mother was wounded by life and, in the eyes of the world at least, she never healed. I know it is hard to believe, but it seemed enough for her that she had me. I was her present, her future, her everything. Given what happened to my father, she didn't believe all shall be well. But she made sure *I* should be well. And I am. After all, didn't I meet you?'

Fleur did cry and fished in her pocket for a paper hanky. Perceval handed her his pack. She took one, wiped her eyes, and blew her nose as delicately as she could.

As she did, he hummed 'Chabadabada ... Ba da ba da da da', and Fleur looked at him searchingly.

'I didn't explain things properly which is normal for me. I didn't mean to play on your emotions.'

Fleur waved away his apology, telling him not to be silly. 'What is the tune you were humming just now?' she managed to ask.

'It's the theme from the old French film *Un Homme et une Femme*. My mother loved French music. Well, she loved all music, full stop. I used to think it was just another song. I remember her humming it. *"Chabadabada ... Ba da ba da da da"*. Always like that, no words. I thought it all there was. And I didn't understand. As a kid I never asked.'

Noisy laughter, screeching and cheering at the bar interrupted him. Fleur grimaced as though the screech had hurt her eardrums.

'I could never get the tune out of my head. It's so simple and yet so wistful. For me just a tune, but for my mother I sensed it was something she was *feeling*. Then at university, I was invited to the Film Soc which was showing *Un Homme et Une Femme*.' Perceval decided not to tell Fleur who'd invited him, a young woman he'd met at a student party who'd told him he reminded her of a young Alain Delon. He hadn't known of Alain Delon. When he'd checked up on Google, he'd been flattered. He discovered later her appreciation of Alain Delon didn't go far when it came to the flesh and blood Alex Perceval. 'Do you know the film?'

Fleur shook her head, her eyes still red and slightly puffed, 'No,' she mumbled.

'It's the story of a widow and a widower, both grieving the

deaths of their spouses. They meet, grow close emotionally, but memories of their former loves pull them apart. I realised that, for my mother, the music was like a lullaby for the life she'd lost. It was comforting to know you *could* find love again, but even more wonderful to know you'd *already* found it, once. And that once was enough. Was that not love indeed?' Perceval finished off his beer and pushed the glass across the table. 'When I saw the film, I think I finally knew my mother, at least what love meant to her. That's what I was trying to tell you in my clumsy way. It's how I feel when I look at you. It's what I meant when I gave you the knot.'

Fleur finished her wine and set down the glass firmly. 'Let's go, Alex,' she said. 'I think we should be alone. Alone together.'

Much later, Perceval woke with a start. His leg had slipped from under the light duvet and he felt the cold. He drew back under the covers as best he could and his movement disturbed Fleur who nuzzled closer to him. Perceval brushed some hair off her forehead, and she mumbled something but didn't waken. As a lover's bed it wasn't much. But it didn't matter. It was her and it was him, tangled up together.

In the last few days, among new people, strange faces, other minds, he'd encountered life embraced and life shunned, faith lost and faith found, compassion given and compassion denied, the past mourned and the future dreamed. Do good all your life and one wrong condemned you forever. Do wrong all your life and one good deed betrayed and then saved you. These things he'd learnt. You could suffer the pains of a wounded land and pine for its natural healing. You could suffer the pains of a wounded land and wish to build it anew. These things he'd also learnt. The Lord wasn't sleeping and there was no way back, no possible return, to *before*. Of that he was convinced.

He'd drawn The Fool from Jo's Tarot pack. Hadn't she told him to be optimistic, not to be fearful, not to be weighed down by old times, and to trust his instinct? At least that's what he thought she'd said, even though he hadn't believed it was possible for him. Now he could believe it. He *wanted* to believe it. In fact, he wanted to feel just like he did right now, forever. He squeezed Fleur tighter, and she moaned contentedly, still deeply asleep. He would be going with Fleur to Chester. He was going to meet her parents.

Perceval knew he'd never fought hard for much in his life. He'd always been someone without qualities, incapacitated by complexity and choice, uncertain, insecure, indecisive, and uncommitted. But he would fight hard for Fleur. It wasn't complicated. It was a simple choice because, really, it wasn't a choice at all.

Epilogue

Emrys, like the good old soldier, did turn up on time. He wore a sharp suit, breasted medals and a tan beret. A large man in physique and in humour, he was the model of a former Welsh Guardsman. 'Everything looks in good nick to me,' he said approvingly. He'd given *Knight Errant* a thorough look over, inside and out, and tested the engine.

'Good enough to have survived me,' Perceval replied.

Emrys appreciated the jest and they shook hands, completing the handover.

Perceval collected his rucksack and got Fleur's bike off the boat. The three of them went together from the basin towards the centre of town. Emrys was heading to Market Street where his comrades were mustering before marching to Centenary Square. After they'd shaken hands again in parting, Perceval asked Fleur if she minded stopping for a moment at the war memorial. 'My father wasn't military. He was police. But he did give his life for our country. And my mother too, in a different way.'

'Of course, Alex, and I can say a prayer for Hywel on the high seas.'

As they stood in silence, Fleur's free arm linked through his, Perceval thought of his father and mother.

The car, an old Skoda Superb estate, dented in places, was parked some way outside the town centre. There was no cycle carrier on the back, but the rear seats had been folded down. Perceval helped Fleur bundle the bike into the cavernous space along with his rucksack and her backpack. They needed to take a roundabout route to avoid the parade in Llangollen but soon reached the main road to Chester.

'You're not anxious about today, are you?' she asked him. 'I hope you don't think I've pushed you into something?'

'Quite the opposite. I like the idea of Sunday at the Stephens'. It has a nice ring to it, don't you think, rather like an old English film, you know, a stylish comedy of manners.'

She considered the words for a moment. 'Too funny, Alex. *Sunday at the Stephens': The Movie*. I'll be the sophisticated, modern gal, you know, the one in the designer silk dress with a cigarette holder and a glass of champagne, like in an episode of *Poirot*.'

'I'll be the unconventional, as well as the incomprehensible, oik, who says things like *ats us nai so it is*,' Perceval said, putting on a strong Belfast accent.

'What on earth does that mean?'

'In your posh and received pronunciation, Fleur, it literally means "That's us now". But it can mean many things, like "That's the job finished" or "We've arrived" or even "nothing can beat this moment".' He looked at her. 'You know, it's what I said to myself when you came into the tearoom at Trevor.'

'I mightn't have said it, Alex, but I certainly thought it.'

The Stephens' home was a striking nineteenth-century detached house, standing in its own well-manicured lawns with a long gravelled driveway. There was mock Tudor half-timbering on the upper floor over a stylish tiled porch. Perceval was impressed and about to say something complimentary as Fleur pulled up at the adjoining garage. But she raised a hand to stop him. 'No, Alex. Let me. *Ats us nai so it is*. I've been waiting to say that for the last half hour.'

'Spoken like a true native. Your parents really will throw me out for giving you bad habits.'

'Come and *meet the parents*,' she said, taking him by the hand.

'Do you think they thought that selfie with me on one knee was a marriage proposal?' Perceval joked.

Fleur stopped, turned slowly, and looked at him as if something had just dawned on her. 'Gosh! I wondered what mum's text meant this morning. She mentioned something about the "big day". I thought she was talking about today, you know, you coming here for the first time. Oh, Alex, this is going to be soooooo embarrassing.' Perceval was panicked for a second. 'Oh, the look on your face, Alex, I'm so disappointed in you. And I'm only joking, of course. Come on. Let's get the introductions over with.'

While Fleur had been showering on *Knight Errant* earlier that morning, Perceval had consulted Google on how to address parents who were both doctors. He'd been advised to ask his girlfriend (which he had done) and if still uncertain, to begin with a polite, neutral approach (no names, just 'pleased to meet you'), to be warm and engaging ('so grateful for the invitation'), and if necessary, to 'test' the use of Dr (as in 'Dr Stephens, Fleur has told me a lot about you') and ultimately to follow the lead of his hosts. He hadn't found it much help. It had only confirmed what a minefield this introduction might be for him. When Fleur opened the front door into the hallway and announced their arrival, his mind went blank.

The Stephens, mother and father, appeared almost immediately, as though they had been waiting impatiently for their arrival. Mrs Stephens looked like an older Fleur, still a slim figure, hair greying naturally, dressed in a cream silk blouse, pale-blue cardigan, and matching blue linen trousers. Mr Stephens was tall and powerfully built, a former rugby player Perceval imagined, balding with silver hair close-cropped, wearing an open-necked white cotton shirt and khaki chinos.

The mother took the initiative and greeted Perceval warmly. He took her hand and couldn't help saying, 'Pleased to meet you, ma'am.' To the father's equally friendly greeting, he said, 'Pleased to meet you too, sir.'

Fleur laughed and explained the reason for her hilarity. Perceval blushed, thinking he'd made a fool of himself yet again.

'Well, I think it's charming, Alex,' her mother said. 'You'll have to forgive Fleur. She can be very tiring sometimes. "Manners are not idle, but the fruit of loyal nature and noble mind". That's what your grandmother used to say, Fleur, and she was right. You should take heed.'

'Hear, Hear!' the father joined in.

Perceval handed Fleur's mum a box of chocolates and small bouquet of flowers he'd bought at a filling station on the way. Fleur had told him it wasn't necessary, but he said he'd feel uncomfortable, as well as churlish, turning up empty-handed. He had the impression she appreciated his sense of doing the right thing. And that was that. The ice was broken. He was embraced warmly, their conversation eased by mention of cricket and the Sleeping Lord. Fleur's brother, Jacob, was also introduced.

'Alex asked me if I should address you as "Your Holiness", you know,' Fleur told him.

'Welcome to Stephens' Manor,' Jacob said languidly. 'And I must apologise for my little sister and commiserate with you, Alex. Fleur, I shall treat that comment with the contempt it deserves. And what damage did you do to my car this time?'

He asked Perceval about his canal journey and Perceval mentioned Julian of Norwich without going into the details of the story Bors had told him. Jacob recounted her parable of a little hazelnut in which she saw three divine truths. 'That God made it,' he said, 'That God loves it. That God looks after it.' Jacob was an easy talker and easy listener. He would make a perfect vicar, Perceval thought, and wondered what the priestly equivalent of a doctor's 'good bedside manner' might be.

Lunch was excellent, traditional English roast beef, roast

potatoes and Yorkshire pudding. Listening to the light-hearted conversation, enjoying this food, sipping the delicate red wine, feeling welcome, already a part of this family circle, above all, having Fleur beside him, Perceval considered things couldn't get much better than this. If this time was his little hazelnut, he hoped God had made it, hoped God would love it and that God would look after it. *Before* be damned. *Now* was the life.

When lunch was over, Perceval helped with the washing up, which was done in familial relay. Mr Stephens arranged the pots, trays, dishes and cutlery at the sink, Jacob did the washing up, Fleur and Perceval did the drying, and Mrs Stephens put everything away.

'You must think it an imposition, Alex, to be invited to lunch and then have to help with the dishes,' Fleur's father apologised.

'Not at all,' he answered with a straight face. 'It's always been my ambition to be part of a synchronised dishwashing team.'

They laughed at his joke and Fleur seemed pleased by how well Perceval had adapted to their household rituals.

Later, Fleur and Perceval went for a walk through the orchard at the rear of the house, crossed a meadow and entered a bowery hollow. She raised the matter of him coming with her to Oxford and staying for a few weeks. Perceval had anticipated this possibility. He didn't want to say goodbye, knowing he would probably be besieged (if not as Fleur had experienced it) by his insecurity and doubts. Yet if he went with her to Oxford, he feared he'd only get in the way and become a nuisance. Furthermore, he didn't want to jeopardise the goodwill of her parents. They were obviously proud of their daughter's academic achievements, keen it seemed, for Fleur to carry on the family tradition. Perceval had no idea if they expected her to join their 'practice' or even if such a thing existed these days. At the back of his mind was the worry, despite all the goodwill they'd shown him this day, they might regard his relationship with their daughter as a threat to her future career, distracting her from study or, even worse, disrupting her life entirely with some foolishly romantic scheme like giving it all up to be a water gypsy with him.

Perceval didn't mention any of these things but insisted, though he'd love to go with her to Oxford, her studies had to come first. He said he had his mother's affairs to settle and the house to sell but promised to visit her as soon as possible. And since he had experience, and good references, he would look to get some temporary post, possibly in the university's administration. 'Then I won't be your shadow or, what's worse, a burden to you.' Though she denied his arguments vigorously in principle, Fleur put up no serious protest to them in practice. On reflection, she admitted later, he was probably right. She must have mentioned this conversation to her parents, for they alluded to it after dinner when inviting Perceval to spend Christmas and New Year with the family. 'And I can promise you plenty more synchronised dishwashing,' her father joked.

That night, Perceval appreciated the delicacy of the decision not to put him and Fleur in the same bedroom but to give him the spare room beside hers. Family honour was served, social propriety maintained, while youthful desire was implicitly acknowledged. No need for creaking floorboards as he tiptoed along the landing in the dead of night. Everyone said goodnight with arrangements for the morning already made. Jacob would drive them to the railway station at Chester, where Fleur would catch her train to Oxford, and Perceval his train to Liverpool. Reaching their separate bedrooms, Fleur whispered to Perceval that she'd come to him later.

When all was quiet, she stole in, wearing a white knee-length towelling bathrobe. 'All clear,' she whispered, turning on the table lamp and sitting on the bed beside him. 'I have something for you.' Out of her pocket she took a small heart-shaped amethyst and held it in the palm of her hand for him to see. 'You've tied the knot. We've met the parents. Now I'm giving you my heart.' Fleur placed the stone in his hand, closing his fingers over it. 'When I was a girl, I collected gemstones and crystals. This one represents love and sincerity. Keep it with you and never lose it.'

Perceval put the stone in the pocket of his jacket which he'd hung on the chair by the bed. Fleur took off her bathrobe and slipped in beside him. She turned off the lamp and, in the darkness, they held each other like a promise.